Glacier Blooming

Edie Claire

fourth of the **Pacific Horizons** novels

Dedication

For the scientists who developed Aimovig™. After a year of chronic migraine, it's really nice to have my brain back.

Acknowledgments

Many thanks go out to Gustavus's own Katherine Hocker, who agreed to take me on a birdwatching hike only to spend all morning sitting in her car in the rain answering such questions as "Do bears ever break into freezers on people's porches? Why did that moose have a collar on? How can you possibly stay sane in the dark all winter?" – all of which she answered with sporting good cheer. I do hope that I have managed to capture some semblance of the spirit of this special place in these pages. (By the way, if you're selling real estate near the Nagoonberry Trail, call me.) Thanks also go out to Jan Barber, MSN, for answering all my nursing-related questions, and to Kathy Ke, MD, who generously attempted to help me understand how a character with Mei Lin's background might experience the world. Rest assured, any factual mistakes in this book are my own errors and not theirs.

Prologue

Chicago, Illinois, Twenty Years Ago

Margot drew in a ragged breath as she faced the man in the hospital bed. He looked pale and miserable, both of which could be expected after emergency surgery to remove multiple bullets from his chest and shoulder. He was hooked up to a half dozen tubes and wires that were in turn hooked up to an assortment of blinking, beeping machines. But at least he was finally conscious. They needed to talk.

"I won't go with you," she announced, fighting to sound firm despite the obvious tremor in her voice. She had no wish to be cruel, but under the circumstances, she was running short on sympathy. He had gotten them all into this mess, and as usual he was leaving her to get them out of it. And she would. She would do what was best for their sons, because the boys were all that mattered. Their father's feelings weren't something she could afford to consider anymore. "I won't do it," she repeated without the tremor. "Because it isn't fair. To me or to the boys."

"Margot," he answered in a voice that was disturbingly weak. "Please. I love our sons."

She pursed her lips in determination. He would not sway her, dammit! "I know you do, Stan. But you don't love me. You can't even pretend anymore. You think that doesn't matter?"

He winced, squirmed on the mattress, then winced even more. She knew he had to be in pain, despite the narcotics he was receiving. Watching him suffer made her horrible task that much more horrible. "Margot," he rasped desperately. "Please. This isn't about us! We have to protect the boys."

How dare he! "It wasn't me who put them in danger in the

first place!" she erupted, surprised at the unleashing of her anger. Yelling at a man in a hospital bed was despicable, but her simmering fury was difficult to contain. "This is your mess, Stan! *Yours*. And I won't let you ruin our sons' lives with it!"

Her voice cracked on the last words, and she fought hard not to cry. Never in a million years could she have foreseen such an outrageous end to the fairy tale of her youth. She'd been a starry-eyed idiot, a newly graduated hospital pharmacist who'd left her rural home in British Columbia to work in the hip and bustling USA. She'd wanted excitement and passion and she had found more than she'd ever wanted of both. Her chosen prince, a dashing trauma surgeon, had fallen for her charms at first sight, and the whirlwind courtship that followed had left her giddy with girlish ecstasy. It had also left her pregnant. And though the couple had married and had a second child, nothing after "I do" had been at all as she'd imagined.

"You don't understand," he pleaded, his striking pale-blue eyes attempting their usual bewitching. "Once we're all out of danger, you can blame me until the day I die. But all that matters now is keeping the boys safe. Whether we proceed with the divorce or not, the two of them will still be targets. That's how these people work, Margot. They go after your vulnerability."

His patronizing insulted her. "Oh, I do understand," she replied coolly. "Better than you think. All this has given you the perfect opportunity to play the big hero, hasn't it? And we both know how much you do love that! But this time, Stan, you're going to put your boys before yourself. Do you hear me? You don't *have* to give these people a reason to retaliate! All you have to do is keep your mouth shut, and I can take the boys back to Canada with me, safe and sound. And you can go wherever the hell you want."

His eyes widened with alarm. "It's not that simple," he insisted. "They're not going to leave me alone just because I *promise* not to say anything! They're not going to stop until I'm dead, Margot. And if they can't find me, they'll go after you or the boys to force me out of hiding. They'd find you all in Port McNeill in a heartbeat!"

Hot anger flared within her. The best solution for the boys was obvious, but he couldn't see it. His mind could only conceive of scenarios in which he played the starring role. "Have you thought for one second about how this grand scheme of yours would affect our sons?" she shot back. "Have you even considered *their* needs, their futures? If we run away with you, they lose everything! Their home, their school, all their friends, even their own identities! They would have to change their names and lie to people about their background. They could never even see their own grandparents again! Have you thought about that? My parents? Yours? Summers in Juneau, holidays on Vancouver Island? This is our boys' whole world we're talking about!"

He stared back at her helplessly, his face wracked with pain. "Of course I've thought of that. But there's nothing else we can do," he pleaded. "The three of you won't be safe unless you go with me. They'll never believe I'm not a threat!"

Stupid, idiot man! "Not as long as you're alive, no."

His pale eyes flooded with sudden understanding. And fear.

"If you'd died on that operating table," she said slowly, "the boys and I would be fine. Isn't that true?"

He made no response.

"You think I don't understand the situation, but you're wrong," she continued, calming her voice. She had his full attention now. "I understand perfectly. Two lovely gentlemen laid out all the options for me a little while ago. The fact is, no matter what kind of deal *you* make with the authorities, you can't take our boys with you without my consent. And I will not consent. I won't do that to them. They can have you and me both, living together in a miserable alliance in some faraway place with fake identities — in which case they lose every other thing they've ever cared about. Or they can keep every person, place, and thing that they love... except you."

A film of fluid obscured his eyes. He blinked, but it didn't help. A single tear rolled down each cheek and dripped onto his pillow.

His obvious grief shook her. Damn him for making this so hard! He did love his sons. And they were crazy about him, too, God help her. But like everything else in Stanley's life, he kept his children in a distinct mental compartment, to be taken out and played with when convenient. She occupied a similar box herself, although the hinges on its lid had grown rusty from disuse. They had never been the family she had longed for, and now they never could be.

"You don't *have* to testify against these people in court," she continued. "If you tell the authorities everything you know, even off the record, they've agreed to falsify a death certificate and set you up with a new identity. Everything about your condition has been held in strictest confidence since you arrived at this hospital; the only people who know that you survived the surgery are the staff, the authorities, and me. So when you're well enough, you can slip out of here and go wherever you want. Alone."

Tears continued to roll down his cheeks. Margot's own eyes flooded when she realized that one of his arms was immobilized and he seemed too weak to lift the other. He couldn't wipe away his own tears! "The boys would..." he began. But he couldn't finish.

Margot's composure crumbled. She had loved this man once — loved him with an all-consuming passion that had made her throw good sense to the wind. She loved him still, in a pitying, sentimental sort of way. But the passion had died a long time ago, and she knew that he had never loved her. They were so different in temperament, so divergent in values. If not for the pregnancy, they would never have married. She would have seen through him in time.

She pulled a tissue from her purse and wiped his cheeks, then did the same to her own. She took another ragged breath and spoke to him more gently. "Everyone will have to believe that you died of your injuries, including the boys. We can't trust them not to let something slip; they're too young. I know this will be hard on them. They do love you, Stan. But they'll need to grieve either way. Because whether you're still breathing or not, you can't be a part of their lives anymore. You just can't."

Not after this, she left unsaid. There was no need to heap additional guilt on him. He'd had enough to answer for even before this particular jaunt to Chicago had exploded in violence. She knew that neither the flying bullets nor the nightmare now ensuing was strictly his fault, but she had worried too many hours, lost too much sleep, and put the boys to bed alone too many nights to divorce this watershed event from everything else he had put her through.

"Can I see them again?" he begged. "One more time?"

She tensed and shook her head. Could he possibly make this any harder? "They'll be told you died in surgery," she explained. "The official story needs to be that you never regained consciousness after the shooting. You understand why."

His eyes closed as he nodded. His wounded body trembled, and Margot felt his pain. His chest and shoulder might burn and throb, but nothing could touch the agony of losing a child. As small a part of his life as the boys had been, she knew he would miss them desperately. Always.

"I'm sorry, Stan," she said sincerely. "I really am. If I could wave a magic wand and make all this go away without anyone's getting hurt, I would. But for their sake, this is the best I can do. I'll always do what's best for them. You know I will."

He gave another slight nod, and as she looked down at the closed eyes in his pale face she was overcome with emotion. This would all be so much easier if she could hate him. She could hate him for pretending to be something he wasn't, for roping her into his realm before she understood, before the naive girl she had been could see the demons that drove him. But she couldn't hate him. Every once in a while, he'd been a damned good father.

She leaned down and kissed him tenderly on the forehead.

"Goodbye, Stan," she whispered.

His eyes flew open, but she found her own unwilling to meet them. She turned away and walked out of the room.

Chapter 1

Southeastern Alaska, Present Day

Mei Lin shut the door of the house, turned, took two steps toward the Subaru Forester that was parked in the gravel driveway, stopped short, and shrieked.

Approximately seven hundred pounds of adult female moose was standing by the driver's side of the car. The shaggy, gangly beast swung its elongated nose toward the interloper and gave the human what could only be described as a bored, derisive look. Then the cow lowered her head and returned to munching on the bushes.

"Oh, please!" Mei Lin begged in a whisper as she slowly backed up again. "The GusMart's going to close!"

The moose did not appear to care. Her giant brown lips continued to strip the tender green leaves from their stems. Her lower and upper jaws slid sideways as she chomped and chewed. She had to splay her front feet to reach down to the bushes, which made her look comically awkward even without the gaudy red plastic collar that ringed her thick neck.

"Number Twenty-Two," Mei Lin mumbled as she reached the relative safety of the doorway. "It figures."

In the tiny town of Gustavus, Alaska, which occupied the flatlands at the tip of a coastal peninsula roughly 45 miles west of Juneau, one could run into a full-grown wandering moose any day, at any time. It was also not unusual to run into one wearing a GPS collar, since the movements of the local herd were being tracked as part of a research study by the state Department of Fish and Game. What was unfortunate for Mei Lin was that this particular moose, known to locals because she was one of the few that spent her summers in town as well as her winters, was less shy of people than she should be. Not only did Twenty-Two have a penchant for cultivated flowers and gardens, she also had the annoying habit of parking herself in the human spaces that harbored them and not budging again until she was damn good and ready.

Seeing the humor in her situation, Mei Lin grinned, pivoted, and reached for the doorknob. Then she caught herself, and her smile faded. Sharing such escapades with her employer had become second nature to her. But Elsie Dunn was no longer resting behind the giant picture window in the master bedroom upstairs, admiring her sweeping view of the Salmon River and the cold waters of Icy Strait in the distance. Elsie's funeral had been three days ago.

Mei Lin struggled to overcome another bruising wave of sadness. If Elsie were alive, she would certainly tell her young caregiver to knock off the melancholy and move on. The ninety-one-year-old's peaceful death had come at the end of a long battle with heart disease, and the only surprising thing about her passing was that it hadn't happened sooner. Mei Lin had served as Elsie's live-in nurse for the last seven months, and she knew better than anyone how much of a miracle it was that the frail old woman had survived through the spring, much less halfway through summer. But knowing that didn't make Elsie's home — a spacious, modern two-story with large windows and decks for year-round wildlife watching — seem any less empty now. Mei Lin might have started out as hired help, but over the long, dark winter, she had come to love her patient as a dear friend.

Now, she missed her terribly.

Mei Lin leaned back against the house and glanced at her watch. The moose had moved a few steps, but she was still grazing within six feet of the driver's side of Elsie's Subaru. It was Saturday, and the GusMart would be open only another fifteen minutes, after which it would close until Monday morning. You couldn't buy groceries anywhere in Gustavus on a Sunday, with the exception of whatever premium-priced delicacies Lesley and Kate had in stock at the Cafe Herbivore, and Mei Lin was out of milk, yogurt, and granola. Besides which, she had a serious craving for chocolate.

"Please move, moose!" she exclaimed in frustration.

The cow did not acknowledge her existence.

Mei Lin resolved to wait it out. She'd had plenty worse problems, after all. One year ago, she had been broiling in the July heat of Dallas, Texas, living in a poorly air-conditioned tin can of an apartment with three other nurses, eating reheated frozen entrees and sleeping on an air mattress. The only wildlife she saw between her high-rise apartment and the medical complex where she worked were garbage-eating pigeons and swarming blackbirds. The state did have other wildlife, of course, but being both broke and without a car made accessing such wonders difficult. If you'd stopped her then and told her that one year in the future she would be carrying bear spray in her purse and cursing at a moose in the driveway, she would have laughed out loud.

Mei Lin had never considered herself "adventurous." At the tender age of two and a half she had been adopted as an orphan from the Chinese province of Gansu and brought halfway around the world to Maine, where she had bonded quickly with her new parents and older sister and had learned a second language within months. But as daring and dramatic as all that sounded, she had zero memory of any of it. In her perspective, she was a timid hometown girl who until recently had spent her entire life within a fifteen-mile radius of Portland, Maine. It had taken all the guts she could gather to leave the only home she'd ever known and move down to Texas two years ago. And look how that had turned out!

The moose raised her head. She seemed to catch an interesting scent on the breeze. Without another glance at her human observer, she swung her giant nose toward the river and ambled off across the meadow.

"Thank you!" Mei Lin praised, creeping slowly around the back of the Subaru as the moose moved away. She slipped into the driver's seat and shut the door. The animal, which had stopped again thirty yards distant to munch on another cluster of bushes, twitched her oblong ears in response to the noise, then went back to eating.

Mei Lin started up the car and backed out. She still had ten minutes. She could make it.

Barring uncooperative moose or deep winter snowdrifts, it didn't take long to get anywhere from anywhere in Gustavus. The town of just under five hundred people consisted of two main roads that connected the town center with its airport and ferry dock, and — ten miles through the woods to the northwest — with the lodge and visitor's center of Glacier Bay National Park. The flat plain on which the town was built had an interesting geologic history, having been covered by glacier floodwaters only 150 years ago. Everything Mei Lin could see now — both the dark, moss-covered forests and the fields full of wildflowers — had regrown only after the ice and water had receded up into the bay.

Mei Lin rolled down her window to enjoy the sensation of the cool, moist air rushing past her cheeks. After a year and a half of inhaling the smelly haze of urban Dallas, she couldn't seem to get enough of the pure stuff. She glanced to the northeast and smiled. The weather was clear enough today to see the snow-covered Chilkat Mountains in the distance. Since they were frequently obscured by fog, she relished every peek.

Elsie's house was located exactly three minutes from the GusMart, and Mei Lin passed only one other vehicle on the way. She recognized the beat-up little Ford immediately as one of the fleet of second-handers belonging to Ron's Rentals, the only car-rental business in town. The Ford broke down less than most of Ron's other offerings, but even tourists who got stuck with the Spider (a particularly dilapidated conversion van with so many cracks in its windows it looked like it was wrapped in a giant web) were never stranded long. Every citizen of Gustavus, including Mei Lin herself, had picked up some tourist from the roadside at one point or other and given them a lift back to Ron's, where customers were assured of another set of wheels, an apologetic smile, and quite likely some fresh-caught fish as consolation.

Mei Lin passed the other driver with the mandatory local wave, which consisted of a brief lift of the fingers off the wheel along with a nod of acknowledgment. The fact that the tourist made no response indicated he hadn't been in town long. Gustavus was a friendly place.

The parking lot at the GusMart was packed, meaning that all three spots directly in front of the building were taken. Mei Lin pulled the Subaru off to the side of the lot and rushed in. She didn't want to make Ed Hanover stay late.

"Hey there, Mei," the storeowner called out as she blew by the checkout stand. He chuckled at her obvious haste. "Don't bust an artery now! You're fine. I'm not going anywhere."

"You deserve a weekend as much as anyone else," she called back. "I'm sorry. Twenty-Two held me up a bit, but I'll be quick, I promise."

Ed laughed again. "Ah, good old Twenty-Two. No hurrying that one along, for sure. Is this all for you, Stanley?" Not recognizing the name, Mei Lin looked up at the elderly customer who was checking out. She assumed he was a local, but she didn't know him. The area had a fair number of residents who kept to themselves, some of whom lived in remote cabins under primitive conditions. Stanley appeared to be one of them. The fabric of his shirt, shorts, and socks seemed indelibly entwined with dirt, his scruffy gray hair and beard hung to his shoulders, and his presence suffused the entire front section of the store with the pungent aroma of man-sweat and wood smoke.

"That'll be all, today. Thanks, Ed," the customer replied. Mei Lin perked an eyebrow. She'd expected to hear the succinct, rough dialect one usually associated with an antisocial backwoodsman, but this individual sounded more like a college professor. She was studying his mud-crusted hiking boots, which looked to have been expensive originally, when she noticed the wound. A nasty laceration curved along the man's calf just above the sock line. The cut had been stitched closed, and capably so, but Mei Lin didn't like the look of it. The gash appeared to be a few days old, and its edges had begun to redden and puff. She thought she saw a disturbing yellowish tinge to the swelling as well, but from where she stood, it was difficult to tell.

She took a step closer. As a nurse who specialized in caring for the elderly, she could no more ignore such a sight than a veterinarian could ignore a starving kitten. But before she could reach the man to introduce herself, she was interrupted.

"Mei Lin!" a female voice cried out behind her.

She turned to see Carol McRoberts, who managed many of the vacation rentals in town. Carol was a strong, big-boned woman in her early fifties with carrot red hair and very pale, freckled skin — all of which seemed to perfectly suit her environment. She had been Elsie's closest neighbor and friend for decades, and she had welcomed Mei Lin into the community with open arms, treating her more like a daughter than a friend's employee.

"I'm so glad you're still here," Carol exclaimed, folding her into a hug. "Every time I see you it makes me smile."

Mei Lin hugged her back, even though the women had just seen each other yesterday. A wave of melancholy surged up out of nowhere, and Mei Lin's eyes watered. "I can't stay much longer. But Elsie made me promise I wouldn't leave until I'd picked all her nagoonberries."

Carol chuckled, her light hazel eyes brimming with emotion. "She was a wily old coot, wasn't she? It did bother her that you might leave before seeing Alaska at its best. She told me once that keeping you around through the summer was as good an incentive as any for her to keep breathing."

Mei Lin swiped at her tears. She knew the truth of that statement. Elsie had chattered all winter about how her New England nurse — who had arrived in the dark of January — simply *must* stay on long enough to see the wildflowers bloom. But as soon as the blue lupine and pinkish-purple fireweed had begun to unfurl, Elsie had mysteriously switched to talking about her nagoonberries. And even in her last days, just as the rare wild berries were beginning to ripen in her meadow, she'd started bragging on the huckleberries, which wouldn't hit their prime till August. "I'll be staying through the middle of the week, at least," Mei Lin answered. "Her lawyer wants to talk to me before I go, and he can't get here till Tuesday."

"Please don't rush off. You know you're not imposing on anybody," Carol insisted. "Elsie wanted you to enjoy the house, and surely it'll take a little time to find another job? Oh, and by the way, you'll have the place to yourself this weekend. The guest house isn't rented out till Monday."

"That's fine," Mei Lin said without concern. Elsie's guesthouse was a small, separate structure nestled in a grove of trees off the main drive. Since it was Carol who checked people in and out and took care of any problems they might have, the renters never bothered Mei Lin one way or the other.

She looked back toward the checkout and was discouraged to see that while she had been distracted, the man with the wound had left. She finished her conversation with Carol and opened the door of the store to look for him, but he was nowhere in sight, and one of the parked cars was gone. Feeling guilty, Mei Lin collected her groceries and brought them up to the register. "Who was that man who just left, Ed?" she asked as she placed her items on the counter. "I hoped to talk to him." She explained why.

"His name's Stanley. Stanley Smith," Ed answered as he manually punched the price of her items into the register. "He lives in a cabin up past the Torpins' place, off a dirt track. Been around a year or so, but he only comes into town every few weeks. Keeps to himself, you know."

Mei Lin digested the information. Her concern was not assuaged. "I hope he's getting that leg tended to. Did he mention if he'd been to the clinic lately?"

Ed shrugged. "Couldn't tell you. I don't know him past a little chitchat, but he seems a decent enough sort. Smart, always real polite to everybody. That'll be twenty-two dollars and twenty-eight cents, please."

Mei Lin paid the grocer and thanked him. She started to step out, then turned around. "What does his truck look like?"

Ed shook his head. "Doesn't have one. He walks. Jesse Torpin says you couldn't get anything with four wheels up the track to his place anyway, not anymore. Hasn't been kept up in years, and now there's trees down and all. When Stanley needs to haul things, he pushes a wheelbarrow out to the road."

"You mean he walked all the way here on that leg?" Mei Lin asked, alarmed. "And he's walking back home with his groceries?"

Ed gave his head another shake. "Nah, Jim gave him a ride as far as Jesse's place. Sometimes I run him up there myself when he's got a lot to carry. There's always somebody around."

"I see," Mei Lin said, still troubled. She thanked the grocer again, apologized for keeping him late, and carried her bags to the car. The town had only one resident medical professional, a nurse practitioner named Sandra Gruber. Sandra handled everything from chronic illness in the locals to the cuts and scrapes of the many tourists who descended on the National Park every summer, and her outpatient clinic was invaluable to the community. Cut off from inland roads by ice-covered mountains, the town of Gustavus was accessible only by boat or plane. Residents who could afford it bought specialized insurance that would pay to evacuate them to Juneau in an emergency; but if the weather was bad, it wasn't unusual for someone with severe abdominal pain or even a broken bone to wait hours for transport.

Mei Lin continued to fret as she drove back to Elsie's house and put her groceries in the fridge. She knew, rationally, that being an RN didn't make her responsible for the health of every person she ran into. Then again, it wasn't as if she had anything else to do right now, was it? She headed toward the phone. If Stanley Smith had been to see Sandra recently, Mei Lin could stop worrying. But she had only taken a step when she realized that by now the clinic would be closed for the weekend, and nobody bothered the overworked nurse practitioner after hours unless they had a true emergency. Mei Lin's question would have to wait.

She made herself a cup of Elsie's favorite wild blueberry tea and took it out onto the house's rear deck. The open-air balcony, like the master bedroom and its prized picture window, looked out over the meadows that flanked the broad, shallow Salmon River. Mei Lin sat down on the loveseat rocker and made note of the patch of dark brown that was moving through a thicket of trees a hundred yards downriver. Number Twenty-Two hadn't strayed far.

She had come to appreciate this view every bit as much as Elsie had, but since the older woman's passing, the house had felt painfully empty. Swallows chirped in the meadow and the caws of seagulls drifted up from the harbor, but as soothing as those sounds were, Mei Lin missed hearing the creak of Elsie's bedsprings, the tinkling of her little call bell, the warm cackle of her laugh. Elsie's near-constant need for care had kept Mei Lin too busy to think about her own problems, and in this oasis of tranquility she had almost managed to forget them. But since Elsie's death, every moment of idleness invited bitter memories of Texas.

Mei Lin let out a sigh. She had never been one to bask in negativity, but happy thoughts seemed harder to come by lately. Very soon she would have to leave this place. Leave it... and start all over. She should be excited about that, and optimistic about her future. She used to be excited and optimistic about everything. But that was before—

The letter!

Nausea swelled within her as she remembered the correspondence that had arrived the morning of Elsie's funeral. Mei Lin had shoved it in a drawer unopened, then forgotten it. She set down her tea and hastened toward the desk in the kitchen. The letter was still in the drawer, exactly where she had left it.

Huffington Fuller, LLC: the law firm representing the skilled care facility in Dallas where she had last been employed. A nursing home that had made the local news after two women on its staff were arrested. A nursing home that faced multiple lawsuits.

She tore through the envelope and unfolded the letter. *As a material witness to the pending case of Gonzalez vs. Silverson Elder Care Center, we are writing to inform you that...*

Mei Lin dropped into the chair. She read on. It was all happening pretty much as the lawyers had predicted. Most of the families affected couldn't prove anything, and their cases had been dropped by their law firms. But the Gonzalez family was following through. Their attorney had filed a claim against the nursing home for wrongful death in civil court. There was still a good chance that the facility's parent corporation would choose to settle. But if not, Mei Lin would almost certainly be subpoenaed as a witness.

She refolded the letter and dropped it on the desktop. "A witness for the plaintiff," she muttered. The law firm defending her previous employer had asked her a minimal number of questions and seemed to take her cooperation as a given. They would be surprised to discover that her sympathies lay entirely with the Gonzalez family.

The familiar tension returned to her shoulders, and her head began to ache. She closed her eyes and massaged her temples. She never wished to set foot in the state of Texas again, for any reason. But going there for the purpose of reliving one of the worst experiences of her life in front of a judge and jury was too horrifying to contemplate. She had dodged one bullet already when the accused staff members had copped plea deals to avoid a criminal trial. But it seemed as if the civil suit would hang over her head indefinitely.

You'll be fine, she assured herself, using the simple words that had always been her mantra. The platitude brought her little comfort now; that it ever had was a testament to her naiveté. She used to be a cheerful, unflappable idealist, the sort of person who soothed other peoples' worries with a hug and a smile, and perhaps a dish of ice cream. But that was before Texas, before the idealist in her had gotten both smacked down and whopped upside the head. Before she'd slunk away from her troubles, battered and ashamed.

These last months in Alaska had been happy ones. But she was painfully aware that all along, she had been hiding. Hiding not from her ex-fiancé, or from the law, or from any other outside party. Mei Lin Sullivan, coward extraordinaire, had been hiding from herself. She didn't need anyone else to judge her, to tell her what an incredible idiot she'd been, or to question her fitness for her chosen profession. She could do that all by herself.

She just wasn't looking forward to it.

Chapter 2

Thane Buchanan watched out the airplane window as the jet curved to the east in its approach to the Juneau airport. He could see the ice fields shining white as they splayed over the mountaintops ahead, and as the plane continued to curve around and descend he was treated to an exceptional view of the Mendenhall Glacier dipping into the clear waters of its lake below. Only rarely had he landed in the capital city when visibility was this good. It was cloudy or foggy most days in Juneau, but being a Vancouverite, the change to him was marginal. He had always loved southeast Alaska. He didn't get up here nearly often enough since his grandfather had died; airfare was too blasted expensive. But he had no regrets over his sudden impulse to jump on a standby this morning. Never in his life had he felt such a strong urge to run away screaming, including that time at Glendale Cove when he'd been charged by a mother grizzly. In that case, running would have been a bad idea. In this case, it was his best option for sanity.

Even as he reveled in the raw beauty of the vista below him, he could not erase last night's debacle from his memory. The scene had been replaying itself in his mind all the sleepless night before. He still had trouble believing it had happened.

He and Vanessa had gone out to eat together at one of his favorite restaurants near the University of British Columbia, as they had done several times before. The only difference was that they usually split the bill, whereas this time she had insisted on treating him. But before they even had a chance to order, unfathomable words had started tumbling from her mouth. He'd been so dumbfounded he was pretty sure his mouth had hung open. Multiple restaurant patrons had turned to stare in their direction...

Vanessa was giggling at him. Her cheeks flamed with red

and her dark eyes twinkled. Her normally pale skin glowed, and her entire face was luminous with pleasure. "Don't say anything!" she warned through her smile, punctuating the point by touching a perfectly manicured fingernail to his lips. She squiggled in her seat with excitement. "Not a word! Not yet. I've thought all this through very carefully, and I absolutely forbid you to answer me now. In fact, I'm declaring a 48-hour waiting period." She glanced around at the people watching, then giggled and squiggled again. "Oh, isn't this *fun!*"

Thane didn't say anything. He couldn't think of a single phrase in the English language that addressed such a situation.

"Well?" she twittered expectantly. Aren't you going to put it on?"

He looked down at the thing that was clutched between his thumb and forefinger. He couldn't remember taking it from her. The second she'd explained what it was, his brain had gone numb.

An engagement ring.

He stared at the odd little device. It was metal. Part of it was black and part of it was shiny gold, the two colors alternating in a wavy geometric pattern. The design reminded him vaguely of the portable toilet in the construction zone by his apartment building.

"I know this isn't exactly *conventional*," Vanessa chirped. "But I saw it and I just thought, 'it's so *you*,' you know?"

Thane did not know. He had never worn a ring in his life. He had the same relationship with jewelry that he did with Vanessa. Both were beyond his scope of comprehension.

She laughed with delight, then grasped the ring herself and pushed it over the third finger of his left hand. "It fits perfectly!" she exclaimed, clapping her own hands under her chin. "I knew it would! I said 'give me the biggest size you have,' and they did!'"

Thane stared down at his hand. He was a big guy, so of course he'd have big paws. They were also weathered and callused, which made the thing on his finger look completely ridiculous. Not that he gave a rat's ass how he looked, but the bauble in question somehow made him feel like he had a loop of rope around his neck.

He started to pull the ring off.

"No, no, no!" she interrupted in a high-pitched squeal, clutching his hands with her own small, pale ones. Her ruby-painted nails dug into his skin as her eyes darted around the room self-consciously. Then her attention returned to his face, and she lowered her voice to a purr. "Please, Thane. You need to understand that I've thought this through very thoroughly already. I've examined all the angles and I've made my decision. I realize you haven't had as long to think it through as I have, which is why I totally don't want to pressure you. What I want is for you to wear this ring, and look at it, and think about it, for *at least* forty-eight hours. Before you say anything. Anything at all. Okay?"

She was still clutching his hands like a vise. If his skin was any less rough, her claws would have him bleeding now. He recovered the use of his jaw, then attempted to respond. "Vanessa, I—"

"No, no!" she interrupted. "I only want you to promise me one thing, love. I want you to promise me you'll *think* about it. About everything I've said. And I want you to promise you'll leave that ring on your finger while you do. I want you to see it there, every time you look at your hand, and think about what a wonderful thing a marriage between a man and a woman can be. Will you promise me, Thane? Please? Will you promise me just this *one* thing? Out of respect for all the years, for everything we've been through together?"

Thane was pretty sure she was asking for at least two things. He was also pretty sure that somewhere inside that inscrutable brain of hers, a screw had finally come loose. But it was true that they'd been through a lot together, ever since they'd been teenagers growing up in the mill town of Port McNeill on the rural north end of Vancouver Island. It was also true that she appeared to be one hundred percent, drop-dead serious about wanting to marry him. No matter how bizarre the circumstances, only a total jerk wouldn't take that as a compliment. Vanessa was a good-looking woman. She was also reasonably smart, aside from the insanity thing, and it wasn't as though she were a bad person. Surely he owed it to her to at least let her down gently.

"I'll think about it," he heard himself croak. And think he would. It would take every minute of the next forty-eight hours to come up with the appropriate words to turn her down. He sure as hell couldn't say what he was really thinking. "That's... all I can promise," he finished.

"And the ring!" she squeaked, her face lighting up even more. "You'll keep it on? Oh, please, *please*, say you will, Thane! It means so much to me!"

He felt his chin nodding in agreement.

The imaginary noose cinched tighter. Involuntarily, he pulled his hands out of hers and fingered his throat.

Vanessa popped up in her seat, leaned forward, and gave him a perfunctory peck on the lips. "Yes!" she declared loudly, all smiles. "I'm *so* happy! Remember, not a word more about it for the rest of the weekend. We can order our food now. Would you like your usual? The pulled pork?"

Thane found himself nodding again. He hadn't felt so taken off guard at any previous point in his thirty-four years. He was a capable, independent man, a veteran outdoorsman who could and did handle himself in rugged Canadian outposts in every season of the year. How had he gotten himself into such a ludicrous situation with a woman? There was no excuse.

But he could always go for pulled pork.

The plane touched down on the tarmac and bounced roughly, shaking Thane out of his reverie. He hadn't told Vanessa he was clearing out for the weekend. He'd merely left a note on his door, having no doubt she'd find it within hours. She lived in the same apartment building and found cause to "drop by" frequently.

The plane slowed to a crawl, then began to taxi, and like

most everyone else on board, Thane reflexively pulled out his phone. Then he reconsidered. He'd told Vanessa in the note that he'd be out of cellular range for most of his trip, but she would doubtless have already started blasting him with gushy, emoji-filled texts. He repocketed the device without turning it on. When he got to his final destination, he would email and tell her he'd arrived safely. Then he'd chuck the damn thing in his luggage for the duration.

He relaxed into his seat, looked out the window again, and allowed himself a smile. If he was running away from his problems, he didn't care. It felt too good to be in Alaska again, and this particular visit was long overdue. He had one and a half precious days to hang out with his favorite mentor, enjoy some of his boyhood haunts, and scope out job possibilities.

He would enjoy himself while he could.

Chapter 3

Mei Lin sat on the deck with one of Elsie's many reference books spread out in her lap. It was an atlas of the United States, complete with topographic and climate maps. Ready or not, she could put off finding other employment no longer. As tempting as it was to accept Elsie's offer to stay and enjoy the rest of the short Alaskan summer, Mei Lin had to get back to work. She needed the money.

Elsie had paid a generous wage in addition to room and board, but even that windfall had failed to dig Mei Lin out of the chasm of debt she'd acquired in the Lone Star State. She had trusted the wrong person, and she had gotten burned. Such a mistake could happen to anyone, but for her it was merely number three in a string of four grave misjudgments — all of which had charming smiles and carried Y chromosomes.

Mei Lin didn't want to think about that. Yes, further analysis of her missteps was needed; but surely that process could wait until she'd found another job? Never mind that she'd taken on this job with Elsie specifically for that purpose. She'd figured that burying herself on the frozen plains of Alaska — preferably with no eligible males around — would offer the perfect opportunity for self-reflection and soul searching. It would certainly make good penance. No other nurse, or even nurse's aide, had been willing to relocate to a tiny, isolated town in the middle of winter to care for a dying woman alone in her home — particularly not in a climate where gray skies brought almost constant rain or snow and daylight lasted a whopping six hours!

But Gustavus had surprised her. Far from making Mei Lin suffer, the picturesque, friendly little town had lulled her into a fantasy world. Between the towering white peaks above and the icy blue waters below, the savage beauty of Alaska had made her past seem more like a bad dream than reality. Which meant that instead of spending the last seven months working through her issues, she had been shamelessly relaxing into bliss.

"So, where would you like to live next?" she asked herself out loud, interrupting her own guilty thoughts. "The Pacific Northwest, maybe?" Any landscape that reminded her of Alaska appealed. She used to find wet weather dreary, but now she associated cloudy skies and precipitation with friendly people and unlocked doors. Why not Seattle? Or perhaps Portland, Oregon? As much as she had always loved New England, she couldn't return home now without feeling like a dog with its tail between its legs. And any place hot enough to remind her of Texas was Out with a capital O.

Gravel crunched loudly in the driveway, and Mei Lin's spirits leapt. She loved having visitors. Elsie had encouraged friends to drop by anytime, particularly after she became bedridden; and since Elsie had a lot of friends, traffic at the house had always been steady. The fact that people kept dropping by even after the funeral moved Mei Lin to tears. She set the book down and walked around to the front balcony.

Carol McRoberts parked her Honda CRV near the guest house and hopped out with a wave. "I lied to you, Mei Lin," she called out cheerfully. "Got a renter after all! Friend of Dave Markov's. Shouldn't give you any trouble."

"That's fine," Mei Lin called back as yet another vehicle started down the drive. She expected to see the aforementioned tourist in one of Ron's rentals, but when a familiar red pickup passed by the guesthouse and kept coming, she smiled and walked down the outside steps to meet the driver. "Hey, Bill!" she greeted happily.

"Hey, there," the tall, middle-aged man answered as he stepped out of his truck. Bill Hoskins ran a charter boat business, and Mei Lin knew him well. His wife Jeanie, the head librarian in town, had been another of Elsie's closest buds. "Looky here what I brought," he said with a grin, extending a bundle wrapped in brown wax paper.

"Oh, my," Mei Lin said cheerfully, even as her heart sank. "Is this what I think it is?"

"Fresh sockeye," he replied, handing it over. "Caught it myself earlier today. Now you can get cooking and have a party."

"That's so sweet of you! Thank you." Mei Lin mentally reviewed her available freezer space. There was none. Half the town had been in the habit of bringing Elsie food, usually way more than both she and Mei Lin could eat, and the deep freeze was now full to the brim with fish and game. Mei Lin had hoped to clear out some of the backlog by feeding people after the funeral, but it was no use; the townsfolk had brought more food to that event than they had consumed during it, so now even Elsie's regular freezer was packed with casseroles, soups, and desserts.

"It's nothing. Enjoy," Bill said, getting back in his truck.

Mei Lin waved goodbye as he turned the vehicle around and drove away. He had to pull to one side of the drive as the iconic Spider van squeezed by on its approach to the guesthouse. Ron's Rentals was clearly down to the bottom of the barrel, but that's what happened when one showed up in Gustavus on a Saturday in July without making reservations.

She took the bundle inside, laid it out on the counter, and unwrapped it just enough to take a peek. *Oh, dear.* It was a ridiculous amount of fish. Bill had already cut off the head and tail — the weight she felt was all salmon steaks. Plus fins and scales, of course. She had no more idea how to cook such a beast than she did how to field dress a moose. She could cope with small pieces of deboned fish, but whenever Elsie had wanted wild-caught salmon, Carol had taken it home and prepared it for them.

Mei Lin rewrapped the bundle and headed back outside to offer it to Carol for her own dinner, but by the time she reached the driveway, the CRV was already pulling out. The idea of scraping scales off the sides of a recently living fish made Mei Lin queasy, but she couldn't let the food go to waste.

As much as fresh sockeye cost in restaurants, that would be criminal.

She turned towards the guesthouse and started walking. Whoever Carol had just installed there, it was highly unlikely they'd thought to pick up groceries before the GusMart closed. And tourists had to eat something, didn't they?

She knocked on the green-painted door. The guesthouse had one bedroom, a small living room with a couch, a kitchen, a bathroom, and a screened porch in the back. It was less than elegant, but well kept and weather tight.

The door opened almost immediately. Mei Lin took a half step back as the entry filled with the broad shoulders of a very large man. He was young, early thirties perhaps, with a full head of thick, wavy dark hair and a rugged-looking beard to match. His tree-trunk legs were encased in worn jeans; his muscular torso, in a plaid flannel shirt and battered fleece jacket. If he were carrying a giant ax over one shoulder, he'd make the quintessential picture of a lumberjack. An uncommonly attractive lumberjack.

"Hello," he said affably.

Mei Lin assessed the stranger. After getting ripped off by Jeremy, not to mention what she'd lost with the other three, she had vowed that forevermore she would ignore her basic instincts about men. Her intuitive judgment could not be trusted; therefore, all future character assessments must be based on cold, hard facts.

She did her best to look at the man objectively. He was a human of imposing size and strength, and if he so chose, he could break her in half like a twig. That alone should make her treat him with caution. Right?

She tried to make herself wary. She imagined the man menacing her, stalking her, even breaking down her door with a bloody hatchet. But those images just seemed silly. He was terribly cute, and he had such an honest smile! His whole countenance was open and guileless, and his eyes practically twinkled with kindness and good nature. How could she help but like him?

Well, help it! she berated herself. Hadn't she liked Jeremy immediately, too? And Josh? And Travis and Anthony? If she traveled back in time and met Jack the Ripper she'd probably invite him in to tea. And yet...

Her agony of indecision lasted only a second before, mercifully, she remembered Carol's comment about the renter being a friend of Dave Markov. *Huzzah!* That fact qualified as objective information, and any friend of Glacier Bay's chief ranger had to be all right. "Hello," she replied with a smile. "My name's Mei Lin. I'm staying up in the main house, and a very nice fisherman just gave me this salmon which I have no idea how to fix and couldn't eat all of if my life depended on it. I don't suppose you'd want to take it off my hands, would you?"

The big man looked at her as if she had offered him gold, frankincense, and myrrh. The shock and delight on his face was almost comical. "Seriously?" he replied. "You don't want it?"

Mei Lin shook her head. He had amazing eyes. Light bluish gray in the center, contrasting with a ring of much darker blue around the edges. Their gaze was piercing, projecting both warmth and charm. "Please, take it. It's sockeye, fresh caught." She held out the bundle. "You know how to cook it?" She realized too late how stupid a question that was. The man looked like he could survive in the wilderness by catching rabbits with his bare hands and roasting them over an open flame sparked by rubbing two sticks together.

He laughed out loud. It was a booming, merry laugh that lit up his whole face. He took the bundle from her and weighed it with his hands. "Oh, I think I can figure out something to do with it. *If* you can round up a couple more people to help me eat it. I'm only staying till tomorrow, and there's enough here for four people, at least!"

Mei Lin grinned back. So he was gregarious, too. She liked that. "Tell you what," she offered. "You just met Carol — she lives right around the bend and I'm sure she'd appreciate a meal she didn't cook herself. If you can fix the salmon, I've got a fridge full of side dishes I can reheat. Then I'll invite her and her husband over and we'll have a feast on my porch."

The man smiled broadly. "Sounds awesome! I saw a grill out back here, didn't I?"

"You did. And you'll find your kitchen stocked with oil and spices. Carol always makes sure of that." Mei Lin paused as the nagging voice in her head castigated her again. Was she being too trusting? Would further verification be wise? She'd felt no hesitation when she'd invited him to a neighborly dinner on her porch, but her feelings weren't supposed to matter. Her feelings couldn't detect a cannibal on cocaine. "So, Carol says you know the Markovs?"

"I do," he assured. "When I was a kid I used to spend at least a month every summer in Juneau with my grandparents. Dave worked for Fish and Game, and he had my dream job. I wanted to *be* him, so I kind of made myself his shadow." He chuckled at the memory. "Dave took it well, I have to say. He's been a real inspiration to me. And Mary's the best, too. I usually stay with them when I visit, but I didn't realize they've got their daughter and grandkids staying there now."

Mei Lin nodded, feeling gratified. He clearly did know the Markovs. Dave and Mary were unfailingly kind and generous people, as evidenced by the fact that they had invited their twice-divorced daughter and her three children to cram into their relatively small house indefinitely. "Dave is sort of an in-law of mine," she explained. "He's my brother-in-law's uncle." And she had reason to be glad that he was. If Dave hadn't mentioned Elsie's plight at a family gathering in Anchorage, Mei Lin's sister Ri wouldn't have heard about the job, and Mei Lin would never have experienced the exquisite taste of a nagoonberry.

"Small world," the man said pleasantly, not sounding particularly surprised. Then he seemed to remember that he'd never introduced himself. He shifted the bundle under an arm and extended a hand. "I'm Thane, by the way. Thane Buchanan. Very nice to meet you, Mei Lin."

They shook. His grip was firm and strong, and he had remembered her name correctly for more than three seconds. Her thoughts began to waft in a biological direction, but she quickly reined them in. On that score, if no other, she actually *had* been accomplishing something. There had been no man in her life for eight months now, and she was proud of that.

Shortly after her breakup with Travis — otherwise known as disaster number four — her mother had sat her down for a "little talk." An invitation which, coming from Julie Sullivan, licensed psychotherapist, was akin to saying, "My God, you need help!" Theramom had proceeded to ever-so-gently point out that Mei Lin had not been without a boyfriend for more than a few weeks since... wait for it... *the spring of ninth grade.* What that fun-fact said about her, Mei Lin still wasn't sure. But her stint in Gustavus had at least broken the pattern. "Nice to meet you, too," she returned in a neutral tone, stepping back.

"So, what time should I have the main course ready?" Thane asked.

She looked at her watch and came up with a time. Then she bid him farewell and left. After a quick call to Carol to confirm the event, she settled back on the loveseat and reopened the atlas. "A smaller town on the Washington coast, perhaps?" she suggested to herself. Fortunately, a qualified RN could get a job almost anywhere...

Her mind drifted. She had never thought about it before, but all her exes had been short. Downright puny, actually. What was up with that? Did she gravitate toward diminutive men because she herself was petite? Was she graciously leaving the taller men for taller women? Or was she subconsciously afraid of muscles? She frowned. If the last was true, it would make her even more of a coward than she thought. Perhaps she simply didn't find the hulking, super-masculine type attractive? She mused over the prospect of dating a man who could lift the bumper of a car.

Her thoughts went biological again.

Nope! Absence of attraction was not the reason. So why had she avoided men who were physically strong? She certainly hadn't managed to avoid the bullies, whom she knew from personal experience came in all shapes and sizes. Could it be that, deep down, she knew she was destined to be manipulated, and that the best defense she had was to stick to men she could arm-wrestle?

Mei Lin returned her attention to the atlas. Concerted self-reflection was all well and good. But some revelations were just too damned depressing.

Chapter 4

Mei Lin leaned back in her chair and enjoyed the expressions of satisfaction on her dinner guests' faces. Thane had seasoned and grilled the salmon to perfection, and the variety of leftovers she had reheated had been a hit. Carol and John McRoberts, both salt-of-the-earth Alaskans, had taken to Thane immediately, and vice versa. The three of them had had a marvelous time swapping stories about their mutual friend Dave and the Juneau of years gone by, and several hours had passed in a blink. Before Mei Lin knew it the couple was rising to leave, despite her invitation to stay longer. She'd been enjoying the camaraderie immensely, even if she hadn't added much to the conversation.

"Don't feel like you have to rush off, too, Thane," Mei Lin implored as her other guests departed. He had risen from his chair and clearly planned to follow the couple out. "I'd love to hear more about your work."

He studied her with surprise, and she felt a quiver of self-consciousness. She hoped that hadn't sounded like a come-on. She truly was just enjoying having company. The evenings had been long since Elsie died, and the last thing Mei Lin wanted tonight was more opportunity for introspection. Besides, she'd never met anyone from Western Canada before, and his background as a wildlife researcher intrigued her. She returned to her chair and sat down with a chuckle. "When I first got here, I was so freaked out about the bears that I was afraid to walk out the door by myself! I'm better now. A little, anyway."

The awkwardness passed as Thane smiled and sat back down across the table from her. "You're not alone. Never mind how rarely humans get attacked, when people know bears are out there, something primal kicks in. But you do get used to it.

Back on Vancouver Island, we've got bears, wolves, and cougars all three."

Cougars? Mei Lin was secretly glad she hadn't been hired to work on Vancouver Island. She'd had a hard enough time wrapping her head around the carnivores that roamed Gustavus. Back in Maine, she'd come to accept the theoretical presence of black bears and coyotes, but the idea of giant grizzlies and packs of stealthy, lean wolves prowling about the house still spooked her. "Black bears or grizzlies?" she asked.

Thane's eyes twinkled at the question, and the corners of his mouth tugged up, making his beard twitch. He was clearly passionate about his profession. "Black. The islands in the Georgia Strait aren't big enough for both species to coexist. Occasionally, grizzlies will swim over from the mainland; but when they do, we relocate them. Otherwise they'll drive off the black bears and screw up the ecosystem."

Mei Lin imagined sunning herself on an island beach and looking up to see a grizzly's nose poke out of the ocean. *Pass.* "I've never seen a grizzly," she admitted. "And I really don't think I want to, at least not unless it's on the other side of a very thick pane of glass. What's your thesis about?"

Thane's cheeks turned a peachy-rose color, and she wondered for a moment if she was being too flirty. The man looked every bit as excited as if she had ripped off her top and asked him to stay over. But no, it was her question about his work that had pleased him, and since her interest in the topic was genuine she refused to fault herself. He had mentioned during dinner that he was working on a master's degree in wildlife conservation, and she would have asked him about it then if the group conversation hadn't taken another tack.

He cracked a guilty grin. "Before I answer that, it's only fair to warn you. I've been told that once I start talking about bears, it's pretty much impossible to shut me up."

Mei Lin laughed and took another sip of the excellent wine Carol had brought over. He could talk all night as far as she was concerned. Everything about his company was delightful.

"I'll risk it. Fire away."

"I've been studying the effects of commercial wildlife viewing on bear behavior," he began. "Specifically, how grizzlies who are habituated to the presence of people in certain areas at certain times respond to humans in other, unexpected situations..."

Mei Lin fought hard not to grin as he continued. Although the words he was saying sounded loftily academic, his face was shining with the same wild enthusiasm a small boy might show while jumping in a fresh pile of dirt. She could see how much he had enjoyed romping with the grizzlies of Knight's Inlet. The data crunching and scholarly writing that had followed were mere necessary evils. The more Mei Lin listened, the harder it became to picture him living on a college campus in metropolitan Vancouver. It was easier — and strangely appealing — to imagine him curled up in some mountain den.

"So what did you conclude?" she asked when she finally found a chance to break in. "Do the habituated bears act differently than other wild bears do?"

The sparkle in his blue eyes dimmed a bit. "Well, about that," he said sheepishly. "My results were inconclusive. The sample size was limited, and the animals had the gall to act inconsistently. All I could really conclude is that individual bears have distinct personalities, and that some will respond differently than others in the same situation. Not a whole lot of help when you're trying to come up with practical advice for an industry!" He chuckled. "As you can probably tell, I'm no academic. I'm just getting the piece of paper for job advancement. That's one of the reasons I came up to see Dave this weekend. He's got a lot of connections in Fish and Game and the National Park Service both."

"Wait," Mei Lin asked, confused. "Aren't you Canadian? Can you even get a job with the U.S. Park Service?"

He smirked. "Ah, but I have a secret weapon: dual citizenship. My mother is Canadian, but my dad was American. I was actually born in Seattle; we didn't move to British

Columbia until I was thirteen."

Mei Lin took note of the past tense in referring to his father. She always listened closely for such cues when she was getting to know someone. Any knowledge that would help her keep her foot out of her mouth was welcome, since it spent a good deal of time there, regardless.

"Living in two different countries and feeling at home in both... that would be nice," she mused. "I was adopted from China, and when I was growing up, my parents put a lot of effort into trying to help me connect with that heritage. But being Chinese never seemed real to me. It was just something I studied at, like math or history. I've always *felt* like any other kid from Maine. What's the other reason you're here this weekend?"

Thane blinked at her, and it took a second for her to realize that he wasn't responding to the whole Chinese thing so much as to her switching subjects so abruptly. She had a tendency to do that. "Other reason?" he repeated.

"For coming up here," she explained. "Besides seeing Dave Markov."

Thane's gaze shifted to his lap, and he seemed suddenly uncomfortable. His right hand crossed to his left and fidgeted with the odd ring he wore. Noticing the repeated gesture, Mei Lin couldn't help but wonder if it was a wedding ring. Not that it mattered to her, of course! She wouldn't have noticed the ring at all if Thane hadn't seemed so uncomfortable wearing it, and if the style of it had even remotely reflected his personality. There was a story there, but she knew the ring was none of her business. Come to think of it, neither were his reasons for traveling to Alaska. "I'm sorry," she apologized. "You don't have to answer that. My sister is always telling me I ask overly personal questions. It's a compulsive thing. When people interest me, I can't seem to help myself."

Thane relaxed again. "Oh, don't apologize. I don't mind the question. It's just that..." His eyes stared off into the distance as he continued to fidget with his hands. Then he seemed to make a decision. He jerked upright in his chair and fixed her with a determined look. "Look, we're essentially strangers, right? You've known me for" — he glanced at his watch — "less than five hours, and after tonight we're probably never going to see each other again. Right?"

Mei Lin's eyebrows lifted. She had no idea where he was going with this. "Agreed."

"Then can you answer a question for me?" he asked. "I know this sounds weird, but the thing is... I really need the opinion of someone who doesn't know me. Someone without any preconceived notions."

"Sure," Mei Lin replied.

He looked at her hopefully, then pushed back his chair and stood up. He pulled the ring off his finger and plunked it down on the table in front of her. "Speaking as a virtual stranger," he began, "what do you think of this?"

Mei Lin's gaze moved from his face to the ring, then back again.

"Please, don't try to guess what I want to hear," he begged. He stepped away and started to pace. "I'm not an easy person to offend. Even if I was, we're never going to see each other again, so what does it matter? Just give me your honest opinion. Your knee-jerk reaction."

Mei Lin was near bursting with curiosity, but with an effort, she streamlined her thoughts and tried to follow his directions. She picked up the ring and turned it over in her hands, trying to study it objectively. She searched for some facet of the jewelry that could possibly appeal to such an earthy, no-nonsense, muddy-boots-and-jeans kind of guy, but she could not. Even the least style-sensitive human on the planet could look at this weirdly shaped, elaborately patterned ring and hear it screaming, "Look at me! I'm a metrosexual!"

She shot another glance at the man who'd been wearing it and knew that if she didn't watch herself, she was going to fall out of her chair laughing. But she did watch herself, because however he had acquired something so obviously, ghastly inappropriate, he was taking the situation seriously. "Well, uh..." She cleared her throat. "I suppose my first thought is that it doesn't look like you. But taste in jewelry is a subjective—"

"I knew it!" he bellowed, smacking his palm on the table so hard the wine glasses jumped. "Sorry, sorry," he apologized quickly, grabbing the table again to stabilize it. "But I knew it! I *knew* that even a stranger would know better!"

His face was suffused with joy. Mei Lin was baffled. "This is *good* news?"

"Hell, yes! It means I'm not losing my mind!" He dropped back into his chair so heavily that the deck shook. "I was beginning to wonder. But I'm not crazy. She is!"

Mei Lin forgot about not asking personal questions. "And 'she' would be..."

"A woman I've known since we were kids," he explained. "It's supposed to be an engagement ring. She said she thought it was perfect for me! Do you believe that?"

Mei Lin blinked. This was getting odder and odder. "So... let me get this straight. You're *happy* that your fiancé is crazy?"

"No, no," he protested. "She's not my fiancé! I never said I would marry her."

Mei Lin must have frowned a little.

"It's not like that!" he insisted, jumping out of his chair again, his face indignant. "You have to understand! I never even asked the woman out on a date, for God's sake. We're just friends. That's why this is all so insane!"

Mei Lin was trying to understand. Really, she was. "Define 'friends.'"

His crossed his arms over his chest defensively. "Don't look at me like that! I didn't say 'friends with benefits.' I said *friends.* Period!"

Now she was really confused. "So why ask her to marry you?"

"I didn't!" he shouted, raising his palms. "*She* asked *me!*"

Mei Lin's good humor returned. Watching a man who bristled with brute strength and oozed raw sex appeal argue so vehemently in defense of his virtue was really too funny. "Surely we're talking *some* benefits..." she teased.

He let out a growl. "I'm telling you, no! No benefits! I have not even kissed the woman since we were seventeen years old!"

Mei Lin could help herself no longer. She cracked up laughing.

"And before you ask," he continued gruffly, though his smiling eyes belied any real ire, "kissing was as far as it went back then, either! Now do you believe me? Is this woman crazy, or what?"

It took a while for Mei Lin to compose herself, particularly after he sat down and started laughing with her, at which point she actually did fall off her chair. He helped her clamber back into it, and then she dabbed under her eyes with her napkin, certain that her mascara was smeared.

Thane let out a long, exhausted sigh, then poured himself some more wine. "I know it makes no sense. And I wouldn't blame you if you didn't believe me. I wouldn't believe me, either. Trouble is, there's nobody I can talk to about this who *will* believe me. Vanessa's very attractive, and I can see how other people might think we were dating. We live in the same building, but only because when I moved to Vancouver two years ago, she gave me a lead on a neighbor's apartment. And since we live close, we do go out to eat together sometimes, and every once in a while we'll catch a movie or something. But our relationship has never crossed the line. I swear."

He shot Mei Lin a sudden, anxious glance. "And *not* because I'm not attracted to women!" he clarified. "I'm just not attracted to her."

"If you say so," Mei Lin said impishly. The man was entirely too much fun to mess with. "But... you did just describe her as 'very attractive.'"

"I meant to someone else!" he bellowed, but the look he threw her was playful. "Okay, fine, you want to know what the problem is? Aside from the fact that Vanessa is nuts, I'm not attracted to her because she reminds me too damn much of my mother. There! Are you satisfied?"

Mei Lin fell out of her chair again.

This time Thane refused to help her up. Instead, he picked up his glass and downed his remaining wine in a gulp. "Yeah, yuck it up," he admonished, even as he chuckled. Mei Lin crawled her way none too gracefully back up to the table, and he began to explain. "Our families are neighbors back in Port McNeil. Our mothers have been friends for decades, but now that Vanessa's an adult, she and my mom are like clones of each other. Every time I go home for a visit, I'll catch the two of them together, smiling and whispering. And then the second I walk over, they clam up! Do you have any idea how disturbing that is?"

Mei Lin tried to imagine her own straitlaced, schoolteacher father secretly colluding with her jerk of an ex-fiancé, but no image would come. The two men had mostly ignored each other. "That would be... unsettling," she conceded.

"They even look alike!" Thane said with a wince. Then his eyes widened. "Wait. I didn't think... What if Vanessa goes blabbing to our families? What if she tells everyone we're engaged?"

"Why would she lie?" Mei Lin asked reasonably. "More to the point, if you have no intention of marrying her, why are you wearing her ring?"

He dropped his head in his hands with a groan, then parted his fingers just enough to peer out from one eye. "To answer the first question — I have no idea why Vanessa does any damn thing she does. And as for the second question... she begged me to wear it for forty-eight hours before giving her an answer, and I was too flabbergasted to argue with her. I just got the hell out of there."

"You mean you took the ring and walked out on her? Without saying anything at all?"

"Well, no. I finished my sandwich first."

Mei Lin exploded into laughter again, and after another moment, Thane joined her. Despite her merriment, she was impressed at his apparent honesty. Only a man who took his promises seriously would wear a ring he hated purely to humor a woman he thought was crazy. "I'm sorry," she apologized again, feeling guilty for her lack of self-control. "I really am. I know this isn't a joke to you."

"S'okay," he replied, wiping his eyes with a finger. "I needed to laugh. It's really the only sane response."

Mei Lin had to agree, but she didn't say so.

In the silence that followed, she realized it was growing late. The air had become chilly and the summer evening had entered its twilight phase. She looked out over the meadow and subconsciously scanned the silhouette of tall grass and bushes for any movement. She and Elsie had occasionally spotted black bears this time of evening, either eating berries or, if the tide was low, trundling toward the beach. "So, if you don't mind my asking... What's your plan?"

He scoffed. "My plan? Well, my first choice would be never to go back to Vancouver, but I suppose that could be considered cowardly."

Mei Lin nodded. Nothing short of a subpoena would ever get her back to Texas, but they were talking about him. "And your second choice?"

He sighed. "I suppose I should just bite the bullet and tell Vanessa the truth. Do I even have another choice?" He threw her a beseeching look.

She shook her head. "Not that I can see, no."

"I'm guessing she won't take it well."

"Probably not," Mei Lin commiserated. "I'm sorry. I do have a suggestion, though."

His eyes locked on hers like a lifeline. "Please," he begged. "Anything."

Mei Lin picked up the ring from the table. "I assume you plan to wear this until you see her again, since you promised?"

He nodded his head, even as he frowned at the thought.

"Then wear it on your right hand," she advised, giving it back to him. "And maybe on another finger. She'll notice the change right away, and it may keep her from getting her hopes up. In the meantime, other people won't get the wrong idea."

"Brilliant," he praised. He tried out the ring in several locations, then decided to leave it on his right index finger. It still looked ridiculous, but at least it didn't look like a wedding band.

He rose to leave again, and this time Mei Lin didn't stop him. She thanked him for grilling the salmon and walked him to the bottom of the deck stairs. "Well, goodbye, virtual stranger I'll probably never see again," she said cheerfully as he stepped down onto the driveway and headed toward the guesthouse.

"Goodbye," he replied, his blue eyes twinkling again. "And thank you."

Chapter 5

Despite joking to the contrary, Mei Lin did hope she would run into Thane Buchanan again. But when she arose the next morning, she was disappointed to find that he had already checked out of the guesthouse. She suspected he would be up at the park with Dave for most of the day, until the two flew on to Juneau. But lacking any plausible excuse for driving to the park herself, she spent the cool, rainy Sunday alone, job-hunting over Gustavus's frustratingly slow wifi. By nightfall, the quiet of the empty house had become maddening.

She was lonely, and she was annoyed that she was lonely. What self-sufficient human being couldn't spend one full day by herself without falling into a funk? Her introverted sister, Ri, could live alone on a boat for a month and be happy, but Mei Lin had always been a social creature. She had never thought of her extroversion as a weakness, and she didn't want to now. She had enough weaknesses to deal with already.

She slept fitfully that night, dreaming of mixed-up pills, a nurse aide in handcuffs, and a wound on an old man's leg that wouldn't stop oozing. She awoke Monday morning still restless, and as soon as regular business hours began, she hopped in Elsie's Subaru and drove straight to the medical clinic. There was nothing she could do about her first two nightmares, but she could certainly address the third.

The parking lot of the facility was nearly full, which wasn't surprising for a Monday morning. She parked at the far end of the lot and hurried in, shamelessly hoping to find enough chaos to justify an offer of assistance. She wanted something useful to do — preferably in the company of other humans. But when she opened the door, she found the small waiting room perfectly in order, with a few adults sitting and staring at their phones while two children played at the Lego table. "Hello, Mei

Lin. What brings you here today?" the receptionist asked.

Lilly Rogers was a local girl a few years out of high school. She had no medical training that Mei Lin knew of, but she did help the nurse practitioner with various office tasks. Right now she was simultaneously greeting newcomers, holding the phone to her ear, and installing a new toner cartridge in the printer. "I just wanted to talk to Sandra briefly," Mei Lin explained, feeling petty for wishing the girl was a little less competent. "It's about another patient of hers that I ran into over the weekend."

"Sure thing," Lilly said cheerfully. "You can go on back now if you want to. She's in the lab."

Mei Lin slipped behind the desk and around the corner to find the nurse practitioner dipping a test stick into a urine sample.

"Hello, Mei Lin," she greeted. Sandra Gruber was somewhere around sixty, had spent over twenty years working for the army, and appeared impossible to shock, offend, or surprise. She handled any and all afflictions and emergencies with brisk efficiency and imperturbable calm, and Mei Lin was in awe of both her competence and her confidence. Unfortunately, Sandra also intimidated the hell out of her. "Something I can do for you?"

"I have some information for you, actually," Mei Lin replied. She talked fast, since she knew the other woman's time was valuable. She explained that she had run into Stanley Smith in the GusMart on Saturday and then described the condition of his wound. "I just wanted to make sure he hasn't skipped any follow-up appointment he might have had with you."

Sandra shook her head as she read the test stick and wrote some notes in a chart. "He hasn't followed up because he never came to me in the first place. He isn't my patient."

Mei Lin sucked in a breath. Sandra had been running the clinic for over a decade; she knew all the residents of Gustavus. There was no point asking if she'd made a mistake.

"I've heard of him," the nurse practitioner elaborated. "But he's never come in."

"I wonder who stitched him up, then. Do you suppose he was treated in Juneau or somewhere?"

Sandra gave a shrug. "Could be. Could also be that he stitched himself up."

Mei Lin tried not to look horrified. "People do that?"

"Sure. A suture kit is standard first aid in the backcountry."

An image of the injured leg loomed large in Mei Lin's mind. "It's just that the stitches were so even," she muttered. "I was sure a professional had done it."

"You think it was infected?"

Mei Lin hesitated. Once upon a time, she hadn't second-guessed her every professional impression and decision. But once upon a time was before Texas. "I didn't get as close a look as I would have liked," she hedged. "But my suspicion is that if he isn't on antibiotics, then he should be, and soon."

Sandra frowned. "That doesn't sound good. Still, if he isn't asking to be treated, we can't force the man."

Mei Lin's pulse quickened. She had seen infected wounds before. Even with prompt treatment, they could be extremely painful. Without treatment they could lead to sepsis, which could be fatal, particularly in the elderly. "If he's hoping he'll get better on his own, and he doesn't, he won't be able to ask for help. He won't be able to walk that far."

"You may be right about that," the nurse practitioner conceded. "Why don't you give the Torpins a call? I'm sure Jesse wouldn't mind going up and checking on him."

Mei Lin relaxed a little. "Good idea. I'll do that."

"Hang on." The nurse practitioner walked to a nearby shelf, counted out some capsules, and sealed them in a paper envelope. "Take these to Jesse," she ordered, writing down some instructions and then handing the packet to Mei Lin. "I don't know Stanley Smith, but I've known plenty like him, and I can tell you right now there's a good chance he won't agree to come to me for treatment, even if he's on his deathbed. I'll go up to him if he'll have me, but if he won't, tell Jesse to leave these. It may be all we can do."

Mei Lin studied the other woman's stern face with appreciation. Prescribing medication to a patient you've never seen went against pretty much everything medical professionals were taught — except the part about saving a life in an emergency. Sandra was putting herself at risk for a stranger, and Mei Lin respected that. She took the packet and slipped it into her pocket. "I'll walk up there with Jesse myself," she decided. "And I'll do my best to get Mr. Smith to agree to treatment, one way or the other."

Sandra's lips curved up slightly, which was as close to a smile as the woman got. She gave a nod as brisk as a salute, then popped back into the clinic's exam room.

Mei Lin returned to her car and drove toward the Torpins' place. She knew vaguely where it was, having been there twice before, but in both cases it had been dark and someone else had been driving.

Her heart warmed at the memory. Winter in Gustavus, much to her surprise, had been a social whirlwind. The locals responded to the long stretches of darkness by finding creative excuses to get together, scheduling everything from church and community events to informal potluck dinners that rotated to different people's houses. Elsie hosted a group of friends at her house every week, and in return she and Mei Lin were frequently invited elsewhere. Elsie rarely felt up to going out in the cold, but often when she declined an invitation someone else would miraculously appear at the house to sit with her so that her nurse could go. Mei Lin had been deeply touched not only by how well the small community cared for Elsie, but how they also took Mei Lin's own needs into account. Far from feeling isolated "in the middle of nowhere," she had had a perfectly wonderful winter getting to know an entire town.

She paused at a fork in the road and considered, then took a guess and turned the Subaru to the left. Getting lost didn't concern her much. There were only so many roads in Gustavus, and if she accidently wound up in someone else's private drive, she had a good chance of knowing the family.

After a few minutes, the road she was traveling dead-ended at the Torpins' place. "I knew it," she lied, parking the car and waving to the two young boys who played with a dog in the clearing. She hopped out, greeted the friendly lab, and proceeded to the door. "Hello!" she called, knocking lightly on the metal frame of the screen. An interior door stood open already. "It's Mei Lin Sullivan."

Within seconds, a thin blonde in her early thirties appeared at the door, struggling with a wiggly infant on her hip. "Mei Lin?" she said with surprise. "What brings you out here? Come in!"

"No thanks, Amanda. I don't mean to trouble you," Mei Lin said quickly, noting the bags under the mother's eyes. The baby whined and balled up her fists in a cranky gesture. "I know you're busy. I was hoping to catch your husband at home." She quickly explained her concern for Stanley Smith.

"Oh, dear," Amanda said with distress, switching the baby to the opposite hip. "Jesse's not here. He's running a fishing charter for Bill Hoskins today. I just saw Stanley on Saturday, but I didn't notice anything wrong with him. He doesn't have a phone up there, you know. There's no electric or water, either."

Mei Lin tensed. Stanley Smith was hardly the only Alaskan to make do with a woodstove and an outhouse, but such conditions did not bode well for sanitary wound care. "How long a walk is it up to his place?" she asked.

"Half an hour, give or take," Amanda answered. "I'd walk you up there myself, but I've got the kids. I'm sure Jesse would be happy to go with you when he gets back, though."

Mei Lin debated. Later today might be fine. They might go up and find Stanley Smith healing nicely and annoyed at being bothered. But her gut was screaming otherwise. It had been two days already since the wound had been in the state she'd seen it, and she had no reason to believe he'd received any treatment since.

Her gut might have a lousy track record. But it refused to be ignored.

"If you think I can find the place," Mei Lin announced, "I'll go on up now."

"Oh, the trail's easy to follow," Amanda assured, walking out with the baby still on her hip. She pointed to a gravel track that branched off from the main road to form a narrow, treeless lane. The gravel quickly petered out, obscured by tall grass and weeds, and bushes encroached from the woods on either side. The "road" that remained was barely wide enough for an ATV, but a trail of beaten-down grass indicated a recently used footpath.

"Just keep walking, and you'll wind up at the cabin," Amanda explained. "Can't miss it. A brown dog will probably come out to meet you; don't worry, he's a lover. The trail's used by all sorts of other critters, though, so if I were you, I'd take bear spray." She looked up at the sky. It was gray, as usual, but not particularly threatening. "And your rain gear, of course. Remember, there's no cell reception back there. How long do you think you'll be?"

"I have no idea."

Amanda's lips twisted. "Tell you what. If you're not back by the time Jesse gets home, I'll send him up after you."

Mei Lin nodded. "Sounds like a plan. Thanks." Amanda took the baby back into the house, and Mei Lin extracted her boots, rain pants, and jacket from the Subaru. Then she donned the small pack that held her water bottle and clipped her bear spray onto a belt loop. Nobody needed to remind her about the latter. She wouldn't walk fifty yards from her car without it.

She set out on the trail, which like all of Gustavus was mostly flat. The walking was easy; even in those places where the lane was blocked with fallen branches and trees, she could easily pick out Stanley's most recently bushwhacked detour. But as the sound of the Torpin boys' play faded out behind her, she felt a growing sense of unease. She wasn't used to being in places with no other people. Particularly places in which the closest person could be farther away from her than the closest carnivore. The Alaskan rainforest was objectively beautiful, but this deep into the woods, the plethora of tightly packed tree trunks hemmed her in like a silent army, and the thick understory of ferns and devil's club seemed tall enough to conceal a half-grown elephant. Anything or anybody could be lurking within feet of her... and how would she know?

A shiver rocked her shoulders, but she tried to think positively. She rooted the image of a stalking wolf out of her imagination and replaced it with a picture of Thane Buchanan, his booming laugh resounding through the forest as he walked the trail ahead of her, telling tales of wild British Columbia. She smiled, feeling instantly more at ease. How fun it would be to have this adventure in the company of someone like him! Someone naturally in tune with the great outdoors. Someone strong and capable...

A sudden wave of guilt dampened her happy thoughts. She'd been crowing about having gone so long without a significant other, but that achievement came with a big fat asterisk. Alaska might be full of men, but the ones who lived permanently in Gustavus were either old enough to be her father, already married, or still in high school. Until Thane Buchanan came to dinner, she hadn't spent more than ten minutes with any semi-eligible male since her plane landed.

She sighed to herself, then just as quickly frowned and set her jaw. So what? However it had happened, she *had* been single all this time, and she had been able to function just fine, had she not? She hadn't pined or sulked or felt incomplete... she'd been busy with Elsie, and she'd been perfectly content. So there! She pressed on with determination, and her unease soon gave way to exhilaration. *Mei Lin Sullivan, backcountry woman!*

A year ago, she wouldn't have dared take such a trek by herself. Her family would be impressed, especially her intrepid sister. Ri Sullivan-Markov had lived in Alaska for a couple years now and was working on a master's in marine biology at the state university in Fairbanks. Mei Lin smirked to remember how she had taken on the Gustavus job assuming that she and her sister would get to see each other often. Naive "mainlander" that she was, she hadn't realized that no road connected the two cities and that flying commercial was expensive, required two stops, and took all day. She'd actually seen Ri and her husband Wolf only once, in May, between the end of their classes and the beginning of their summer fieldwork. And even that get-together probably wouldn't have happened if her Alaskan brother-in-law didn't know several pilots.

Mei Lin chuckled at her ignorance. She'd had no idea what she was getting into when she came to the land of the midnight sun. But she had no regrets, either.

Something lying on the ground stopped her short. *Scat.* A pile of animal droppings, dark with berry juice and riddled with tiny seeds. She looked around. A bear had definitely been here. But when? She had learned much from Elsie's nature books about how to identify wild creatures by their scat and tracks, and she'd enjoyed practicing her skills at the beach and on the Nagoonberry Trail. But in those places, she had at least some chance of getting cell reception.

"Hello?" she called out uncertainly. The pile look reasonably fresh, but under no circumstances was she checking its temperature. She listened for a moment, but heard no rustling of bushes or snapping of twigs. The only sounds she heard were the wind in the trees and the occasional chirp of a forest bird. *You'll be fine,* she assured herself. The scat could have been there for a day or more. She pushed forward, but decided she should probably sing something while she walked. She was as tone deaf as a stump and never, ever sang in front of people, but presumably the bears wouldn't mind. As long as they heard her coming — all the nature books insisted — they would do their best to get out of her way.

She continued down the trail, alternating pop songs with some of her favorite musical theater numbers, fudging the lyrics she couldn't remember. The rain held off, and she was enjoying herself. But eventually her repertoire ran thin, and during a period of silence when she was trying to think up another song, she heard a noise.

It was a crackling sound, like a twig breaking. It was followed by a steady thudding and a rustling, both of which were coming from the direction in which she headed.

Mei Lin froze. The sounds grew steadily louder. She could see nothing moving, but the trail curved ahead, leaving only a dozen yards or so visible. Whatever was making the noise, it was coming closer. And it was coming closer fast.

Her heart skittered. She reached down and unhooked the can of bear spray from her belt. She pulled off the safety clip and stretched out her arms, aiming the nozzle down the trail.

Most bear charges are fake-outs, she reminded herself. *They veer off at the last second. Wait until the bear is in range to spray...*

Her pulse pounded in her ears, nearly overwhelming the rustling and the thudding. She saw movement in the tall grass around the curve.

Whatever was coming would reach her in seconds.

Chapter 6

Don't look it in the eye!

Then where CAN I look?

Only pull the trigger when it's within thirty feet and you're sure it's headed for you...

Wait... how far is THAT?

Keep it together — you'll be fine!

I am SO going to pass out...

Mei Lin couldn't breathe. Her arms trembled so violently the spray can jerked around in the air in front of her. Holy crap! She couldn't hit the side of a barn!

The grass ahead swayed and bent. A ball of brown fur shot into view and hustled toward her.

It was a medium-sized dog.

Mei Lin let out her breath with a gush and dropped her arms to her sides. Her jelly legs bent beneath her and she dropped into an ungraceful squat. "Oh, my God," she cried aloud as the dog ran past. It then reversed course, wiped out on its side, got up, and scrambled back to her. "You scared me!" she chastised.

The dog slowed. It covered the last few feet between them in a submissive crouch, its tail wagging limp and low. "It's okay," Mei Lin said immediately, stretching out a hand. "I didn't mean to scare you, either." She gulped for breath as the dog gave her a sniff.

"Why didn't you bark?" she asked with surprise. The dog must have come running when he heard her singing. Most dogs would be barking their heads off if a stranger approached their home in a remote area. This mutt went belly-up the second she started petting him. "I guess security's not your cup of tea," she teased.

The dog seemed pleased; but his self-indulgence lasted only a moment. Then he scrambled back to his feet and began a frantic pacing. When Mei Lin rose, he ran back the way he had come. She watched as he disappeared around the bend. Friendly as his greeting had been, the dog was agitated.

She continued walking down the lane after him, but her progress was evidently not fast enough. The dog reappeared, this time stopping short about ten feet in front of her. His brown eyes locked on hers, and he issued a single, sharp bark.

Mei Lin felt a tingle of anxiety sweep up her spine. The dog was happy to see her and would doubtless have been happy to see anybody. But something in his canine body language told her he was on a mission. An urgent one.

Not liking the images that popped into her head, she began to move faster. The dog took off again, doubling back periodically to make eye contact before tearing off into the weeds once more. Mei Lin checked her watch. She'd been walking half an hour already; Stanley Smith's cabin had to be close.

The dog had been absent for some time when Mei Lin finally caught sight of a structure ahead. She broke into a jog and followed the trail to where it opened out into a large clearing. Centered in the open space was a weathered but solid-looking wooden cabin with both a stone chimney and a stovepipe emerging from its roof. Several smaller outbuildings also dotted the clearing, which was bordered on its far end by a shallow stream.

Mei Lin could see neither the dog nor his owner, but the cabin's front door was ajar. She was apprehensive; the homestead was unexpectedly quiet. "Hello?" she called. "Mr. Smith? Are you here?"

The door moved a little, and the brown dog squeezed through the opening and stepped out onto the sheltered front porch. He looked at her, wagged his tail, and gave another understated woof.

Mei Lin felt a prickling on the nape of her neck. "Mr. Smith?" she called again, stepping closer. No sound came from inside the cabin. The dog remained on the porch, watching her.

He pranced a bit, then dipped his head and crouched, almost as if he wanted her to play.

She suspected the dog wanted otherwise. She suspected he wanted her to come inside the cabin.

When she reached the porch steps and started up, the dog pushed his way inside the door and disappeared. She heard a snuffling noise, then a plaintive whine.

"I'm coming in now," she called nervously. She reached the door and peered inside, but in the dim light beyond she could see nothing but wood-plank flooring.

Steeling herself, she grabbed the knob and pushed. The door moved only an inch, then hit something. The dog squirmed back out, bumping Mei Lin's legs and stepping over her feet. She pushed again, but the door didn't budge. Whatever was blocking it seemed to be at floor-level. It wasn't the dog.

She turned sideways and attempted to squeeze through the opening, but it wasn't wide enough. She backed up, braced her hands on the frame, and gave the door a solid butt-smack. Something heavy scooted along the floorboards, and the opening widened another three inches. She squeezed inside.

Her eyes took a few seconds to adjust to the dim light, but when the shape on the floor became visible, her stomach gave a lurch. "Mr. Smith!" she cried, dropping to her knees by the motionless figure. The older man was lying on the floor behind the door. Mei Lin reached a hand to his neck and felt for a pulse.

Thank God. "Mr. Smith!" she called again, patting his cheek. His pulse was rapid, his face flushed. She moved her hand to his forehead to confirm the obvious: he was burning up with fever.

She glanced around. His cabin consisted of a single room. Three of the walls had windows, but all of the curtains were pulled shut. She got to her feet and pulled them all back, letting in as much light as possible from the cloud-covered sky. The back wall had a large, open fireplace in which a black kettle hung over a nearly extinguished fire. A bed jutted out into the room, its sheets and blankets bedraggled and trailing onto the floor. Near where the man had fallen, a tin bucket lay on its side.

Mei Lin examined him as best she could and determined that although he was feverish and dehydrated, he was not in severe straits... yet. He was in a daze, but not unconscious. His breathing was regular and he showed no obvious signs of low blood pressure. His most immediate need was for water.

She rose and checked the kettle, figuring he must boil his water to sanitize it. The kettle was still warm to the touch, but bone dry. He must also keep a supply of cooled water... but where? She located a plastic water container near the woodstove, but a quick push of the spigot confirmed that the dispenser was empty.

Had the poor man been forced to drink warm water directly from the kettle? If his fever had come up quickly when his supplies were low, he could easily have gotten too weak too fast to replenish what he was drinking.

She headed to the porch, the dog prancing at her heels. In addition to having a stream nearby, the cabin was set up with a rainwater collection system. One large wooden rain barrel at the edge of the house was connected to a downspout, while another closer to the door was smaller and made of plastic. The near container was about half full, but Mei Lin had no way of knowing if its contents had been boiled already. Most likely they had not. Mr. Smith probably brought batches inside with the bucket and poured them in the kettle, then after boiling, used another bucket to refill the inside dispenser. He'd probably been heading outside for more water when he collapsed.

She removed her own, nearly full water bottle from her pack and walked back inside. She returned to her patient, got down on the floor, and attempted to prop him up and raise his head. He moaned slightly as she moved him.

"Hello, Mr. Smith," she greeted calmly as she lifted her

water bottle to his lips. "I brought some water for you. Do you think you can drink it?"

The process was slow and frustrating. The man's mental state was bleary and he seemed unable to speak or even keep his eyes open. But at least he was conscious, and after some time and effort Mei Lin managed to get him to drink. Unfortunately, the water she had brought was not nearly enough.

She let him rest a minute while she took stock of the situation. Would it be quicker to boil water in the fireplace or on the stove? She touched the surface of the stove, found it cool, and decided on the fireplace. She filled up a bucket with water from the plastic container on the porch and poured it into the kettle. Then she brought in more firewood and kindling and revived the dying blaze.

"Now," she said loudly, hoping that talk might help to revive him as well, "let's get you a little more comfortable." She found some small towels, wetted them with water from the rain barrel, and began to sponge off his face and limbs. He was frighteningly warm. Mei Lin had no thermometer, but experience suggested his fever was well over a hundred degrees. At the feel of the cool liquid on his skin, his eyes fluttered, and his limbs began to flail. "No, no. Just relax for now," Mei Lin soothed. "No need to get up yet." As he became more alert, she alternated sponging him off with helping him to drink. By the time her water bottle was empty he was able to open his eyes, but he still made no effort to speak.

"Do you think you can make it back up onto the bed, with some help?" she asked. From what she could see of his leg in the shadow of the door, the cut had indeed become infected. The entire line of stitches was swollen and puffed, and he flinched violently whenever his calf was touched or bumped. She couldn't make out the wound's color and was anxious to get him off the floor and into better light. His bed was in a brighter area and a propane lamp was mounted on the wall beside it.

His hazy eyes looked from Mei Lin to the mattress a few feet away. Then he nodded, seemingly understanding. She moved behind him and hooked her arms under his, then braced her feet and attempted to lift him. He was able to pull his feet under him and assist her, although he tensed whenever the infected leg bore weight. It was an awkward dance, but eventually they managed to move him over and up onto the mattress.

While the man rested from his exertion, eyes closed and breathing heavily, Mei Lin turned on the propane lamp and studied him more closely. His age was hard to determine. His gray hair and beard were thin, his skin was heavily weathered, and he sported an unusual number of healed scars. His muscle tone was still quite good, leading her to believe he was no older than his early seventies and up to now had been in reasonably good health. But the current condition of his wound was troubling. The tissue around the stitches was grossly swollen and discolored — bright red with a sickly yellowish tinge — and the lower end was draining a small amount of pus.

"Your cut is infected," Mei Lin told him as she straightened the sheets and arranged his limbs more comfortably. "You need medical attention, and immediately." The man made no response. "Can you hear me?"

He nodded slowly, but declined to open his eyes. Mei Lin took his vitals again and felt an unfamiliar sense of professional panic. She had faced many clinical situations that were at least as dire as this man's, and not once had she lost her cool. But never before had she been so completely alone, with no staff, no supervising MD, and no option of calling an ambulance.

She knew what needed to happen. He needed IV antibiotics and fluids, perhaps even surgical drainage of the wound — none of which she had the equipment to provide. She could run to the Torpins' place right now and have Amanda call for help, but she feared what would happen in the hour or so he would be left alone. As bleary as the man was, he could burn himself with the heating water in the kettle or even stumble into the fireplace. She could put out the fire before she left and carry some water back with her from the Torpins' house, but she couldn't carry much, and any delay on her part could be disastrous. With his fever raging and no clean water to drink, his condition could deteriorate rapidly.

She made a decision. He needed more water, and he needed it now. He also needed the antibiotics and acetaminophen that were in her jacket pocket, but he couldn't swallow them until he was more alert. Her best course of action would be to boil up a supply of water as quickly as possible, rehydrate him to the best of her ability, and try to get a dose of medication in him. Then, and only then, could she leave him alone long enough to go for help.

She moved to the hearth and stoked the fire. Once upon a time, she thought she would enjoy working more independently. She had liked the thought of being a decision maker as well as an order taker, and immediately after nursing school she'd entered advanced training to become a nurse practitioner. She had envisioned herself as a Sandra Gruber type, providing care to geriatric patients in areas where MDs were scarce.

Texas had changed her mind.

Mr. Smith let out a mumbling sound and thrashed. "Don't take them," his rusty voice croaked. "Don't. I can't—"

Mei Lin left the fire, collected more cool rags, and pulled the only chair in the cabin up to his bedside. "Easy," she said softly as she sponged off his forehead. "Lay still for now. No need to get up."

In his delirium, he appeared oblivious. "My boys... No, please... I need... you can't! No!" His agitation increased. His eyes remained closed, but his face was a mask of anguish. "My boys," he repeated, rocking his frame restlessly from side to side. "No!"

Mei Lin felt a stab of pain in her heart. She watched helplessly, her cool cloths no match for his self-imposed nightmare. Whether he was remembering a past horror or fearing a future one, she had no idea. Either way, he was clearly suffering. "Your boys are here," she soothed, knowing he would remember none of this later. "They're fine, I promise. You rest now."

His thrashing movement began to slow. Mei Lin looked anxiously toward the kettle. Had water ever boiled more slowly?

Her patient mumbled something else. She couldn't understand him, but the look of agony on his face had been replaced with a small smile. "*My* boys," he said clearly.

Then he lapsed back into sleep.

Chapter 7

"It's smaller than I remember," Thane said as he looked through the glass display case at the Mendenhall Glacier visitor's center in Juneau.

"Yeah, well, you're bigger than it remembers," Dave Markov quipped beside him.

"No doubt," Thane laughed. He had not been inside the visitor's center for a very long time. The bear in the display was a taxidermist's rendering of an animal that had been killed in a car accident in 1998. It had been preserved and mounted here because it was a "glacier bear," a recessive color morph of the local subspecies of black bear. Glacier bears had "blue" coats, shades of silver and gray that glistened in the sunlight, and they were extremely rare.

"Sometime before I die, I'm *going* to see one," Thane asserted.

Dave, a thin, nearly bald man in his late fifties, chuckled sadly. "Yeah, well, you'd better get working on that. As many bears as I see around the bay every year, you'd think I'd have run into one by now. But no. I'm beginning to think there are fewer glacier bears than there used to be. With the ice fields melting, the subspecies are mingling more. Eventually that'll dilute the gene to nothing."

Thane didn't disagree, although he wished he could. He hated the thought of the glacier bears dying out. Some of his fondest memories from childhood were of the times his father and grandfather had taken him and his brother to Yakutat, a small fishing village on the coast between Juneau and Anchorage. Yakutat had the highest density of glacier bears in the region, and for Thane and Jason, the trip was like a pilgrimage. His grandfather had been telling stories of the legendary bears since their dad was a kid, and searching for a "blue bear" was a family obsession. They never saw one, on that trip or any other, but the quest was always fun.

"I remember the first time I saw this display," Thane said as he reflected. "My dad had just died. I felt bad that he never had the chance to see it."

Dave put a hand on Thane's shoulder, as he'd been doing since Thane was a gangly boy of fourteen. Dave had had to reach up to do it, even back then. "I'm sure he's seen plenty of them. What good is heaven without bears? Too boring."

Thane smiled gratefully. The bear in the display was posed as if it were walking, its neck extended and nose in the air, sniffing the breeze. One front paw was raised, as if it had just smelled something and was about to stand up on its hind legs to see it. Its coat was a light silvery gray over the back and around the neck, its legs and head were dusky, and its paws and muzzle were brown. How many times had Thane's father tucked him and Jason into bed with stories of hiking through the Alaskan bush and meeting up with a bear just like this one?

If Thane could move up here and work out of Juneau, he'd have at least some chance of seeing one someday. But Dave was right — it was a long shot. Even back when the blue-coated bears were supposedly more common, many people, including Thane's grandfather, spent their whole lives in the area without ever coming across one. Today, naturalists and photographers came to Yakutat and Glacier Bay from all over the world to try their luck. But even on those rare occasions when a blue bear was spotted, the exact location of the animal was usually kept secret. The photographers were proprietary with their wares, and as for everyone else — well, the prospect of such a rare pelt inevitably attracted trophy hunters, and no one wanted that. Not even other trophy hunters.

"We'd better head out to the airport now," Dave suggested.

Thane nodded, then reluctantly turned from the display. He hoped he would be back soon. His friend had gone over and above in assisting with Thane's job hunt: they'd spent Sunday morning meeting Dave's current coworkers with the National

Park Service at Glacier Bay, Sunday night hanging out with his former coworkers from the state Fish and Game office in Juneau, and this morning meeting up with some of the local Forest Service rangers. Making a side trip to Mendenhall Glacier had been pure indulgence on Thane's part, and Dave needed to drop him off at the airport and then fly home to Gustavus himself.

"Yep, let's hit it," Thane agreed. He tried to speak with the same cheerful, optimistic tone that had come so naturally to him all weekend. But as his return to Vancouver — and Vanessa — drew nearer, cheer was harder to come by.

Mei Lin looked at her watch, guiltily wishing for a storm to blow up at sea that would force Jesse Torpin to end his fishing trip early. Morning had turned to afternoon, and with each passing hour her internal debate over whether to stay or go for help had grown more difficult. Stanley Smith's fever raged on. It took constant attention to get him to sip as much water as possible during his lucid periods, and he still wasn't cogent enough to safely swallow the pills he needed. Over and over she weighed the chances of getting him hydrated with oral fluids against the risk that more appropriate IV fluids, no matter how fast she ran through the woods, would take too long in coming.

She continued to replace the wet cloths on his face, arms, chest, and legs with cooler ones, and kept a close watch on his level of alertness. He had been dozing uncomfortably long now, and she was glad when his eyelids fluttered. "You need to wake up, Stanley," she urged. She usually addressed her patients as Mr. or Ms. until she knew them better, a show of respect most people appreciated. But since he was delirious, she thought his first name might be more effective. "You need to drink more, all right?"

His head moved back and forth on the pillow, his eyes still half-lidded. "Don't kill me," he murmured. "Don't shoot... I can't save him. I can't! Leave them alone!"

Mei Lin attempted to soothe him, but he only grew more agitated. "Bombs... the children! No, no more. Too much blood. Butchers! They don't care... Can't somebody... can't anybody feed them?"

He had been babbling similar phrases for hours, and Mei Lin couldn't help but be affected by the horrors he must be imagining. He spoke of violence that sounded like a war zone: destruction, disease, dismemberment, and death. He seemed particularly affected by the plight of nameless children and he became angry at any mention of food. He was old enough to have fought in the Vietnam War, but Mei Lin heard nothing specific to confirm that's where his mind was. Once or twice he spoke of the heat, but he also mentioned sandstorms. Eventually she had given up any attempt to make sense of his ramblings and focused on getting him back to the present. Waking up feverish and miserable with a stranger in his house would not be pleasant, but with such scenes constantly playing out in his mind, the real world should be a comparative utopia.

"Open your eyes, Stanley," she ordered. "Can you hear me? Stanley?" Her heart skipped a beat as his eyes fully opened and his thrashing ceased. His gaze roamed aimlessly in the air for a moment, then came to rest on her face. His eyes struggled to focus.

"Wang Li?" he rasped.

Mei Lin grabbed the pills off his side table, determined not to miss an opportunity. "My name is Mei Lin, and I'm a nurse," she replied. "You've got a nasty fever right now. Can you sit up and drink a little for me?"

She helped him to prop up, and he cooperated beautifully. She raised the cup to his lips and he put his hands over hers, then gulped. After a few seconds, she pulled the cup away. "Do you think you can swallow some pills?" she asked. "It's really important that you take this medication as soon as possible."

He continued to stare at her, though it was clear from his constant blinking that he could not see her well. "They found her body on the rubbish heap," he said miserably.

Mei Lin's insides twisted. It was bad enough to have a raging fever and a throbbing leg... why must the poor man remember such horrible things in the midst of it? "Can you take this?" she asked, placing a pill in his hand and closing his fingers over it. To her delight, he raised the tablet to his lips and reached out his other hand for the cup.

"Perfect!" she praised when he'd swallowed the antibiotic. He had no idea how significant that small action might be to him. "Now, another one," she prompted. He took the second half of the dose with equal ease and she prayed he wasn't allergic. He was in no state to be interrogated about his medical history and at this point she had only the one option. Thankfully, the drug Sandra Gruber had prescribed was relatively unlikely to cause a serious reaction.

Mei Lin decided to go for broke. She had no idea how much longer he would be even this alert. "Now, just one more, and you'll be done," she encouraged, extending an over-the-counter fever reducer. When he swallowed that pill, too, she felt like jumping for joy. "That's wonderful!" she praised instead, smiling broadly.

He glanced down toward his swollen leg. "Hell fire," he mumbled.

"Yes, I'm sure it feels like that," she sympathized. "Your cut has gotten infected. But you're going to be all right. Do you think you can drink some more?"

Stanley managed a few more sips, but his spurt of energy quickly waned. He lay back on his pillow and stared at the ceiling. "I didn't mean it. I'm so sorry. It was all my fault!" His voice rose in anguish. If he weren't so dehydrated, Mei Lin suspected his reddened eyes would be teary.

"It wasn't your fault," she said automatically. "It was an accident. Nobody's blaming you. Rest now. Everything will be better soon."

Her words seemed to soothe him. His eyelids closed, his muscles relaxed, and within a minute he was snoozing again.

She put down the cup, rose, and stretched her limbs. Her patient was nowhere near out of the woods, but if he continued to drink and take the medication, he at least had a fighting chance.

She looked down at the dog, who had collapsed on the floor beside the bed shortly after she arrived and had remained in a dead sleep ever since. Had the frightened mutt been up all the previous night, watching over his master and waiting for help? If so, she was honored by his vote of confidence.

A smattering of raindrops struck the roof of the cabin, and she glanced out the window. Within seconds, a deluge followed. "Oh, no. I didn't really want it to storm!" she lamented, crossing to open the door and look out. All day the sky had settled for an innocuous light gray, but now it had darkened to a threatening slate color, and the rain it was producing was not the usual soft trickle, but a steady downpour.

She cursed beneath her breath. Nothing prevented her from going for help in the rain, but if it continued falling this heavily, the low visibility and slippery footing would slow her down.

"Run!" Stanley yelled, making Mei Lin jump a foot. "Run, now!" She closed the door and whirled around to see him thrashing again. Before she could move even the few feet to his bed, his arms flailed so wildly that one of his hands struck the water pitcher and knocked it off the table. As precious sterilized water began to pour out onto the floor, Mei Lin made a dive for the pitcher and righted it, only to receive a glancing blow to the head from the hard plastic cup that flew through the air next.

"Cut it off!" he yelled, sitting up and gripping his knee above the swelling. "Cut it off, now!"

The awakened dog ran circles around Mei Lin's feet, whining with distress. A crack of thunder split the air, and a dazed Stanley reacted by swinging both legs off the bed. "Get down! It's the Ruskies!"

So much for leaving him by himself. "Easy, Stanley," Mei Lin soothed, approaching him with caution. "Everything's going to be all right."

She prayed she wasn't wrong.

Chapter 8

Thane plopped down on one of the many large logs strewn across the beach that edged the University of British Columbia. The spot was one of his happy places. Here he could watch for orcas, listen to the gulls, and gaze across the Strait of Georgia toward Vancouver Island, the place he'd called home for the majority of his life. He didn't care much for Vancouver proper, or for any other large city, but if he had to spend two years in academia, UBC was a good place to do it. The campus incorporated the Pacific Spirit Regional Park, an urban wonderland of relatively undisturbed forest, as well as the stretch of beach he was enjoying now. Whenever he'd had his fill of confining walls and artificial light, he had always been able to take a hike. Literally.

Still, he was glad his time in the city was coming to a close. He was ready to get back to the real world and real work, and he had high hopes of landing a job in Juneau with the folks at Fish and Game. The current mammal biologist was retiring, and as far as Thane could tell, no shoo-in was waiting. There would be plenty of applicants, as always, but with his freshly minted research degree and Dave Markov's recommendation, Thane thought he stood a decent chance. He certainly hoped so, because none of the people who held the equivalent positions in Western Canada were retiring anytime soon.

As soon as he turned in the final revisions to his thesis, he could move up to his grandparents' place in Juneau, establish Alaska residency, and get the ball rolling. But first, he had to deal with Vanessa.

Even the thought made him wince. He'd managed to avoid her thus far, but only by coming straight to the beach from the airport. As soon as he returned to their mutual apartment building, the agony would begin. She'd been texting him all day, asking when he would get home. He'd been intentionally vague about the timing, but such tactics rarely worked with a control freak like Vanessa. She had probably already checked the flight schedules.

He envisioned her driving around the faculty lots, looking for his car. The possibility was not as far-fetched as it sounded. She was employed by UBC herself, in human resources, and she seemed to know where he usually parked, as well as where he liked to hike. But he knew she would never follow him down to Wreck Beach. For one thing, it was "clothing optional," which made her uncomfortable. But what she really hated was the 473 steps it took to get here from the main campus up on the cliff.

He heard a ringtone noise and tensed. His mother was calling. Vanessa, he could put off for a while, but ignoring a call from Margot Tremain had only one result: greater grief down the road. He had been relieved not to hear from her all weekend, since he suspected she already knew about Vanessa's proposal. Her calling him now was not a good sign.

"Hey, Mom," he said as jovially as possible. "What's up?"

"Nothing, dear. Just the usual," Margot said crisply. For a woman who'd spent nearly all her adult life in a mill town like Port McNeill, her speech was oddly erudite. Thane had never understood why she bothered. She'd been a respected pharmacist at the district hospital for years; everyone knew she was smart and professional. Nevertheless, she had always placed a high value on both speech and poise, much to the chagrin of her two laidback sons. "I was calling to see how you are," she explained. "Is anything exciting happening?"

Oh, yeah, she knew, he thought. "I just got back from Juneau," he answered. "I spent some time with Dave. It's looking pretty good for a job up there."

She was silent for a moment. Despite her desire to sound like a woman of the world, Margot Tremain had no desire to live anywhere besides Vancouver Island, and she would prefer that Thane and his brother lived there, too. Preferably with wives of her choosing and litters of grandchildren. Thane would be perfectly happy on the island if he could get a better job, and he looked forward to having a family someday. But his mother's frequent intrusions into his personal life were not appreciated. "So far away?" she lamented.

"It's two short flights. You used to love going to Juneau."

She made no response to that. She never liked to talk about the time before his dad died. "Well, what's happening in Vancouver?" she baited. "Anything new?"

Thane stifled a sigh. No way was he saying anything to his mother before he spoke with Vanessa. He owed the woman who had proposed to him that much. "Nothing to speak of. How's the *Sparecrow* coming?"

"Slowly," Margot answered, referring to his stepfather's newest boat-rebuilding project. *The Crow* had been Doug Tremain's pride and joy as long as Thane could remember. But if one boat was good, two was better — particularly for a restless retiree with plenty of time on his hands. "Your father is determined to get it in the water this summer, but I have my doubts."

Thane tensed. He was never quick to anger, but his mother had a gift for pushing his few hot buttons. The way she said "your father" in reference to Doug was one of them. Thane had nothing against his stepfather; they had always gotten along well and were genuinely fond of each other. But there was an unspoken message of insistence in his mother's tone, a demand that her sons forget they ever had *another* father.

Thane would never forget. He had been thirteen when Stanley Buchanan was kidnapped from outside a medical conference in Chicago and then ruthlessly murdered. For the sensitive young teen, losing the father he idolized had been a crippling blow. But his mother's behavior at the time had unsettled him further. Margot had grieved openly at the funeral, accepted by one and all as the hapless victim, the bereft and suffering wife. Only Thane had seemed able to see that her copious tears were disingenuous. His mother's unspoken animosity towards his father had been always been plain to his eyes; in fact, fear of their divorcing had nagged his entire childhood. He was disturbed and confused by her theatrics; but even as he tried to give her odd expression of grief the benefit of the doubt, the weeks that followed had brought even stranger behavior. Margot had grown increasingly tight-lipped at any mention of her late husband, until one day it seemed she no longer wanted to remember him at all. Worse still, she hadn't wanted his sons to remember him, either. Within months she had uprooted them all to begin a new life in Port McNeill, wiping away the past as if everything the boys had experienced in Seattle was a misery better left forgotten.

"Listen, Mom," Thane said as amiably as he could fake. He wished he could purge his soul of the bitterness it still carried, but dredging up the old wounds never ceased to affect him. "I've got to get going. I'll come up and see you guys in a week or two. Okay? Tell Doug I'll give him a hand with that boat."

His mother agreed and got off the line. But she did not sound happy about it.

Thane rose and began walking up the beach, picking his way over the stretch of smooth gray boulders that were not yet covered by the incoming tide. His mind was troubled, as always happened when he revisited that part of his past. Whatever excuses he might make for his mother's behavior after the tragedy, her refusal to acknowledge her sons' right to remember their own father confounded him. The rapid disposal of Stanley Buchanan's belongings and the disappearance of his photographs from their walls and mantel were hardly subtle gestures on Margot's part. Nor was the immediate resumption of her maiden name. When she had married Doug a year later, her usurpation of the simple phrase "your father" had added insult to injury. But any protest from her sons had been willfully ignored.

Thane's stepfather, in contrast, had been a model of parental concern. Doug had explained to the boys that their mother avoided the subject because talking about their father was too painful for her. He assured them that they could always talk to him; that although he had never met their father, he knew Stanley must have been a wonderful person, because he'd raised such incredible sons.

Yes, Doug Tremain was a fine man. He'd made all their lives easier, in many ways. But Thane's good relationship with him had no bearing on whether he missed his own father.

"There you are!" a chipper female voice called out, driving a chill down Thane's spine. He looked up.

No. He could not believe it. Was Vanessa really so desperate for his answer that she had trekked down 473 stairs to a beach she hated when she knew it was 473 steps back up again?

Holy hell. He had underestimated her.

"I'm so glad I found you!" she cried, moving toward him. She stepped up on a rock and teetered precariously before catching her balance. She was wearing heels.

Thane suppressed another sigh. If he hadn't witnessed a good chunk of the process himself, he would never believe that Vanessa had been raised on the rural end of Vancouver Island. "Stay there," he insisted, holding out a palm. "I'm coming."

She clapped her hands gleefully. "I've missed you so much!"

Thane could think of no honest, yet kind reply. It was time to get this nightmare over with.

Chapter 9

Behind the omnipresent clouds, the Alaskan sun was well on its way down to the horizon from whence it came when Stanley Smith's fever finally broke. An exhausted and relieved Mei Lin smiled as she placed a hand against his forehead and felt the difference. After so many fitful hours of shaking and sweating, he was at last sleeping peacefully. She was hopeful that he was responding to the antibiotic and that, when he woke again, he would be lucid enough for her to leave him for a while.

She stood up and stretched, then realized how hungry she was. If she didn't eat something before running for help, she might very well collapse on the way. Turning towards the wall by the stove, she examined the contents of the cabin's built-in shelves. Fixing a proper meal from the dried beans and bags of rice and pasta was beyond the scope of her patience, but as soon as she found a tin of granola she poured out a serving and began to munch. The shelves were stocked with dehydrated milk, pancake mix, jerky, oils, honey, spices, and an assortment of nuts and dried fruits. A half bottle of vodka sat covered with dust, indicating that Stanley probably wasn't a drinker.

Mei Lin heard a noise behind her. She turned to see her patient raised up on his elbows, blinking at her in confusion. "Who are you?" he croaked.

She crossed to his bedside and sat back down. His eyes focused on her face, and she felt a fleeting sense of recognition, though she couldn't think who he reminded her of. "My name is Mei Lin Sullivan," she answered. "I'm a registered nurse." *And sort of a nurse practitioner,* she failed to add. She had earned the appropriate master's degree, completed the necessary clinical work, and even passed her national exam. The only credential she lacked was state certification. "The wound on your leg has gotten infected, and you've had a high fever. How are you feeling?"

He continued to stare at her, confused. "Leg hurts," he said with effort. "Thirsty."

"Not surprising," she said pertly, propping up the pillows behind him and then reaching for the pitcher. She poured him a cup of water. "As soon as you're able to drink by yourself, I'll run to the Torpins' place and we'll figure out how to get you to the hospital. Do you have insurance that would cover an emergency evacuation?"

He reached out a shaky hand, took the cup she extended, and pulled it to his lips. His movements were slow and awkward, but eventually he drained it dry. "No hospital," he rasped, his eyes closing again.

Mei Lin felt a flicker of panic, but tried not to show it. "Nobody likes the hospital, Mr. Smith. But if this infection spreads to your vital organs, your situation could get very serious very quickly. Your life could be in danger."

His eyes opened again, but his expression conveyed more vexation than fear. He attempted to pull his head and shoulders up off the pillow, presumably to get a look at his leg for himself. Mei Lin put an arm behind his back to support him and pulled away the sheet. One dose of antibiotic had made no difference to the wound's grisly appearance — if anything, it looked worse. The entire back surface of his calf was red and firm with swelling. The edges of the cut were threatening to separate, and a whitish-yellow discharge oozed out the seam.

He made a sound of disgust and fell back onto the pillows, weakened even by the brief effort of leaning forward.

"You're only doing as well as you are because you've got one dose of antibiotics in you," Mei Lin explained, covering his legs with the sheet again. "But you need to be in a hospital."

She ticked off all the reasons why, explaining the gravity of the situation as simply and as sensitively as she could, but he did not appear to be listening. Whether he was unable to stay awake or was blocking out the unwelcome information, she couldn't tell. "Mr. Smith," she tried again. "I need to leave you alone for a little while to bring help. All right?"

He spoke without opening his eyes. "No hospital," he repeated, weakly but clearly. "You're a sweet girl. But if I die, I die."

Mei Lin stared at him in surprise. She was not unsympathetic to a patient's right to refuse treatment, even if that meant hastening death. She could imagine several end-of-life scenarios where she might choose the same option herself. But Stanley Smith was no hospice case. He was an otherwise healthy man who, before this injury, had probably been more physically fit than the majority of men his age. As far as she could tell, the infection was the only thing that stood between him and another ten or even twenty productive years of life.

"Sorry," she said firmly. "No one dies on my watch unless they're already terminally ill." *Except for Mariel Gonzalez,* an inner voice taunted. A flash of pain shot through her, but she gritted her teeth and tried to ignore it. "At least let Nurse Gruber and I treat you at home while you think about it. We can get you fully rehydrated, clean that wound up, and make sure you get the proper antibiotics and pain relief. You'll be much more comfortable."

His eyes remained closed, but he shook his head slowly. "Don't bother."

Mei Lin's concern grew. He was falling asleep again, and if his last words to her were to refuse treatment, he would put her in a terrible ethical bind. "Mr. Smith!" she ordered, squeezing his shoulder. "I need you to stay awake!" But it was no use. She could tell from the limpness of his muscles that he was no longer hearing her. She slumped back in her chair with frustration. She could only hope that the next time he woke, he would be thinking more clearly.

She rose, put more water in the kettle, and stoked the fire. She'd been doing so continuously in order to replenish his reserve of clean drinking water, but the process was painfully slow. *Everybody's going to die sometime, and there's not a damn thing you can do about it,* a grating voice echoed in her brain. She wasn't sure what had reminded her of Tina Booras, RN, unless it was the red-hot glowing wood she was poking at. The woman's image did have a certain association with eternal hellfire in Mei Lin's mind.

Mrs. Gonzalez seems very agitated and she's sweating profusely, Mei Lin had reported to the oncoming charge nurse as she finished documenting the symptoms in the patient record. *But she doesn't have a fever, and there's no history of similar symptoms. Should I call Dr. Castille before I go?*

No, the more experienced, middle-aged nurse had replied with a sigh. *Let me have a look at her first, then we'll see. She's a bit of a hypochondriac, you know.*

Mei Lin had not been pleased by that response. Tina had a warped definition of hypochondria, which Mei Lin had pointed out before. Hypochondriacs were people who imagined symptoms for illnesses they didn't have. The patients at Silverson Elder Care all had genuine medical issues, which was why they were in a skilled-nursing facility in the first place. Besides which, Mrs. Gonzalez was not "imagining" perspiration so heavy her sheets needed to be changed.

But Nurse Booras was in charge for the next eight hours; Mei Lin's shift had ended at eleven. She'd left the facility that night both concerned and puzzled, but confident that whether the charge nurse put in an emergency call or not, Dr. Castille would sort things out in the morning. Mei Lin had documented her concerns appropriately and the geriatrician was highly regarded. By the time Dr. Castille made her rounds, however, Mrs. Gonzalez was dead.

Mei Lin turned away from the fire. Her heart felt like lead. Why did she keep doing this to herself?

"Stanley?" a man's voice called from outside the cabin. "Mei Lin?"

The dog jolted up from a sound sleep and ran to the door, and Mei Lin hastened across the cabin to open it. The dog raced out with her behind him. "Jesse!" she exclaimed, her heart lightened. "You can't imagine how happy I am to see you right now!"

Jesse Torpin, a strapping man in his mid-thirties, took a second to greet the ecstatic dog before looking up at Mei Lin. Jesse had light blond hair and an unshaven face that was coarse rather than handsome, but his easy manner and friendly smile showed his warm heart. "I'm glad you're all right," he said with relief. "Amanda was getting worried. She figured something had to be wrong with you or Stanley, one or the other. How is he?"

Jesse stepped up to join her on the porch, and the dog nearly tripped him twice, stepping on his feet and bumping up against his wet rain pants. "Easy, Kibbe," he soothed, pronouncing the name KIB-ee. "What's gotten into you, boy?"

"His master gave him a scare," Mei Lin answered, explaining what she had found at the cabin.

"How is he now?" Jesse asked. "Does he need a medevac?"

"Yes," she answered. "But he's refusing treatment."

Jesse swore under his breath, then took off his wet things and headed inside. Mei Lin followed him into the cabin, where Stanley continued to sleep peacefully. Jesse felt the older man's forehead. "Doesn't seem too bad."

"He took a dose of antibiotic that Sandra sent up with me, as well as a fever reducer. But that was before he was alert enough to argue about it."

Jesse sighed and stepped back. "You know, most people who live alone like he does move up here to get away from everything. They don't want interference in their business, no matter what. When Stanley first moved in he was depressed as hell — I half expected he'd take a pistol to his head before the first snow. But when Ed's dog had that litter, he got all excited — he was the first one in line for a pup. Since then he's been different. Cheerier. I started thinking maybe he was feeling better, that he might be thinking twice about living like he does. I guess I was wrong."

"You could still be right," Mei Lin said optimistically. "I can't believe he really wants to die. Certainly not like this."

Jesse shrugged. "He's a hard one to get to know. We only see him when he's making a supply run. He never comes down just to socialize, but if the boys are out when he comes through he always stops to toss a ball with them. He's tough to figure. Friendly enough, but doesn't like to talk about himself."

Mei Lin was puzzled. A person didn't withdraw from nearly all human contact without a reason. "Do you know if he has any family?"

"Not that he's ever mentioned to me," Jesse answered. "Amanda asked him once if he had any kids or grandkids, and he said no. I asked point blank when he first moved in if he wanted to give us a name or a phone number to keep handy in case anything happened to him, and he said no to that, too. Didn't seem interested in the 'what-ifs.'"

Jesse cast a long, sober look at Stanley, then turned back to Mei Lin. "Well, how can I help here? You want to take off and let me stay with him overnight?"

"No," Mei Lin said without thought. "I can stay. He needs a trained nurse, whether he wants one or not."

Jesse seemed surprised. "You sure you're okay being out here all by yourself? I mean, I've got no reason to believe Stanley's dangerous in any way. But we don't really know him."

Mei Lin smiled. "Actually, I have quite a bit of experience when it comes to dealing with the old and the cantankerous. This one is far too weak to pose a threat to me, even if I did think he was dangerous, which I don't. I'll be fine." She shoved aside any nagging concerns about her poor character judgment, knowing that her assessment in this case was not all subjective. She knew that Stanley Smith spoiled his dog and played ball with children. After spending all day in his cabin she also knew that he wasn't a drinker, that he possessed no drugs, porn, or unnecessary weapons, and that his favorite books were a world atlas, a dictionary, and a Michael Crichton novel signed by the author. No, she wasn't afraid.

"He's lucky to have you around," Jesse praised. "Not just any nurse would have hiked out all this way on a hunch. And you were right about his condition, besides."

Mei Lin wished she had been wrong. "If you could let Sandra know what's going on and ask her to come up and check on him tomorrow morning, that would be great. In the meantime I'll keep him comfortable and try to get another dose of antibiotic in him."

Jesse looked at his watch. "I can make another trip up. You'll need a decent dinner and something to sleep on. Anything else I can bring you? Amanda can drive over to your place and pick up anything you need."

Mei Lin nodded with appreciation. She had the feeling she was in for a very long night.

Chapter 10

Vanessa sat curled up on the far end of Thane's couch, sobbing. She'd gone through half a box of tissues already and showed no sign of stopping.

Thane was at a loss. He had tried to explain, in as gentle a way possible, that he did not return her feelings and did not want to marry her. That feat would have been difficult enough if he didn't also have to convince her that they'd never actually been dating in the first place.

"It's just that I thought marriage was the direction we were headed," she gulped, repeating the same argument she'd brought up multiple times already. "If you didn't feel the same, you should have told me ages ago!"

Thane found himself wishing for a false fire alarm. A tornado warning. An air raid siren. Anything that could spare him further such agony. He truly didn't know what to do for the woman. If anyone else — and he did mean *anyone* else — was this distraught in his presence, he would pull them into his arms for one of his famed Buchanan bear hugs. But not Vanessa. She had already misinterpreted catching a movie and eating out as foreplay; if he so much as touched her arm she might slap him with a paternity suit.

"I've explained it every way I know how," he replied tiredly, wishing to hell they had started this conversation in her apartment, so that he could leave. He'd made his answer clear almost an hour ago now, but she showed not the slightest inclination of moving from where she sat. "I'm sorry if there was a misunderstanding. We should have talked more all along, I guess."

"I talked plenty!" she spat back at him. "All you ever do is listen!"

Now, there was a complaint Thane hadn't heard before.

Under the circumstances, any new material was welcome. But he had no intention of rebutting. He just wanted to wrap things up. "I'm sorry," he said for the fiftieth time. "I understand if you're upset with me. But I can't change the situation. We can continue to be friends if that's what you want. It's not like I'm trying to avoid ever seeing you again." He stopped himself for a moment, assessing the truth of that statement. Never seeing her again did sound appealing. But since he had no hope of achieving that outcome, he wasn't lying, either. Their parents were neighbors — they couldn't avoid each other forever if they tried. "I'm just making sure we're on the same page," he finished.

She raised her head from her hands and sniffed. "So you think maybe our relationship could turn into more... over time?"

Thane resisted a strong urge to yank his hair out by the fistful. "No," he said firmly. "That's never going to happen, Vanessa. I hope you can accept that."

"Do I have a choice?" she screeched. On the upside, she also stood.

Thane shot up along with her. "I think it would be better if we both had a chance to cool off," he suggested mildly, walking toward his door. "We can talk more later if you like."

Assessment: False. He would avoid further discussion at all costs. If you waved a plane ticket in his face, he would jump on the next jet to Siberia. He felt slightly guilty for lying to her, but after blinking back at him for a second, she did start moving toward his door, so he kept his mouth shut.

"I don't know what your mother is going to say," she repeated. Whether Vanessa intended the statement to be a threat, he wasn't sure and didn't want to know. Since he didn't respond to threats, he didn't respond at all. Instead, he opened his door for her.

Her face suffused with indignation, and she opened her mouth as if to repeat something else. But then, abruptly and mercifully, she pursed her lips and stomped out.

Thane quickly — but softly — closed the door behind her. He heard a muffled cry of anguish, then a stifled whining noise that gradually petered out as she moved toward the elevator. And then, finally, everything went quiet.

He stood at the door a moment, breathing deep. Then he marched into his bedroom, pulled his luggage down off the shelf, and started packing. He could finish the final revisions to his thesis anywhere as long as he had his laptop and the internet. There were a few loose ends he needed to tie up on campus, but those could be settled in a day. Then he was out of here. His lease ran out in a couple weeks anyway.

He paused, wondering suddenly if his impending departure was what had nudged Vanessa into lunacy. She had been quirky as a girl and was erratic as a woman, but her behavior the last week defied explanation. She'd been flirty with him ever since he moved to Vancouver, but he had never responded and she had never pressed the issue. In fact, she had gone out of her way on several occasions to let him know that she was dating other men. The last couple months he'd seen her even less than usual. So where the hell had this come from?

He shook his head. He was moving on. As soon as the tourist season ended, the lakeside bungalow in Juneau that he and his brother had inherited from their grandparents would open up, and he could move to Alaska. In the meantime, he would crash at Jason's place in Tofino. Vanessa knew where his brother lived, of course. But she wouldn't hassle Thane there. Would she?

His gut twisted with misery. All he could do was hope.

Mei Lin lay down on the thick bedroll Jesse had brought, grateful for the small touch of comfort. Amanda had sent up a huge helping of beef casserole, which had been fabulous even at room temperature, and Mei Lin felt as though she could sleep for a week. As soon as she arranged the covers over herself, Kibbe jumped on her legs with enthusiasm, turned around twice, then lay down with his head across her shin.

She scratched his ears with a chuckle. He might be worthless as a watchdog, but the mutt did make excellent company. She was just closing her eyes and trying to relax when her patient in the bed began to mumble and thrash. It was the first Stanley had stirred in hours, and she lay in the dark and listened to see if he was truly awake or only dreaming.

"No use," he muttered, his voice sounding irritated. "Arm's worthless! I'm worthless..." his voice turned despondent. "Let me die. I told you... It was my fault. I didn't..." His mumbling ceased, and his body stilled. He was asleep again.

Mei Lin felt a pang as the guilt in his voice struck a sympathetic chord. So, he had done something he regretted, did he? Something so horrible he felt like he didn't deserve to live.

Yes. She could relate to that.

Stop it! The voices of loved ones echoed in her head. Absolutely everyone had told her that she had nothing to feel guilty about where Mariel Gonzalez was concerned. Even the facility's lawyer had assured her that there was no legal basis under which any of the events occurring at Silverson Elder Care could be laid at her doorstep. And rationally, she did understand that nothing in her professional actions had been inappropriate. But her conscience remained unassuaged.

She listened another few minutes to see if Stanley would wake again. But he remained still. The only sounds to be heard were the huffing breaths of the dozing dog and the quiet patter of raindrops on the roof.

It was ironic that Stanley Smith's talking in his sleep would keep her up, since she was famous for doing the same thing herself. The lifelong habit had merely amused her sister, but it had caused serious trouble with her ex-fiancé. *Who's Ted?* Josh would demand some random morning. *What did you mean by 'leave me alone?' And who were you talking to about a bra?*

Mei Lin's lips twisted into a smirk as she remembered how aggravated Josh would get, particularly when she insisted she had no idea what he was referring to. She wasn't lying to him;

she rarely remembered her dreams. But the insecure Josh had always been sure she was hiding something.

Evidently she and Stanley Smith had two things in common: sleep-talking and a nagging sense of guilt. Was it remorse that drove him to refuse treatment? Did he truly want to die?

She mulled over the possibility, wondering what he could have done that was so terrible. She supposed the thought should worry her — make her concerned for her safety. But no angst presented itself. And within minutes, she was asleep.

It was late. Margot Tremain glanced at her phone again, debating whether to pick it up. Thane wouldn't appreciate her calling him; she knew that. He would consider any expression of concern on her part to be an intrusion into his personal life. And she supposed he would be right. He was a thirty-four-year-old man now; he could do what he liked.

She paced about her living room a moment, then grabbed the phone anyway. To hell with it. What were mothers for?

The number rang three times. He was there; she could sense it. He just didn't want to talk to her. She continued to let it ring.

"Hey, Mom," Thane greeted eventually, his half-hearted attempt at cheer not even close to convincing. "What's up?"

"Don't give me that," Margot protested with frustration. "You know very well why I'm calling. I'm sorry to bother you, but I really can't stand it anymore. Could you please explain to me why you've dumped poor Vanessa after all this time? The girl is devastated. You've been together since high school!"

Her son went silent. She hated it when he did that. He had always been sensitive, a deep thinker and a deliberate actor, but his silences bothered her. She wanted to know what was in his head. "Thane?" she prompted finally.

"Do you really want me to explain?" he asked, his voice at last betraying frustration. "Because I will, but only if you'll listen first before arguing with me."

"I am not arguing with you!" Margot argued. Then,

embarrassed, she shut her mouth.

Another silence ensued. "Are you listening?" he asked.

"Yes, I am listening," she replied. "I'm sorry."

"Except for those few months in high school, Vanessa and I have never been 'together,'" he proclaimed. "We've only been friends. Whatever else she imagines is all in her head. I'm afraid she's becoming delusional."

"How can you say that?" Margot exclaimed, speaking before she could think. Resentment flared and her face grew hot. She wanted to be on her son's side, but the issue of men taking sex lightly hit painfully close to home. Particularly when she'd tried so hard to raise her sons otherwise. "Just because you haven't taken your relationship as seriously as Vanessa has doesn't mean she is unbalanced! Surely you've just miscommunicated."

"There was nothing to miscommunicate," Thane said tiredly. "Nothing happened."

Margot's jaw tightened. If sleeping with a woman was 'nothing,' she had officially failed as a mother. How could he be so callous toward Vanessa when the poor girl obviously loved him so much? She would never have expected this from him. From Jason, yes — she'd known since her youngest son hit puberty that he would be hopeless. But Thane? He'd never acted like this before. He was breaking her heart as well as Vanessa's. "I see you're like your father after all," she muttered.

"Which one?" he replied.

Margot went silent. A wave of guilt washed over her as she realized what she had said. It was unforgiveable of her; she had no right conflating her son's situation with her own, ugly past. No matter what had happened with Vanessa, he didn't deserve that. In truth, Thane resembled his stepfather much more than his own flesh and blood. Thank God!

"I'm sorry, honey," she apologized. "I didn't mean that. You're a wonderful person and you know I—"

"And my father wasn't?" he demanded.

Margot's voice faltered. She hated to be put on the spot. She'd always tried to protect her sons, to avoid their being too badly disillusioned. But she was only human, and Thane's endless questions as a teenager had driven her near to madness. She thought he'd gotten over this childish need for hero worship, but apparently she was wrong. Jason had long since let it go — would Thane never do the same? Why, oh why, could he not be happy with Doug as a father?

"It's just that this situation puts me in a very awkward position with both Vanessa and her mother," she replied in a more neutral tone, changing the subject. "We were all expecting a wedding announcement."

She was not surprised when Thane went quiet again. Her eldest had never been one to argue. His way was to state his piece and, if unsuccessful, to check out of the conversation as soon as possible.

"Well, I'm sorry you're all disappointed," he responded. "But I have to go. I'll talk to you later, Mom."

Margot knew when she was beaten. He would discuss the situation no more. She returned his goodbye, hung up, and let out a long, heartfelt sigh. She would never tell him, but in one critical way, Thane Buchanan was very much like his father.

She could never understand either one of them.

Chapter 11

Mei Lin woke the next morning to a dog stepping on her face. She yelped and sprang up.

"Sorry about that," a voice apologized. "Kibbe wants out. I tried to get up a little while ago, but—"

"Oh, no! Don't do that," Mei Lin protested, scrambling toward the door with the dog dancing at her heels. She opened it, watched Kibbe shoot outside, then turned around.

Stanley Smith was sitting up. The crackers she'd left beside his bed last night were gone. His voice was no longer croaky, but sounded almost normal. All of which was good, but Mei Lin's practiced eyes could see other, less positive signs. His forehead was damp, his face was flushed, and his eyes were bright. He was getting feverish again.

"I'm sorry," he said politely, "but... who are you? How did you get here?"

Mei Lin stepped closer and met his gaze. Despite his fever, she could see in his eyes a certain telltale spark of awareness. She smiled, knowing that for the first time, she was talking to him in his conscious entirety. She sat down in the chair beside him and patiently repeated an introduction of herself and the explanation for her presence.

As she spoke, his blue eyes scrutinized her with a wondrous expression, as if he couldn't quite believe she was real. "I don't know what to say," he replied soberly when she had finished. "You've certainly gone above and beyond for a stranger. I appreciate that. Thank you."

"You're welcome, Mr. Smith," she answered, reverting to the formal address. "I'm just glad you're better." Meeting his eyes produced another vague flash of recognition, which puzzled her. Did he remind her of her father? Stanley Smith was older than Tom Sullivan and looked nothing like him. But there was a certain resemblance in the soft, polite way in which both men spoke. Imagining her own father living off the grid with long gray hair and a straggly beard was difficult, but somehow this man seemed equally out of place.

He scrutinized her in turn. "I think I remember seeing you before," he said thoughtfully. "In the store."

"That's right," she agreed with a smile. Perhaps that was the explanation? She crossed to the table and collected his next dose of antibiotic, as well as a pain reliever. Then she moved toward him and extended the pills matter-of-factly while they chatted. "You gave me quite a scare when I arrived yesterday. Not to mention upsetting poor Kibbe." He took the pills from her hand, and she held her breath. His fingers were warm and sweaty. He desperately needed the medicine.

He cringed. "I feel bad about that. Poor Kibbe. He's such a sensitive soul."

Mei Lin poured a cup of water and extended it. "Does the name mean something?"

He cracked a weak grin. "It's a food in the Middle East, like a meatball. When he was a pup, he used to sleep all curled up — looked just like one." He took the cup and sipped from it, but the pills remained in his hand.

Mei Lin was afraid to speak. She wasn't sure if he'd changed his mind about treatment or if he just wasn't paying attention. He sat still for a painfully long amount of time, not looking at her, before he finished the water. Then he set both the empty cup and the pills on his nightstand.

"Don't forget your pills," she reminded casually.

He settled back onto the pillows. "No, thank you."

Mei Lin sucked in a breath. Clearly, he *was* going to be difficult. She needed to tread carefully and play this right. "Why don't you want them?"

He said nothing for a moment. He avoided looking at her. "It was very nice of you to come all the way out here, Mei Lin. Don't think I don't appreciate what you've done. But you have no need to stay. I can take care of myself, now."

Mei Lin steeled herself. Many of the best nurses she knew handled noncompliant patients with hard-hitting sermons and a touch of intimidation, but she'd quickly learned that her own petite, dimpled-cheeked self was hopelessly unconvincing as a bully. However, she did have other means of influence. "I very much doubt that, Mr. Smith," she said softly. "If you don't take the antibiotic you're likely to get worse. Much worse." She relaxed into the chair and poured herself a glass of water. "But you needn't worry about wasting my time," she continued more cheerfully, taking a sip. "I'm happy to keep you company. Since Elsie died I've been terribly lonely, rattling around all alone in that big, gorgeous house of hers. It just doesn't feel the same without her there."

Stanley threw her an expression of surprise. His forehead furrowed briefly, as if he were trying to figure her out. He had made no complaint of pain or discomfort, but the sheen of sweat on his skin and the tightness in his jaw told Mei Lin that he was both feverish and in significant pain. "What happened with Mariel Gonzalez?" he asked.

Mei Lin choked on her water. She sputtered and coughed for nearly a minute before she could draw breath enough to speak. "Excuse me?"

"Sorry," he apologized, a glimmer of amusement dancing behind his fever-bright eyes. "I didn't mean to startle you. But I was a bit restless last night. And you talk in your sleep. You said something about a lawsuit, and you mentioned the name Silverson. I couldn't help but be curious."

Mei Lin's face flamed with heat. Such a turn in the conversation was not in her plan. When most people talked in their sleep, they garbled out broken phrases and indistinct mumbles. What sick-humored fairy had cursed her and only her to enunciate with perfect clarity while unconscious?

"I'm sorry if I heard something I shouldn't," he hastened to add. "But if you'd like to unburden your soul, feel free. I might not have the greatest reputation as a listener, but at the moment I'm a captive audience."

Unburden her soul? Mei Lin's heart raced. What the hell had she said? And furthermore, why should he care? He had been ready to kick her out mere seconds ago! The man was pure enigma. He had the speech and mannerisms of a professor and the appearance of a hermit — adding fatherly concern was too much contradiction to process.

Kibbe jumped up suddenly, placing his front paws on his master's bed. Stanley cried out as one of the dog's claws raked his infected leg through the sheet, and Mei Lin moved swiftly to push the dog away. "Stay down, Kibbe," she said gently, rubbing his ears. "We can pet you from here."

Stanley's face, which had blanched, gradually suffused with color again. He dropped a hand over the side of the bed and the dog moved toward it for a pat. "It's okay, boy," he rasped.

Mei Lin winced at his tone. The unexpected pain must have been intense. He had broken out in a fresh sweat.

"Talk to me, Mei Lin," he said with an effort, even as his teeth gritted. "Please?" The pills were within his reach, yet he made no move to take them. "I know it has something to do with somebody named Tina. And that the records were changed. And a pill was wrong... that seemed especially upsetting to you."

Mei Lin knew that he was trying to distract her from her goal — and himself from the pain — but she remained too stunned to protest. She had babbled all that... and he had listened and remembered it! There was no other explanation, since Elsie was the only person in Gustavus who knew about Mariel Gonzalez, and Elsie would never have told a soul.

She looked at him thoughtfully, considering the irony at play. Stanley Smith had been a witness to the unconscious overflow of her troubled mind, and she had been a witness to his. In a way, his request seemed only fair. If she was clever, she could use it to help him.

The man before her might be unaccountably odd, but she believed that he was sane and not suicidal in the traditional sense. For all that he seemed *willing* to die if nature dictated, he did not seem overly anxious to hasten the process. Living alone in this cabin for over a year now, he could have ended his life in any number of creative ways at any time. What was he waiting for? Did he truly want to die, or did he only feel as if he *should?*

She refilled his cup of water and handed it over. "I'm afraid I can't speak about that topic, Mr. Smith," she said with an apologetic smile. "Lawyer's advice. We'll have to talk about something else. I'd love to hear more about you and your life before coming to Gustavus. You said some pretty interesting things yourself when you were feverish."

He paled. "Delusional nonsense, I'm sure," he said shortly. "And call me Stanley, please."

She nodded in agreement. He was clearly an intelligent man, and not one easily manipulated. Well, neither was she. At least not anymore. "It didn't seem like delusional nonsense," she said easily. "It seemed more like you were reliving disturbing events from your past."

He looked mortified, and Mei Lin felt a twinge of guilt. She hated to distress him, however necessary it might be. A drip of sweat rolled down his temple and dripped from his cheek.

"Like what?" he demanded, his voice cracking. "What did I say?"

"You mentioned several different events." She grabbed a rag, moistened it with cool water, and touched it gently to his burning forehead. "But your fever seems to be climbing. I really don't think this is a good time to discuss it."

"I feel fine," he lied, even as his shoulders shivered. He made no attempt to stop her ministrations. "Go on, please. What did I say?"

Mei Lin shook her head. "No, Stanley," she said quietly, but firmly. "I won't babble on like nothing's wrong while you lie there suffering unnecessarily. It disturbs me too much."

His blue eyes narrowed, and for a long moment he studied her critically. Mei Lin stared back at him, unblinking. At last, he cracked a smile. Then, unbelievably, he chuckled. "There is more to you than meets the eye, Nurse Sullivan," he said wryly.

Mei Lin grinned back at him. "Likewise, I'm sure."

He scooted himself farther up on his pillows and took a sip of water. "You remind me of an old friend of mine. She was a sweet-looking thing, just like you — so tiny and thin you'd think a gust of wind would blow her over. But put a pistol in that girl's hands..." He whistled and shook his head.

"You mean Wang Li?" she suggested innocently.

His pupils widened in alarm. "Who?"

She picked up his medicine from the bedside table. Then she shrugged. "You brought up the name. You mistook me for her, I think."

"What else did I say?" he asked with a quaver in his voice.

Mei Lin smiled, but said nothing. She extended a hand and offered him the pills.

In the depths of his blue eyes, she caught a flash of anger. But she also saw a glimmer of respect.

Thane was sitting sideways at his accursedly uncomfortable desk when his mother rang his cell phone. The metal desk was jammed into the corner of an office that hosted four graduate students in a space sufficient for one, and he couldn't get his legs under it if he chopped off his feet first. He worked elsewhere whenever he could, but this morning he had data to gather and copies to make. When that was done, he had only to square things with his advisor and pack up. If he was lucky, he could catch the three-thirty ferry out of Horseshoe Bay without a reservation. Then he could dump his stuff at Jason's and lay low for a while.

"Mom?" he said with less deference than usual. "I'm sorry, but I'm super busy here."

"Well, you'll have time for this," Margot replied. Her voice sounded strange, and Thane stopped what he was doing. "I want to apologize," she continued. "Vanessa called me last night, and we had a long talk. I had no idea..."

An uncomfortably long pause followed. Thane waited it out, saying nothing.

"Clearly I had no idea what was really going on between the two of you," Margot continued. "Although I don't know how I could, since you never tell me anything! But when I pressed her, she admitted that you're not... well, that you haven't been—"

Thane spared his mother the awkwardness of finishing that sentence. "I told you that yesterday," he reminded, his voice gruff. He did appreciate his mother's willingness to apologize. But he wanted this discussion about as much as a mosquito bite in the armpit.

"I know!" Margot said apologetically, letting out a frustrated sigh. "I know you did, and I should have believed you. I'm sorry. What you said just sounded so... well, so unlikely. And it didn't fit at all with what Vanessa has been suggesting all this time, not just to me, but to her family, too. I still can't understand why she would blow the situation so out of proportion!"

"She's not right, Mom," Thane said tiredly. "I'm beginning to wonder if she needs professional help."

"Yes. I think she might," Margot replied, her voice strained. "I'm meeting her mother later. We'll talk about it."

"Good," he replied, genuinely relieved. "I hope you guys can get through to her. Thanks for calling."

Margot Tremain was impervious to hints. "It's just that the poor girl has always wanted to be a mother so badly. And she's concerned about her biological clock..."

Thane winced in agony. He let his mother prattle on for another thirty seconds or so, thanked her again for her apology, then said a firm goodbye.

He set down the phone and buried his face in his hands. He would never so much as eat a burger with a woman again.

Chapter 12

Mei Lin stretched her arms over her head and stood on her tiptoes. The ground outside the cabin was far too wet and mushy to indulge in her usual yoga routine, but considering the scenery, she didn't mind improvising. It was turning out to be a beautiful morning.

No sooner had Stanley begrudgingly swallowed his much-needed medicine than Jesse Torpin had reappeared at the cabin door, this time with Sandra Gruber in tow. As the nurse practitioner introduced herself to her new patient, a relieved Mei Lin had stepped outside. Stanley would be all right now, she was certain. The seasoned ex-military nurse would have the situation in hand in a trice.

Last night's rain had swollen the stream, and Mei Lin smiled to see two bright red fish in its center. They were swimming against the current, but their efforts were only just enough to keep them stationary. They were large creatures, over two feet long, and even though they were in the deepest channel of the stream, the tops of their green fins stuck out above the surface. "Hello, sockeye," she greeted, earning a tail thump from Kibbe, who rested near her feet. She looked down at him and chuckled. Living as the dog did, he had every reason to believe that any words spoken were addressed to him.

She practiced a few more stretches. The meadow around Elsie's house in town was picturesque, but the cabin's setting was even more striking — in a darker, more mystical way. The forest on the opposite side of the stream was so thick with trees and understory that she could see only a little ways into it before the sunlight petered out, leaving nothing visible beyond a greenish-brown haze. The straight tree trunks were so close together a bull moose couldn't walk between them without getting his antlers caught, and an explosion of moss coated every exposed surface with a symphony of green. When the sun shone brightly, she felt as if she were surrounded by a fairy world. But the second the warm beams were blocked by drifting clouds, a shadow fell across the forest, giving it an eerie feel.

She jumped when the cabin door banged shut. Sandra Gruber walked towards her. "This one's all yours," the nurse practitioner announced, shaking her head. "Says he spent his whole life pushing paper for some oil company." Her eyes rolled. "Lying through his teeth. I'd bet any amount of money he's an MD. Probably a surgeon. Arrogant know-it-alls always make the worst patients!"

"I don't— I don't understand," Mei Lin stuttered.

Sandra shrugged briskly. "He's refusing treatment."

Disappointment swamped Mei Lin's previously sunny mood. She'd been so sure that Sandra could talk sense into him! Mei Lin had coerced him into taking two doses of antibiotic, but he needed many more, and her stopgap trickery could only go so far.

Sandra squared the broad shoulders that held her military-grade canvas backpack. "I've left everything he needs, if he chooses to take it. When the pain ramps up, he may well change his tune. I'll be happy to come back if he asks for me, but I can't neglect my other patients. Have a good day." She nodded curtly, turned on a heel, and marched back down the trail.

Mei Lin's head swam. Now what? She wondered if Sandra could be right about Stanley's being a doctor. He was certainly intelligent and well educated. He hadn't asked her a single question about his condition or its prognosis, and his sutures had been sewn with skill. But... any MD would know what an exquisitely painful death he risked by refusing treatment. Stanley couldn't possibly think he deserved that! Could he?

A heavy weight of worry resettled in her middle, but she tried to think positively. At least Jesse was still inside the cabin. Perhaps the friendly outdoorsman could succeed where both women had failed? The two men had known each other for a year now, and they had that male camaraderie thing going on...

She waited at the edge of the stream for some time, throwing sticks for Kibbe and plucking wild raspberries and salmonberries from the sunnier spots. She made no move to enter the cabin, as she was hesitant to interrupt whatever the men were doing. After what seemed like an hour, Jesse emerged and walked toward her. His forehead was creased with concern. "Got Stanley cleaned up a little. He's asking if you'll come back in now — he says the two of you were in the middle of something." Jesse sighed. "He was very polite, but he insisted he doesn't want any more help from anybody. He says he can manage on his own from now on."

"He can't," Mei Lin said.

"I know," Jesse replied. He ran a hand through his shaggy blond locks. "I'm going to come back later anyway — bring him a good dinner. I just wouldn't feel right otherwise, you know?"

Mei Lin knew. She offered to check on Stanley again first thing tomorrow, and they agreed to tag-team visits until he was feeling better. She assured Jesse that she would be fine walking back by herself, then waved goodbye to him as he hurried off to work.

She glanced toward the stream. The salmon had made little progress, despite swimming constantly. What did the poor, tired creatures have to look forward to upstream, anyway? Spawning, followed by death. And those were the lucky ones. The unlucky ones skipped the spawning part. One had to admire their persistence.

She squared her own shoulders, inhaled deeply, and walked back into the cabin. Stanley was propped up in bed looking pleased with himself, and his feverish blue eyes glittered at the sight of her. His long hair and beard had been neatly combed, and he was wearing a fresh shirt. Her nose even caught a spicy scent. She must have looked surprised, because he smiled self-consciously and gave a shrug. "No point in impressing Kibbe.

But I *can* clean up nice."

She smiled back at him. "How very thoughtful of you."

"I'm just glad you didn't leave," he said earnestly. "We made a bargain, you and I. Have a seat."

Mei Lin complied. He was trying to appear casual and composed, but the tightness of his jaw betrayed him. He was nervous.

"I need you to tell me whatever it was I babbled yesterday," he proclaimed. "Please. You promised."

Mei Lin was puzzled. For someone who didn't care whether he lived or died, Stanley seemed inordinately interested in what information he might have passed on to her. Was the man a spy? But no, that was too fantastic. Why would a spy hang out alone in the Alaskan rainforest? He could be a criminal, hiding out from the law. But she didn't believe that either, whether it made sense or not. Perhaps his concerns were more personal. "You mentioned your boys," she offered uncertainly. "Several times. You have sons, I presume?"

Stanley twitched as if she'd slapped his face. For a long, uncomfortable moment, he simply sat and stared at her. "I don't have any children."

Mei Lin could tell that he was lying. She remembered that he'd also told the Torpins he had no kids; but she still wasn't buying. There had been something in his voice when he spoke of *his boys*... something loving and undeniably paternal. Perhaps it was a matter of semantics. "A man can care about kids who aren't his own," she suggested.

He stiffened. "I don't have any children," he repeated. "Biological or otherwise. What else did I say?"

Mei Lin was at a loss. "You talked about people dying," she said soberly. "And about children not being fed. I got the feeling you were in a war zone."

His breathing quickened again. He was definitely frightened.

"There's no reason to get upset," Mei Lin soothed. "I'm a nurse, remember? We're not in the habit of exposing our patients' personal business to the world. I may be horribly nosy, but I'm not a gossip. I respect your privacy."

His expression softened slightly. "Thank you. I appreciate that. It's... well, it's important."

"I can see that." She felt a strong gush of sympathy. Whatever had made this man retreat from society, she believed that he was social by nature. "The thing is, Dr. Smith... you seem troubled. And I *am* a good listener. If you'd like to talk, I promise that whatever you tell me won't leave this cabin."

"Can you just tell me what I said?" he urged. "Everything I said?"

Mei Lin assured him that she would try. Sandra Gruber had been right; he *was* a doctor. Her surreptitious use of the address had slipped right past him. She did her best to recall the content of his ramblings, repeating it all back to him as accurately as she could. He listened intently, making no comment except for an occasional wince. When she had finished, he stared off into space.

"Damn, I've got loose lips," he said finally, sounding disgusted with himself.

Mei Lin poured him another cup of water. "Welcome to the club," she teased. "Annoying, isn't it?"

He almost chuckled. He took the cup from her hand, then faced her suddenly. "You called me Dr. Smith," he accused.

She grinned at him. "Nurse Gruber's hunch. She was right, wasn't she?"

He had the decency not to deny it. He made a harrumphing sound, then drained the cup. He returned it to his bedside table, slid down on the pillows, and looked at Mei Lin with a frustrated expression. "Wang Li was an anesthesiologist I used to work with ages ago," he explained. "She was Chinese, too. But now that my eyes are focused, I can see you look nothing like her. Sorry about that."

"No offense taken," Mei Lin assured, wondering how he had pegged her as Chinese, rather than Korean or Vietnamese or Indonesian. She supposed that more widely traveled people were better guessers. "Were you a military doctor?" she asked.

"Some of the things you said made me think you'd been—"

"Good God, no!" he replied forcefully. "I loathe the damn military. *Any* military."

A pacifist? She got another idea. "Did you work for Doctors Without Borders?"

He stiffened again. Then, after giving her a good, long look that held suspicion, respect, and exhaustion all at the same time, he let out a heavy breath. "No. It was another organization. But the mission was the same."

"War zones," she murmured, remembering some of his more gruesome ramblings.

He nodded. "I was permanent staff for almost twenty years."

Mei Lin swallowed. She could not imagine ever dredging up half as much courage as this man must hold in one pinky toe. "You've been staring death in the face for a good chunk of your life!" she exclaimed. "Why give up now?"

He turned his head away from her. But Mei Lin would have none of it. She moved until her face was back in his line of sight again. "Why are you giving up, Stanley?" she repeated. "Tell me. Why?"

His blue eyes locked on hers, and for a long moment, they stared at each other in silence. Then, slowly, he raised his right arm above the blankets. He lifted his hand and wiggled his fingers. "Because of this," he said bitterly. "*This* was everything to me."

The skin on his arm was deeply scarred, but Mei Lin could see nothing wrong with the limb's function. She waited.

"I was a trauma surgeon," he explained. "And a damned good one, until a car accident left me with nerve damage. For the first couple weeks I could barely move my fingers. I couldn't write; couldn't type. Doing surgery was out of the question. Over time I've gotten some control back, but not enough. I'll never do surgery again."

"You were able to stitch up your own leg well enough," Mei Lin pointed out. "I thought you'd been treated at the clinic."

He huffed out sarcastically. "Yeah, I did a hell of a job on that. Clearly."

"You had no antibiotics."

He shrugged. "I've had worse cuts heal on their own, no problem."

Mei Lin refrained from stating the obvious. He knew perfectly well that his immune system no longer had the vitality of a thirty-year old; he was just loath to admit it. And she could easily envision a man with his credentials and ego being reluctant to seek care from the local nurse practitioner.

He flexed his fingers again. "I can chop wood and run a can opener. I can even throw a few stitches and tie a few knots — at a snail's pace. But I still can't write. I can barely sign my own name."

Mei Lin looked around the cabin. He could probably type now, but with no electricity and no cell service, the only keyboard he could make use of here would be a manual typewriter, which he didn't appear to own. She frowned. Any number of modern accommodations could have allowed him to keep working in some capacity, yet he had chosen not to take advantage of any of them. And while she could understand his being depressed over losing a skill he had worked a lifetime to perfect, he had already reached a respectable retirement age. Needing to feel useful was one thing. Feeling suicidal was another. "Why did you move out here?" she asked.

Stanley looked away again. He put his arm back under the blankets, then shrugged. "I always wanted to live in a cabin in the woods," he said without emotion.

Mei Lin's heart sank. He wasn't going to tell her the truth. At least not yet. She reached out to touch his forehead and was relieved to find his fever down a little. The antibiotic was working. But he had to keep taking it.

"That breakfast Amanda sent up was sheer heaven," he murmured as he settled himself more comfortably in the bed. "If I knew I'd get cinnamon rolls out of it, I'd have cut my leg a long time ago." His eyes closed then, and he remained still. He might be tired enough to fall asleep, but Mei Lin suspected he was feigning. Now that he'd gotten the information he needed, he probably just wanted her to leave.

She looked at her watch. The meeting with the lawyer was this afternoon, and she was hosting it at Elsie's house. She had few responsibilities these days, but this one could not be shirked. She rose, topped off Stanley's water pitcher and supply of crackers, and laid out his next doses of antibiotic. Then she wrote him a note, explaining that Jesse or Amanda would be checking on him later today, and that she herself would be back first thing tomorrow — whether he liked it or not.

As she gathered her things and crossed to the door, a strong wave of apprehension accosted her. Stanley wouldn't take the medicine. She knew he wouldn't. There had to be *something* else she could do! But what?

She contemplated for several moments. Then she walked to the bedside table and penned a postscript.

> *If your fever is down tomorrow, I'll tell you about Mariel Gonzalez. I think you may be able to help me. But it absolutely must stay between us.*

Chapter 13

Margot Tremain's cell phone rang, and she looked down at the screen with a frown. Linda was already late for their lunch date. She was probably calling to make some lame excuse and beg Margot to wait around the cafe another half hour. Which would be annoying, because Margot was anxious to get the awkward conversation over with. Vanessa needed help, and her mother needed to understand that. Linda was a good friend, but Margot would not let her get away with blaming Thane for her daughter's troubles. Margot felt terribly guilty for having taken Vanessa's word over that of her own son, and she was not a woman who was comfortable with guilt. She preferred redemptive action.

The caller was not Linda. The party trying to reach Margot was identified as "Chicago Pol Dep." She tensed. She wanted to believe the call was random... some scam, perhaps, designed to have her wire money to Algeria. But her gut told her otherwise. It had been a very long time since she had communicated with anyone in the Chicago Police Department, but her landline number — which forwarded to her cell — hadn't changed in over a decade.

She huddled down in the booth and cupped a hand around the base of her phone. "Hello?"

A man with a vaguely familiar, gravelly voice identified himself as Lieutenant Baumgarten and asked if he was speaking with Mrs. Margot Tremain.

"Yes," she replied with a tremor. "What is this about?"

The pause that followed was physically painful. "We've spoken in the past, Ms. Tremain, regarding—"

"I remember," she said impatiently. "What is it? Has something happened?" Her heart was beating fast. Fear for Stanley's wellbeing suffused her even as she cursed the man for making her worry about him — again.

"There's no cause for alarm," the Lieutenant said calmly. "In fact I have good news. Tony Russo is dead."

Margot felt numb. The sounds and smells of the cafe still permeated her consciousness, but they no longer seemed real. "Dead?" she parroted. "Are you sure?" Deep in her mind, steel pistols flashed. Voices shouted obscenities; multiple gunshots rent the air. She'd witnessed none of the above, but the images haunted her nevertheless. For half a lifetime they had plagued her, along with a raw, gut-burning fear.

"Oh, he's dead all right," the Lieutenant confirmed with incongruous cheer. "Son of a bitch could escape conviction, but he couldn't escape colon cancer. Figured you might want to know."

"I do," she acknowledged. *Tony Russo.* It was a common enough name. Many men shared it. But there was only one Tony Russo who for the past twenty years had held the power — and the will — to destroy her family's lives. "Have you informed... my ex-husband?" she asked.

"We have not," the Lieutenant replied matter-of-factly. "Do you know how to reach him?"

Margot's face felt hot. "No," she said defensively. "I haven't heard from him in years. Why would I?"

The Lieutenant ignored the question. "Well, that's too bad. I'd have liked to let him know. Your case is one that's stuck with me. A real shame, all around."

Margot had no desire to rehash the past. "Are you telling me you can't find Stanley?"

"The department hasn't kept tabs on your ex-husband for a while now. We know he's back in the country, but his trail runs cold about a year ago. Wish I could do more, but I've got a file on my desk three inches thick. here. We don't have the manpower to track down every person Russo ever had a hold on."

"Of course not," Margot mumbled. It was Stanley's own fault. If he wanted updates, he should have told the department how to contact him. Still... "Can you tell me the last place he was living?" she heard herself ask.

"Officially, no," the Lieutenant replied. "Unofficially, there are indications he was in Alaska."

Margot sucked in a breath. *Alaska.* Of course. "Thank you."

"You're welcome." He paused a moment. "Nothing's ever for certain with lowlifes like Russo, Ms. Tremain. They do have very long memories. But looking back over your file, I can't see anybody your ex-husband was involved with who should pose a threat to you or your sons now. Most of them have been dead for years. Russo was the last of the group to have any real influence."

Margot thanked the Lieutenant again, then hung up the phone and looked around. Everything inside the cafe was the same as it had been five minutes ago. She still hadn't gotten the coffee she'd ordered, and Linda still hadn't showed. But the outside world had changed very much.

Tony Russo and his compatriots were finally all dead. Her sons were no longer in danger. Not the sharp, agonizing danger that had loomed over their heads when she had moved them to Canada; nor even the scant, theoretical danger that had followed them into adulthood. It was over now. All of it.

And Stanley had no idea.

A waitress appeared, set down a cup of coffee, and asked if she was ready to order. Linda appeared at the doorway and waved. A child in a nearby highchair began to scream.

Margot reacted to none of these things. But as she reached for the steaming mug in front of her, she noticed that her hand was shaking.

Mei Lin stood at the edge of the cabin's clearing, staring down the trail. She was not looking forward to the long, lonely walk back to the main road, and her anxiety over the prospect annoyed her. She'd made the trip once already, hadn't she? Besides, she had no choice. She had to get back to town. Elsie's lawyer had requested her presence at this afternoon's meeting; he was flying in from Juneau specifically for the purpose.

She plucked up her courage and started walking. A bird chattered loudly from a branch overhead, and after an initial start at the noise, she smiled. She did like the wilderness. She just didn't like being *alone* in the wilderness. Now, if she was making this same trek in the company of someone like Thane Buchanan...

Her thoughts veered off into a pleasant fantasy that worked wonders for her mood until she realized that her thoughts were once again dwelling on the only eligible man she'd had anything to do with in the last eight months. She blew out a frustrated breath, then plowed around the next bend in the overgrown trail. Thane *was* a uniquely intriguing person, and if she had met him under different circumstances, she might be justified in pursuing his acquaintance. But when she *knew* she was never going to see—

She stopped short. Less than twenty feet ahead of her stood a black bear.

Her body — and her brain — froze. What was she supposed to do? She couldn't remember. Couldn't think!

The bear swung its big brown nose in her direction and sniffed.

Don't look at its eyes! Back away slowly!

Neither of the suddenly remembered directions was easy to follow. Mei Lin's gaze was glued to the end of the bear that held the teeth, and her limbs felt like marble. A crashing sound in the brush terrified her further. *What else? Where?*

Her question was answered as first one cub, then another, popped out of the woods and lumbered up to its mother.

She panicked anew. Mothers protecting their cubs were the most dangerous! She wanted to move backward, but she couldn't move at all. The mother bear continued to stare in her direction, statue-like, while the cubs ambled about without concern. A part of Mei Lin felt like she was watching a nature documentary. The cubs were objectively adorable. One was black like its mother; the other was gray. One pawed at the other's head, starting a play-fight in the middle of the road. The tumbling twosome bumped into their mother's flank.

Mei Lin's feet finally moved a little. She took a slow step back. *Say something. Let the bear know you're not a threat.*

"No problem, Mama Bear," she squeaked out in a faint voice. "Nobody's going to hurt your babies. I was actually just leaving—"

The cubs noticed her. The gray one stood up on its back feet and cocked its head at her, which would have been charming if she were on the other side of a good, stout fence. But she was not. The mother could charge at any time, and as fast as bears ran, this one could be chomping on Mei Lin's neck in less than three seconds. Could she even get her bear spray off her belt in time? She was afraid to reach a hand down. She was afraid to do anything that might further alarm the animals. Her feet kept inching backward. The gray cub sniffed the air. The black cub took a tentative step toward her.

"No, no," she begged weakly. "Stay there, little fella. Don't make your mother kill me. I'm not worth it; really I'm not. I was only passing through. I—"

The mother bear moved. She swung her giant nose away from Mei Lin and hastened into the bushes on the other side of the road.

Oh, my God. She's leaving!

The gray cub came down off its hind paws, then jumped on the black cub's back in a sneak attack. The black cub let out a grunt of annoyance and whirled toward its sibling, teeth bared. The gray cub retreated and bounded off after its mother. The black cub followed.

Mei Lin took a much-needed breath. *Were they gone? Really gone?* Her heart beat like a jackhammer. She'd seen bears before, both here and in Maine, but never at such a close distance — and outside of a car. She felt more than a little light-headed.

How long she stood in the road, trying to calm herself enough to breathe, she couldn't say. But when she finally pushed herself forward to the spot where the bears had crossed the trail, she could neither see nor hear any sign of them.

She pressed forward down the path, her pace brisk. She attempted to sing a counting song from her childhood, but kept forgetting how many ants were marching and which one was tying his shoe. She switched to barrels of beer on the wall, then ran through the twelve days of Christmas. Twenty minutes later she burst out onto the Torpins' driveway with her heart still hammering. No one was home at the sprawling ranch house, so she jumped into her waiting Subaru and took off. With her hands trembling on the steering wheel, she drove home uncharacteristically fast, every cell of her body humming with adrenaline.

She passed no one on the drive, and Elsie's house was quiet. Mei Lin jumped in the shower. Only after turning the heat up and letting the water roll over her head for nearly half an hour did she begin to relax. By the time she had gotten dressed and tidied the house she was feeling nearly normal, and when the first invitees arrived, she had recovered enough sanguinity to recount the episode with humor. Which she did immediately, since the first guests to arrive were the chief ranger of Glacier Bay National Park and his wife.

"I forgot everything I'd ever read about bears!" she laughed as she blurted out the story. "In the critical moment of danger, my mind just went blank. Good thing I never wanted to be a Navy Seal!"

"Now, give yourself a little credit," Dave Markov teased back. "You did the right thing — as soon as it came to you. Most likely it only took a second. Time slows down a lot when you stop breathing."

"That is so true," Mei Lin agreed, still laughing. "And the cubs were so cute! One was black and one was gray. I wanted to ask you about that. The gray ones are pretty unusual, aren't they?"

The ranger's smiling face went white. For a long moment, he couldn't seem to speak. Mei Lin was about to ask if he felt all right when his pale lips began to quiver. "Gray? You're sure?"

She threw a sideways look at his wife. Mary Markov watched her husband with amusement, but said nothing. "Yes, I'm sure," Mei Lin answered. "It was a light, smoky gray color. Isn't that what you call a glacier bear?"

Dave stretched out a hand. With almost comical slowness, he placed it lightly on her shoulder. "Mei Lin," he said vehemently, "I've never seen a glacier bear in my life. They're extremely rare." Then his eyes began to sparkle, his color returned, and the corners of his mouth tugged up into a huge, fantastic grin. "This is huge! A brand new glacier cub? Right here in Gustavus!"

Mary laughed out loud. "Oh, Lord. Now you've done it, Mei Lin. He'll be tromping through the woods twenty-four hours a day now looking for that poor animal!"

"Where exactly did you see it?" Dave asked, ignoring his wife.

Mei Lin explained. Dave went from delighted to downright jittery.

"Now, settle down," Mary ordered. "We're here for a meeting. You are *not* taking off before the lawyer even gets here!"

Dave's face reddened. He looked practically mutinous. "Time is of the essence, woman!"

Mary laughed again, then released her breath with a sigh. "Oh, for God's sake. Fine! You go on. I'll find out what the man has to tell us."

The doorbell rang. Mei Lin turned to answer it, but Dave caught her before she could move. "Do me a favor," he pleaded. "Don't tell anybody else about this. Not just yet. If word gets out, Mr. Smith will be asking for a world of uninvited company. Let me check it out first. Then we can report it without giving away the specifics. All right?"

His earnestness was beyond amusing. "Sure," Mei Lin chuckled. "Whatever you think is best."

Dave shrugged on his jacket and kissed his wife on the lips with a perfunctory smack.

"See you next week," Mary replied drolly.

Mei Lin crossed to the door and opened it to Elsie's lawyer, whom she had met once before. Dave greeted the other man briskly, slipped out around him, and jogged off. Mei Lin would have loved to continue her conversation about the bears with Mary, but several other people were arriving behind the lawyer, and her duties as hostess took precedence.

When all the invitees — which included the heads of the town council and the library board — had arrived, Mei Lin settled everyone upstairs in the living room and introduced the lawyer. She knew that the meeting was important, but no sooner had the man started talking than her mind began to wander. She had no idea that seeing a glacier bear was such a big deal! Would Thane have gone as gaga over her story as Dave had? She dearly wished she could find out. Just imagining the look on his face—

"Ms. Sullivan?" the lawyer called.

She snapped back to attention, embarrassed. "Yes?"

"Mrs. Dunn has specifically provided for you to stay in this house, free of charge, until the end of August."

Mei Lin squirmed with discomfort. She knew that Elsie's offer had been sincere, but she still felt like a squatter. "Yes, she explained that to me. It was very generous of her."

"After that time has elapsed, she has arranged for ownership of the property to transfer to the town of Gustavus, as part of a negotiated agreement with the council to provide housing capable of attracting a qualified provider of hospice services to the community."

Mei Lin blinked. Elsie had said nothing to her about the fate of the house; she assumed it would be sold and the proceeds given to Elsie's favorite charities, since she had no biological heirs.

"If a suitable candidate is recruited and approved by the council, housing will be provided as part of a generous benefits package."

"Oh," Mei Lin sputtered with delight. "How nice! Elsie was always saying what a shame it was that home hospice care isn't available outside of Juneau. What a wonderful idea!"

"Indeed," Carol McRoberts agreed, looking at Mei Lin with a peculiar sparkle in her eye. "There are a lot of people in Gustavus, and on Chichagof Island too, who'd love to be able to finish out their lives in the comfort of their own homes, just like Elsie did. She could afford her own full-time nurse, but she knew most people couldn't. We've tried before to get a practitioner to work out here, but that's easier said than done. Elsie thought that maybe offering a nice place to live would make a difference."

"Oh, I hope so," Mei Lin agreed.

A silence followed. She began to feel a distinctly unsettling vibe, and as she looked around at the familiar faces she realized that every one of them was staring at her. They were studying her with the most curious expressions of... what? Amusement? Expectation?

The lawyer cleared his throat. "Yes, well. The next item concerns Mrs. Dunn's endowment to the library fund..."

Mei Lin stared back at the townsfolk. What exactly was she missing here?

Oh.

Chapter 14

"Dude," Jason responded with a laugh, shaking his head. "I don't know why you're so surprised. I told you that girl was a headcase!"

Thane grumbled. His happy-go-lucky younger brother always seemed to have an answer for everything. What was annoying was how often he was right. "You said that about every girl in the neighborhood."

"And they were all nuts!" Jason insisted. He handed Thane a drink, set his own down on his coffee table, then dropped onto his sectional sofa and stretched into a comfortable sprawl. "I don't know why you keep beating yourself up about this," he said more sympathetically. "Vanessa's always been a flake. That's why you dumped her in high school, remember?"

In truth, Thane could not remember. He looked at his brother quizzically. He and Jason bore little resemblance to each other, aside from what their mother described as "a strong jaw." Jason was above-average height, but his build was slighter and leaner than Thane's own imposing form. The younger Buchanan's eyes were gray, rather than blue, and his hair, although just as bushy, was curlier and lighter in color. In short, he looked like a surfer. Which he was. "I have no clue," Thane admitted, shaking his head.

Jason rolled his eyes. "How can you forget? She staged that whole drama with that equally whacko friend of hers... Nora? Nancy? Whatever her name was, Vanessa had her come on to you, as some kind of test. And the whole time Vanessa was hiding out watching you both!"

A vague memory of stupefied annoyance welled up in Thane's gut. "Oh, right," he drawled, stuffing the feeling back down again. "She apologized for all that later. I think."

Jason laughed out loud. "Bro, you gotta give yourself a

break. Vanessa doesn't deserve your gentlemanly concern. Forget her and move on. When was the last time you went on a date anyway? Met a woman you could really get excited about?"

A flash of shiny dark hair and merry brown eyes teased Thane's brain, and he let out another grumble. He had brought up the subject of women, true, but now he wanted to change it. Jason had no trouble in that quarter. Women always seemed to materialize and — more importantly — conveniently disappear whenever the guy snapped his fingers. "I live on a college campus with forty thousand giggling girl-children," Thane defended, not really answering.

"You live in Vancouver," Jason pointed out. "The third largest metropolitan area in the country."

"So, how's the new Shack coming along?" Thane diverted. "I'm looking forward to seeing it."

Jason eyed him knowingly. Thane had no doubt that the subject of women would come up again, since Jason seemed to think his big brother needed remedial help in this area. Maybe at some point Thane would even listen, considering how tired he was of going to bed alone. But not tonight. "The Pacific Rim Surf Lodge," Jason corrected proudly, "is coming along splendidly. I'll take you out there tomorrow."

Thane nodded. Everyone in the family had given Jason grief when, not long out of college and with a degree in physics and ocean science, he had gone into hock to purchase a collapsing heap known as the "Tofino Surfing Shack." The dilapidated hostel was an eyesore as well as a source of regular complaints for disturbing the peace, but Jason was playing the long game. He had repaired the building with his own hands, raised the rates, and kicked out anyone who annoyed him. Now, several years later, he had raised enough capital to expand. His second building would have twice the capacity and would incorporate a surf school and equipment rental business. He was proving to be a savvy entrepreneur, and Thane was proud of him.

"So, what's this about you looking for a job in Alaska?" Jason asked, taking a swig of his drink. "You really want to move there permanently? Live in Grandma and Grandpa's house? Be an American?"

"We're already American!" Thane protested. Jason had been ten when they'd left Seattle; he should remember growing up in the United States. He should *feel* American, at least partly. But Jason's supposedly better memory had always had holes in it.

Thane sat forward and looked at his brother earnestly. "Mom said something really weird to me yesterday. She was ragging me about the whole Vanessa thing, and she said I was just like my father. She meant our real father, and she didn't mean it as a compliment. What do you think she meant? Have you ever heard her say anything like that?"

Jason shrugged. "She never says anything about him."

Thane sat back with a sigh. His brother's lack of interest in piecing together the past, in trying to get some retrospective handle on their parents' bizarre relationship, shouldn't surprise him. He supposed that Jason's laissez-faire acceptance of their family history was more understandable than Thane's own abiding fascination with it. Thane did wish he could let it all go... just stop bothering to even try and understand. But he couldn't. Not as long as the sickening doubts persisted. Not as long as their mother's strange actions and queer, unintended hints seemed designed to hide something important. Thane wanted to believe that his father was the man he remembered: kind, gentle-natured, and fun-loving. Passionate, optimistic, and full of energy. But what if that wasn't the truth? What if the man he'd spent his whole childhood admiring was a lying, philandering bastard?

A pillow struck Thane squarely in the face.

"Snap out of it!" Jason ordered with a cackle. "Will you stop taking everything so seriously? It's a good thing you came here — I can see that you need me. Give me twenty-four hours, and I'll get you all set up."

Thane raised an eyebrow. "Get me set up how?"

Jason smirked.

Thane opened his mouth to protest, but felt the cell phone

in his pocket buzzing with a call. He shot a warning frown at his brother and pulled out the phone, planning to silence it. But when he saw the name on caller ID he answered immediately.

"Dave!" he greeted with enthusiasm. "What's up?"

"You want me to run up there with you?" Jesse Torpin offered the next morning as Mei Lin stood in his driveway and stared — yet again — at the trail to Stanley's cabin. She had dreamed of bears all night long. Black ones, gray ones, big ones, small ones... they had all looked perfectly friendly until they turned on her and bit her arms off.

She looked back at Jesse eagerly, prepared to do the wussy thing and say yes, when she noticed that he was loading up his truck with fishing gear. "No thanks," she replied, trying hard to sound self-confident. Per Dave's instructions, she hadn't told anyone about the glacier bear.

Jesse walked over closer to her. "I hope Stanley took his medicine, but like I said, he wouldn't make me any promises. He seemed a bit more depressed last evening than earlier in the day, but he did eat a good dinner." He shook his head sadly. "I don't get it. Neither does Amanda. As friendly as he can be sometimes, it sure seems like he moved out there with a death wish."

A death wish.

Mei Lin threw her shoulders back. She unclipped her can of bear spray from its carabiner and took it by the handle. She could do this, dammit.

She said goodbye to Jesse, wished him luck with the fish, and set off. She sang until her voice was hoarse and rotated her head so much she got a crick in her neck, but after a tense half hour she arrived at the clearing. No bears of any description had made an appearance, thank goodness. The only mammal she'd sighted was one skittish red squirrel. The cabin door was standing open as she approached, and Kibbe ran out to meet her. Yesterday, Jesse had rigged up a rope and a broom so that

Stanley could let the dog in and out without having to get up. Mei Lin wondered why the door remained open now. Was Stanley well enough to push it closed?

Hastily she reclipped the bear spray to her jeans and flexed her fingers. She'd been holding the can so tightly that her hand was cramping. "Kibbe, boy!" she cooed as he collided with her shins, then flopped onto his back for a belly pat. "Is your master okay?" She rewarded the dog with a quick rub, then noticed something white lying on the porch. She hurried up the steps to find a piece of note paper, slightly mangled and covered with muddy dog prints, but readable. A glance told her that it was a note to Stanley from Dave Markov. Most likely Dave had left it wedged in the closed door late yesterday.

A fresh sense of dread washed over her. Why was it still so quiet? She stuffed the note in a pocket and walked inside. Stanley was in bed. He appeared to be asleep, but he made no sound. Mei Lin hastened to his side, her eyes searching frantically for signs of movement: a flaring of nostrils, the rise or fall of the blankets above his ribs—

She let out her breath with a gush. He was alive. His jaw was moving. He seemed as if he was trying to talk, but he was only dreaming again.

She opened the curtains to let in more light, then took a closer look at him. His color seemed all right, but he was feverish again, and his sleep was uneasy. His limbs began to twitch, and he made a dull moaning noise. Mei Lin looked at the bedside table. Her own note was there, crumpled into a ball. Last night's medication was no longer present. But this morning's dose remained untouched.

"I'm so sorry," he mumbled suddenly, startling her. She thought for a moment that he had awakened, but he had not. His eyes were still closed. She watched as the wrinkles in his brow deepened. "I'm so sorry, Angela," he mumbled. "I didn't mean it. I didn't... He was..." Stanley's next words were indistinct. He broke out in a fresh sweat and his limbs began to thrash.

"Wake up, Stanley," Mei Lin ordered, deciding that he'd had enough. Her fellow nurses had mixed feelings about awakening residents with nightmares, but she couldn't stand to see anyone suffer from imagined horrors when their waking hours had enough real pain. She collected her rag and moistened it with water, then touched the cool cloth to his brow. "Wake up, now. Dr. Smith?"

His eyes flew open. For a second, they were filled with alarm. Then he blinked and focused on her face. "Mei Lin," he said clearly. "What... what happened?"

The kernels of a theory began to form in her mind. *Angela.* Perhaps she was his Mariel? Whatever he had been apologizing for, the guilt of it affected him deeply. Could the burden be so heavy that it made him wish to die? "Nothing happened," she said gently. "You've just been talking in your sleep again."

Stanley closed his eyes and swore. He looked drained and wretched, but after a long moment he seemed to decide to pull himself together. He sat up higher on his pillows and stared at her accusingly. "By the way... you are an evil person, Nurse Sullivan."

Mei Lin smiled. He was teasing her, which was an excellent sign. "Oh? How so?"

"Don't play innocent with me. You are an extortionist!" Stanley insisted. He reached out for the crumpled note she had left and extended it with a frown. "Taking advantage of a sick man's boredom. For shame! You knew damn well this would irritate the hell out of me!"

Mei Lin grinned shamelessly. "Did I?"

Clearly fighting a grin of his own, Stanley chucked the ball of paper into the fireplace. Given his condition, his aim was impressive. "I took the damn antibiotics. So you'd better hold up your end of the deal."

Mei Lin feigned an innocent dullness. She was good at that. "Oh. But I thought I said specifically that your fever had to be down?"

Stanley glared. "It is down."

"Hmmm," Mei Lin mused, touching a fresh rag to his cheek. "I'm not so sure. Of course, it could just be because your morning dose is late..."

"Evil," Stanley repeated. "Pure evil." He was trying very hard to glare at her, but the spark of amusement in his eyes was hard to miss. He grabbed the pills that were laying out, tossed them in his mouth, and chased them down with a swallow of water. "Start talking," he demanded harshly. "And I mean the whole, ugly story. Everything that happened with Mariel Gonzalez. *Now.*"

Mei Lin's answering smile was hesitant. She felt a pleasant sense of triumph at having gotten two more doses of antibiotic into him. But in her ardor to make a bargain, she had neglected to consider the cost. Not only was Mariel Gonzalez the last thing she wanted to talk about, but once Stanley's bizarre curiosity on the issue had been satisfied, she would lose her only remaining bit of leverage. What happened when tonight's dose came due?

"And don't leave anything out," Stanley qualified.

Mei Lin drew in a breath and resigned herself. A bargain was a bargain.

She leaned back in her chair and started talking.

Chapter 15

Nine months ago, Dallas, Texas

Mei Lin punched a button on the desk phone at the nurses' station, putting the caller on hold. Her heart beat fast. She rose and began walking down the A corridor of the Silverson Elder Care Center.

Julia, the licensed vocational nurse she sought, was one of the few others on this night shift that she knew. Mei Lin's usual shift was three to eleven; she only worked nights when Tina Booras, the usual overnight charge nurse, was off. Tina's frequent vacation, personal, and sick days were supposed to be covered by the part-time RNs who worked weekends — or so Mei Lin had been told at her interview. But in the three months she'd been working at Silverson, she'd been called in to sub for Tina twelve times. She suspected she could say no, but after the debacle with Jeremy, she needed the extra cash. Unfortunately, such shifts tended to be stressful because she was unfamiliar with the night staff. Turnover in Tina's group was so high that her people barely knew each other.

She spotted the back end of the med cart disappearing into a room and hastened her steps. She was worried about Julia. The struggling single mother of four worked the same regular shift as Mei Lin, but the LVN could be found at the nursing home at any time, racking up extra hours. Julia was usually a fount of energy, but in the last week she had seemed increasingly pale and harried, and Mei Lin hated to bring her distressing news.

The thin, immature voice calling on the phone just now had sounded distraught, and the little girl had been sniffling and gulping so much that Mei Lin could barely understand her. What she eventually determined was that Julia's children were home alone, two of them had gotten into a fight, somebody had gotten hurt, and no adult seemed to be around. They couldn't reach their mother directly, since the staff at Silverson were required to keep their personal phones at the nurses' desk, so the girl had nervously called her mother's "emergency number."

Mei Lin entered the room to find the LVN leaning over the bed nearest the door, gently awakening a resident. "Paulina," Julia cooed. "Time for your meds, honey."

"Excuse me. Julia?" Mei Lin interceded, stepping around the cart and into the room. "You have a call at the desk from your daughter. On line 2. She seems very upset, I'm afraid."

"Which daughter?" Julia exclaimed, so loud that both residents in the room jolted awake. "MacKenzie? You mean she called the *desk?* Why would she do that? What's going on?"

"I'm not sure," Mei Lin replied calmly. "You go on and talk to her. I'll take over here."

The too-thin Julia stared at Mei Lin with disbelief for a moment. Then she handed over the glass of water and paper medicine cup she was holding and flew out of the room.

"I'm sorry, Mabel," Mei Lin apologized to the woman in the far bed. "You go on back to sleep, now. And Paulina, you just need to take your medicine and then you can go back to sleep, too."

Mei Lin froze, her eyes fixed on the tablet in the cup. What was this? She checked the medicine administration record. At this hour, Paulina was supposed to receive a single dose of pain reliever. But the small white tablet Julia had put in the paper cup was not the drug prescribed.

Mei Lin picked up the pill and examined it. It was circular and flat, with no manufacturer's markings pressed into it. Paulina had been prescribed a narcotic to alleviate pain in her spine — a tablet with a specific shape and recognizable markings. "I'm sorry, Paulina. Can you hang on a minute?" Mei Lin asked. She unlocked the controlled substances compartment of the cart and checked its contents. Julia had only just started her rounds, and all the doses of narcotic that should still be on the cart were present and accounted for. Paulina's dose had been removed, but it was not in the cup. Its empty wrapper lay on top of the cart.

Mei Lin's pulse quickened as she fit the pieces together. Even if the small white tablet Julia had been about to give Paulina had been accidentally placed in the wrong packaging, the LVN was experienced enough that she should have noticed the difference when she dispensed it. Far more likely was that the real pill had been switched with another — most likely a placebo — after the wrapper had been opened. Julia had stolen a narcotic!

A ripple of panicked horror shot through Mei Lin. Had Julia been planning to switch out other residents' narcotics, as well? Each at the last minute, so that the cart itself would bear no evidence? *Good God!* Had Julia done this before? How many times? How many doses? How many residents had suffered?

Mei Lin turned to Paulina to apologize for the delay, but the frail woman had already fallen asleep again. Like many of the residents on A-unit, she suffered from dementia and paid little or no attention to the pills she was given. Some residents examined their own meds religiously... But Julia knew which residents did not.

Mei Lin dropped the placebo into her breast pocket, pushed the cart back out until the hall, and quietly closed the door. She stood in the hallway motionless. She knew that the opioid in question had a high street value. What she didn't understand was how could Julia do it. The woman had her flaws, and she wasn't terribly intelligent. But she had always seemed devoted to her job. She was one of the hardest-working LVNs Mei Lin had ever known, competent and caring with her residents. How could she secretly allow them to suffer?

Nurse! a man's voice echoed in Mei Lin's memory. *My leg's hurting awful this morning. Can't you give me something for it?*

Miss Mei Lin? Georgia had pleaded. *The medicine isn't working. I told the doctor it's not! I hurt so much. Can't you do something? Ask him again for me?*

It must be getting worse, James had explained to her. *Most of the time it's fine, but every once in a while it aches like the devil...*

Mrs. Santino had said nothing, but her daughter had said plenty. *She didn't have pain like this in the rehab hospital! What are you people doing to her? She should be feeling better, not worse!*

"Oh, God, no," Mei Lin muttered into the empty hallway. This *had* happened before, hadn't it? Julia worked every shift at some point or other... she could easily pocket a pill here or there with no one being the wiser. She was one of the few LVNs that all the charge nurses trusted to dispense! Julia could have been stealing pills for months, years even. And to think that it had been happening on Mei Lin's own watch!

Bile rose up in her throat, and the walls of the hallway began to teeter. Oh, why hadn't she suspected anything? Why hadn't she taken the residents' complaints more seriously, seen the pattern? A crushing weight of guilt fell upon her, but she forced herself to fight it off. She could beat herself up later — right now she needed to act.

Part of Mei Lin wanted to confront Julia immediately, before a single other resident got cheated out of a dose of painkiller. But the scope of this crime went beyond one LVN and her charge nurse. Mei Lin would have to report the incident up the chain, so that the proper legal steps could be taken. The authorities would have to do a thorough investigation, review records, collect evidence...

"I'm going to kill that girl with my bare hands someday I swear to God!" Julia called out as she sailed back down the hall. "Those two fight like cats and dogs and she's bigger than her brother and I just *knew* that something like this was going to happen! And who do you think's going to get the blame if Ricky winds up having to go to the ER someday? Me! That's who! I'll be hauled in for child abuse, when it should be my damn niece who's responsible. Outside with her boyfriend the whole time, do you believe it? And the baby asleep in her crib!"

"Do you need to leave?" Mei Lin asked, surprised to hear her voice sounding more composed than she felt.

"No," Julia answered, barely looking at Mei Lin as she retook the cart. "My niece is on it now, and her boyfriend's an EMT and he says nothing's broken and they're just going to ice it. The baby didn't even wake up. And it's better if I don't go straight home anyway because if I got a hold of Rowena right now I'd likely break her bossy little bones myself!" She put her hands up and took a deep breath. "Don't worry," she assured Mei Lin, forestalling her next comment. "I'm all right. I'm calm. No problem."

Mei Lin put a hand back on the cart handle. "Take ten minutes, Julia," she insisted. "I can do the next couple rooms. Pour yourself a cup of decaf and relax."

The LVN looked hesitant. She did not seem suspicious, but sitting and relaxing was a foreign concept to her. She was the type of energetic busy bee that seemed always to be in motion.

"Five minutes," Mei Lin repeated, faking a smile. "That's an order."

Julia huffed out a breath and whirled away.

Mei Lin moved slowly. She dispensed meds to the next resident at a snail's pace, performing the necessary checks three times over. She knew she was distracted, and she didn't want to make a mistake. Her next step seemed clear. She should report the incident ASAP. The idea that the LVN might steal more pills, even as Mei Lin was on the phone, was gut-wrenching. But any harm from a missed dose tonight could be managed. It was more important that Julia not be tipped off until someone with more authority than Mei Lin could decide how best to proceed.

Her hands shook as she tore open packets and poured water. The course of action before her seemed logical and correct... but something about it still felt wrong. Technically, any suspicions of malfeasance on the part of her staff should be reported to the Director of Nursing. But Silverson's DON was on leave to visit a new grandchild. And the acting DON was Tina Booras.

Deep in the swirling pit of acid that was her gut, Mei Lin

was certain that telling Tina would be a mistake. She felt it deeply, knew it instinctively, even though she could not explain why.

What she had seen tonight with her own eyes implicated no one besides Julia. The LVN was known to have a stressed home life and myriad financial problems — her motivation for such a crime was obvious. But something dark and loathsome kept playing in the back of Mei Lin's mind, and that something involved Tina Booras. Perhaps her own tortured conscience was merely lumping together her greatest moments of guilt, but she could not stop thinking about her last unpleasant experience with Tina... and the death of Mariel Gonzalez.

A few short weeks ago, Mariel had still been alive. The chatty ex-schoolteacher had a wide variety of health problems, but dementia wasn't one of them, and her cheerful attitude had quickly made her one of Mei Lin's favorite residents. Mariel had a large and caring extended family that frequently took her out of the home for day visits, but unfortunately, on one of those visits she took a fall and fractured several vertebrae. Not being a good surgical candidate, she was returned to the home from the hospital with a prescription for pain relief and strict orders for limited movement. For the first few days after her arrival, she appeared as upbeat as ever. But one afternoon, Mei Lin noticed a change. Though Mariel didn't complain, she seemed uncomfortable and lacked her usual vivacity.

By evening it was clear that Mariel was worsening. Mei Lin kept a close watch on her and charted every complaint, but the woman's symptoms were vague and none rose to the level of an emergency. Still, as the end of Mei Lin's shift neared, her concern grew. Mariel had begun to sweat heavily, which she had never done before. Tears rolled down the old woman's cheeks as she told Mei Lin that she didn't want to be a bother, but that she felt awful and didn't know what was wrong with her.

Mei Lin hadn't known, either. She had gone home that night feeling unsettled, even after reporting her concerns to Tina

Booras and confirming that the doctor would examine Mariel first thing in the morning. But when Mei Lin returned for her shift the next afternoon, she was told that Mariel had died. Passed away in her sleep, presumably from a stroke.

"I'm all right now, honest," Julia chirped, interrupting Mei Lin's reverie as she intercepted the nurse in the hallway. "I'm really sorry about all that. It won't happen again, I promise."

"I hope not," Mei Lin replied, unable to avoid a double meaning. "I'm glad your kids are okay."

"Thank you," Julia said pleasantly, retaking the cart and turning it toward the next room. "I appreciate it."

Mei Lin nodded. She walked back to the nurses' desk, her limbs as heavy as lead. She was dropping into her chair when the realization hit. *Anxiety. Restlessness. Inability to sleep. Excessive sweating... increased tear production.* Not the usual set of symptoms that preceded a stroke. But classic for narcotic withdrawal!

She froze in horror. Mariel had been in withdrawal. How many doses of prescription opioid had she missed? It must have been several in a row to bring on such a "cold turkey" reaction. If Mariel did die of a stroke, it was no coincidence — not when withdrawal caused an increase in blood pressure!

Mei Lin spun around and punched at her keyboard. What other symptoms had Mariel shown that night, once Tina Booras had taken over? Did anyone notice her pressure spiking? Did Mariel have vomiting? Diarrhea?

She logged into Mariel's patient record. She had checked for cause of death before, but this time she drilled down and pulled up the nursing notes from that night. Tina's reports held nothing out of the ordinary. Nor, to her amazement, did her own. Mei Lin's pulse pounded in her ears as she searched the now read-only document for words that were no longer there. The symptoms she had recorded... any mention of sweating or tearing... *gone.*

Gone!

Her stomach heaved. This was definitely bigger than Julia. Even if the LVN worked two shifts back to back, she couldn't have stolen enough sequential doses of narcotic to put Mariel into full-blown withdrawal. Nor could she have altered Mei Lin's nursing notes. The only people with sufficient clearance to edit her remarks were the other charge nurses and the DON — and they weren't supposed to do it, either.

The charge nurses. The DON!

Mei Lin's heart could beat no faster. How high up did this evil go? Did it stop with Julia and Tina Booras? Was the DON herself involved? How long had it been happening? To go undetected for any length of time, the stolen doses would have to be coordinated so that no resident suffered obvious symptoms. Had Mariel Gonzalez' death been a rare mistake? Or... God forbid, had other residents gone into withdrawal, only to have their symptoms ignored, their records altered? Had other residents died?

Mei Lin's gaze moved to the phone. She could not call Tina Booras. Nor could she page the Director of Nursing. Not when she had no way of knowing where the corruption stopped. Following the facility's protocol was almost certain to tip off a guilty party, and if the situation became a she-said, she-said Mei Lin would be sure to lose. Her only chance at stopping this horror would be if she went outside the chain of command. Even then, she'd need hard evidence. And if she was wrong, she would never work again.

She breathed deeply and attempted to center herself. She had to make a decision, and she had to make it now. Julia had stolen at least one pill tonight and had not left the building since. Mei Lin was fairly certain Julia had moved no farther than the nurses' station, and all the public areas of the home were covered by security cameras. If the LVN was swapping out the pills at the residents' bedsides, she must be keeping a supply of placebos on her person. Which meant that Paulina's dose of narcotic — and perhaps others — could still be sitting in Julia's scrub pockets.

Mei Lin picked up her cell phone, stepped into a nearby supply cabinet, and shut the door.

She looked up Dallas Police, Narcotics Division. Then she clicked on the number and called.

Chapter 16

Present Day

"What happened?" Stanley asked after Mei Lin went quiet for a while. They were the first words he'd spoken. He'd been listening to her story attentively. "Did they send someone out?"

She nodded. If possible, the rest of her tale was even less pleasant to remember. "They came out, all right. It was awful. Julia went hysterical the moment they asked to speak with her. She refused to let them search her pockets and they detained her until they got a warrant. She had three doses of narcotic and some spare placebos in the front pocket of her scrub top. She was crying and screaming..."

Mei Lin shook her head at the memory. She hadn't seen Julia since her arrest that night. She'd heard that Julia's mother was taking care of the kids, but she still felt sick every time she thought about the children. "The next few hours... days... were a fiasco, as you can imagine. Nearly everyone on staff was questioned, as well as the administrators. I was suspended by the Executive Director, only to have that order rescinded almost immediately. They didn't know what to do with me."

"I can imagine," Stanley broke in wryly. "They should have thanked you. But that's never what happens. Let me guess... you became a pariah?"

Mei Lin nodded. "I wasn't looking for thanks. But everyone at work acted like I was some kind of traitor to the team — as if by going outside the system and calling the police, I had personally made orphans of Julia's children. It was miserable. Eventually I just quit."

Stanley clucked with dismay and shook his head. "You did the only thing you could do. If you'd told your supervisor they would have just fired the people involved and hushed it up.

Then off those nurses would go to steal pills elsewhere."

Mei Lin paused and looked at him. He really did understand, didn't he? Although she had received unqualified support from her friends and family, others in the healthcare field had not seen the issue as so cut and dried. "The Director of Nursing was very well liked," she explained. "No one could understand why I hadn't just reported what I saw to her. There was no evidence she knew what was going on, but she got fired anyway. They said she failed to check references, but really they just needed someone in management to take a fall. The other nurses blamed me for that, too. And in a way, they were right. If I had trusted her and she had reported it herself—"

"*If* she reported it herself," Stanley rebutted. "Handling it internally and hushing it up would have been better for her — for everyone employed there. Don't you see? What you did was put the patients first. Not just your own, but the next ones those two were likely to harm if they weren't arrested. And you know damn well they never would have *been* arrested if you hadn't acted immediately, while the LVN still had the pills on her! The scam could have gone on for years."

Mei Lin's eyes grew watery.

"You did the right thing," he said again, decisively.

"I know," she conceded. "But I still feel responsible for its happening at all — for not seeing it sooner. I worked very closely with Julia. If you'd asked me the day before if she was capable of doing such a thing, I would have said no. I didn't even suspect that Tina Booras had it in her to be so cruel."

His weathered brow creased. "So? You're not a mind reader."

"But I was a manager!" Mei Lin argued, giving voice to her innermost angst. Her family had tried to be helpful, but they didn't understand — they didn't know what it was like to be responsible for helpless patients' lives. "If I can't judge the character of the people who work under me, what good am I? It's all well and good to be a cheerful person with a rosy attitude on life, but what if I'm just plain gullible? Because the handwriting is on the wall, Stanley. I *am* gullible! I *am* too trusting! If I sat here and listed all the times I've gotten burned, just in the last two years—"

He sat up, his expression intent. "So tell me."

Images of Josh, Anthony, Jeremy, and Travis flashed before Mei Lin's eyes. "You don't want to know."

"Yes, I do," he insisted. "I want to know why you *think* you have bad judgment, because I disagree. You knew something was seriously wrong with Mariel Gonzalez that night, didn't you? You also knew something was seriously wrong with me. You were so certain of it that you hiked all the way up here, to a place you didn't know, to help a man who for all you knew could have been an ax murderer."

"Well, wasn't that gullible, too?" Mei Lin challenged. "If you were an ax murderer I'd be dead now!"

He mulled that over. "You took a calculated risk, yes, but the odds were in your favor and you did it for a good cause. What you did took courage, Mei Lin. The kind of courage that way too many people in the medical field today lack."

"You don't know the whole story," she demurred. "I've thought about this a lot, and my mind is made up. I can be a good nurse, but I'm not nurse practitioner material. I'm not even charge nurse material. I'm better off sticking to—"

"You'd be a great nurse practitioner!" he interrupted.

"No, I would not!" Mei Lin argued, her voice rising. How had she allowed herself to get into this conversation? Every second was torture, but her lips kept flapping. "My professional judgment is only part of it. My personal life is a friggin' disaster, and all because I keep trusting people who can't be trusted! I'm just plain stupid about people, especially men. And sooner or later that stupidity is going to hurt somebody else!"

"What makes you think you have to have a perfect life to be a good practitioner?" he shot back with equal volume. "Good Lord, girl! As a man I'm the scum of the earth, but I was still a damn good surgeon!"

Mei Lin got up from her chair. He was poking needles at her

psyche, and she didn't like it. Her mind was made up. "It's my decision," she proclaimed. "I have to do what I'm comfortable with. And as for—" She touched an unexpected object protruding from her back pocket. Anxious for a distraction, she pulled it out and looked at it. "Oh," she remembered, holding it out to him. "Sorry. This is for you. I found it on the porch earlier."

Stanley eyed her suspiciously as he took the note. "This conversation is not over," he warned. He unfolded the paper, held it at arm's length, and squinted. "Dear Mr. Smith," he read aloud. "I'm tracking some wildlife in the area and stopped by to make sure you don't mind me crossing onto your property. Hated to wake you — heard you're not well. Will drop by again soon. Please tell Mei Lin or Jesse if this is a problem. Thank you, Dave Markov, Chief Ranger, Glacier Bay National Park." He lowered his hands to his lap, his brow furrowed. "I've heard of him. He's never bothered to come out here before, though. I wonder what wildlife he's talking about."

"It's my fault, I'm afraid," Mei Lin apologized, grateful for the reprieve. She let out a heavy breath and sat down again. "I ran into some bears on my way home yesterday, and he wanted to check them out. Do you mind?"

Stanley's expression changed from puzzlement to worry. "Check out what? What happened to you? Were you hurt?"

His tone was practically paternal, and Mei Lin was touched. "Nothing happened," she assured. "The bears just sized me up and walked off. Of course, just seeing them that close was scary enough! But that's not why Dave is tracking them." She paused a second. She'd promised the ranger she wouldn't tell anyone else, but Stanley didn't count; it had happened on his property. "He's interested because one of the cubs was an unusual color. Have you ever heard of a glacier bear?"

Stanley's face froze. The color drained from his cheeks so rapidly that Mei Lin leaned forward, fearing he had gone into shock. Was he having a stroke? A heart attack? She grabbed his wrist to take a pulse. "What is it? Are you in pain?"

He stared back at her, glassy-eyed. Then he took in one huge gulp of air, and his color began to return. "Glacier bear?" he repeated hoarsely. He pulled his arm away from her and struggled to fully sit up. "Where was this?" His voice grew stronger. "When?"

Mei Lin studied him in surprise. It took several seconds for her to realize his crisis wasn't medical. He was flipping out over the stupid bear!

She fell back into the chair again and tried to calm her unjustly rattled nerves. What was wrong with these people? You could expect a man who served as chief ranger at a National Park to have a thing about bears... but Stanley was a freakin' doctor! "You scared me!"

"Sorry," he replied shortly, no longer sounding paternal. He'd morphed into a man possessed, just as Dave had yesterday. "Tell me!" he begged. "Tell me everything that happened. Exactly what you saw!"

Mei Lin sighed. She was surrounded by crazies. But the obsession did seem to make the men happy, and with Stanley that could be significant. She decided to indulge him, telling the story of her harrowing encounter in narrative form, complete with hand gestures and a few melodramatic embellishments. Stanley listened with an expression of rapture, interrupting frequently to ask for more detail. But when he seemed satisfied that she'd told him all she knew, he pulled back the blankets and swung his legs off the bed.

"Oh, no!" she protested, alarmed. "Where do you think you're going?"

"Well, *out*, of course!" he declared happily. "I can't very well see this cub for myself if I'm lying around inside, can I?"

Mei Lin shot up and moved around the foot of the bed to block him. "You can't possibly think you have enough strength to go traipsing around in the woods! You still can't even make it to the outhouse!"

Stanley frowned up at her. His breathing was rapid again, and his face was flushed. Mei Lin stared stonily back at him until he gave in and looked away. She knew he hated needing her and Jesse to empty his chamber pot, but he really couldn't walk more than a few steps without his legs giving out. "Okay, so maybe not," he conceded. "But... a glacier bear!"

His tone on the last two words was as reverent as if he were proclaiming the messiah, and Mei Lin rolled her eyes. "Well, if anybody can track down those bears again, it'll be Dave," she assured. "And if you want to get out there yourself, the fastest way to—"

"Well I sure as hell can't just lie in here all day! I can sit out on the porch and keep watch at least, can't I? There's a chair out there. I'll need something to prop up my feet..."

Mei Lin stopped arguing. Why a man who was convinced he had nothing to live for would get so excited about a bear, she had no idea. But if the prospect of spying one of the rare creatures from his porch was enough to motivate him through even one more dose of medicine, she was all for it. She helped him hobble outside, settled him in his plastic Adirondack chair, and scouted around until she found a wooden crate to use as an ottoman. Then she brought out a blanket and covered his legs. It was a warm day for Gustavus — low sixties, perhaps — but the porch was in the shade and the breeze was cool. The whole time she worked, he babbled with excitement, hardly noticing her.

"To think of all the years I've waited to see a glacier bear! Shoot, it's been my whole life! My grandfather saw one once, you know, up in Yakutat when he was a kid. He had cousins that lived up there. By the time I came along there was only Old Reggie left, but he was a character. We never saw a glacier bear, but we sure did try! When the boys were old enough we took them up there too, my dad and me. Such good times! And to think that in all those years, we never saw a damn thing, and now there's a blue cub right on my own property! I can't believe it!"

Despite his still-lingering fever and weakness from exertion, Mei Lin was surprised to hear Stanley flap his lips so carelessly.

When he'd mentioned 'the boys' before, he'd been delirious. Whenever he was fully conscious he had denied having children.

"It's funny," Stanley continued. He looked at her without seeing her, his piercing eyes watching scenes from a lifetime ago. "I used to tell a story just like yours. Well, sort of. It was about a mother bear with two cubs, one black and one blue. There were these two brothers who would go out camping, and more than anything they wanted to see a glacier bear. But no matter how hard they tried, the bears always stayed just out of sight! They're all following each other around, you know, and the cubs are just as interested in the boys because one of them has brown hair and the other blond..." He laughed to himself. "They loved that. And then there was this really funny part where the boys are stringing their pack up in a tree at night — you know, to keep the bears out of their food — but then the cubs figure out that—" He looked around his chair. "Can you grab my binoculars?"

"Where—"

"In the bin under the bed. Thanks. Anyway, so the cubs smell the food in the pack and decide to try..."

Mei Lin let him prattle on as she walked back into the cabin and reached under the bed. She pulled out a plastic storage bin and was surprised to find it full of crossword puzzle books. Had he not said he could barely write his name? Curious, she opened one and saw that the grids were filled in not with letters, but with dots and dashes. *Morse code,* she thought with amusement. Leave it to Stanley... he'd found a way to keep his brain active, even in his self-imposed solitary confinement. She replaced the puzzle book, located the binoculars, and shoved the bin back under the bed. When she returned to the porch he was still talking.

"And then the next day, they decided to kayak to a 'secret island,' but the cubs heard them talking and swam out first, you see..."

She laid the binoculars down in his lap and studied him as

she pretended to listen. His cheeks were a healthier color and his blue eyes held a vibrant new sparkle. The optimist in her couldn't help but smile.

There might just be hope for him after all.

Chapter 17

Margot's heart beat rapidly as she dialed her younger son's number. Jason's hearty, cheerful "Yo" made her smile, even as she fretted. "Hi, honey," she greeted. "I can't reach your brother. His phone's been off for a while and it's got me worried. Is he there with you?" She thought she detected a sigh on the other end, but perhaps she was only imagining it. Something crashed in the background, and the voice swore, even as it remained cheerful.

"Well, his *stuff* is sure as hell here," Jason answered. "Although I swear half of it is mine. Dude never returns anything. Hey! So that's where my pressure shower went!"

"I'm serious, honey," Margot pleaded. "I'm worried. Do you know where he is?"

This time a sigh was definitely audible. "He's on a plane, Mom. Keep calling, you'll get him eventually."

Her pulse increased. "A plane to where?"

"Juneau. I think."

Alaska! But how could Thane have... *no*. He didn't know anything. He was looking for a job up there, remember? Margot tried to calm herself. She was being ridiculous. Alaska was a big state. "But he's all right?" she finished lamely.

"Why shouldn't he be?" Jason returned.

"No reason," she replied too quickly. She was worried about Thane for more reasons than one, but she had to watch what she said. Jason might or might not already know about the Vanessa situation, and if he didn't, it was just as well. As difficult as her youngest son had been to raise, she did take some comfort in knowing that his obliviousness to family drama had left him a relatively happy, unencumbered adult. Thane was another matter. He'd always been more sensitive, which is why she was determined to deliver this latest bombshell about Vanessa in person. "It's just that I haven't seen him in a while... I haven't seen either of you in a while. I was going to drive to Tofino tomorrow, but I guess I'll have to wait. Do you know when he'll be back?"

"Sorry. You'll have to ask him," Jason said blithely, seeming distracted.

Margot was not offended. Her youngest had been in a state of constant motion — and resistance — since toddlerhood, but he was a good son and she knew he loved her. She agreed that she would try Thane again, asked a few questions about Jason's new surf lodge, embarrassed herself by asking about a girlfriend who was apparently now an ex, and then hung up.

Juneau. She hoped that Thane's stay in the city would be brief, because she was anxious to see him face to face. She wanted to get Linda's disturbing confession off her chest. She wanted to sit down with both her sons and have a nice, long chat over a hearty, home-cooked meal. But most of all, she wanted Thane the hell out of Alaska.

Mei Lin felt a twinge of guilt as she sat before her computer and typed the name into the search bar. *Stanley Smith, MD.* It seemed dishonest to do stealth research on a friend, which is how she was beginning to see him. But Stanley was also still a patient, and if she wanted to help him, she would have to understand him better. His excitement over the bear was bound to fizzle out eventually, and if his underlying issues weren't resolved by then, he could drop into another suicidal funk.

She could not allow that to happen.

Stanley had promised her that he would take his evening dose of antibiotic, and this time she had believed him. She had left him in the capable company of Dave Markov, who had shown up at the cabin in a tizzy explaining that on his last foray he had sighted what he believed to be the tracks of a bear sow and two cubs just a few hundred yards upstream. The men had quickly developed a rapport, and as Mei Lin walked away they had been sharing a pot of coffee on the porch, discussing potential bear movements like military commanders strategizing for battle.

She stared at the churning circle on her laptop screen. The wifi in Gustavus was excruciating. But she did credit it with helping break her habit of constantly checking her phone for messages and silly pictures. She still voice-called her friends, but since coming to Alaska she'd spent way more time seeking out the company of other live humans, which she found far more satisfying.

Finally, her laptop screen flashed, and Mei Lin sat up. Her search had produced a long list of hits. Not surprisingly, the name Stanley Smith was a common one, and it was shared by quite a few doctors. She steeled herself for a marathon of churning circles, then began clicking through the entries one by one, checking age and specialty for every possible match. But her effort proved fruitless. There simply was no trauma surgeon, or even general surgeon, who fit Stanley's profile.

She sank back in her chair, frustrated. Given that Stanley had spent a good chunk of his life on foreign soil in underdeveloped areas, she wouldn't expect him to leave much of a digital footprint. But she had expected to find *something*. An archived record of medical school graduation, for example. A donation to his alma mater. A line in a parent's obituary. But... nothing?

She dropped the *MD*. She tried adding *Alaska*. Stanley had never said where he'd lived or worked before going overseas, but his musings about relatives in Yakutat and his familiarity with the rainforest made her suspect he had grown up in Southeast Alaska. Wherever he had lived over the past roughly seventy years, he must have left some trace! Unless...

She groaned out loud. Of course! *Stanley Smith* wasn't even his real name! She pushed back her chair and stood up. She should have known. Had the man not bought a cabin in the middle of nowhere with the intention of hiding from the world?

Spirits flagging, she moved to gaze out the window over Elsie's meadow. A misty rain clogged the air, and no creatures stirred, not even the restless swallows that nested in the eaves. The dutiful parent birds would catch no mosquitos today — not until the rain stopped. *If* the rain stopped. Either way, Mei Lin could draw comfort from the vista. She knew that most people would find such a gray, soggy scene to be depressing. But she found it hauntingly beautiful.

I don't want to leave.

The voice that piped up from her subconscious was faint, but it demanded to be heard. Mei Lin's eyes swelled with tears. She had known this cry was coming. She'd known it the second she'd spied all those job query responses in her inbox... and felt miserable.

She didn't want to leave Gustavus. Not when she'd been so happy here. She was *still* happy here, despite the loneliness of the empty house. But she couldn't stay. She had to have gainful employment. And no matter what anyone else thought, she couldn't—

Her tears turned to sobs. She so hated to disappoint everyone! Her mind kept replaying the faces of her friends at the will reading... so excited, so earnest. They had all been so certain she would make a fine hospice practitioner! The confidence they had shown in her warmed her to her core, even as it made her feel wretched. And Elsie, in absentia, had made her feel worst of all. Dear Elsie, who knew all about Texas and *still* believed in her! Elsie had never directly asked Mei Lin to set up a hospice practice in Gustavus, but ambushing her at the will reading was entirely in character. Besides enlisting half the town to apply peer pressure, the wily old dear had managed to transform what would otherwise have been a friendly suggestion into a dying wish!

Mei Lin chuckled through her sobs. Elsie was a scream. If they'd known each other when Elsie was younger and healthier the two could have had some raucously good times. But Elsie was gone now, and the one thing she had asked of Mei Lin was the one thing she could never, ever do.

She cried harder. Stanley had said that one needn't have a perfect life to be a good practitioner, and Mei Lin didn't disagree. No one was perfect. But nobody, not even her family, knew the whole extent of her stupidity. The gullibility of Mei Lin Sullivan, BSN, MSN, was off the freakin' charts. With men her own age, it was legend-grade. She'd known her ex-fiancé, Josh, for six solid years, yet she'd never really known him at all. She'd thought Anthony to be intelligent, Jeremy to be responsible, and Travis not to be a felon. Zero for four spelled failure by any standard; her only consolation was that with those relationships, the only person hurt had been herself.

Professional misjudgments, on the other hand, carried grave consequences. A poor judge of character made a poor judge, period, *and there would be no more Mariels.* Knowing what she knew about herself, Mei Lin felt morally and ethically obligated to stick to what she was good at: following orders and providing bedside care.

Her sobs subsided as her resolve hardened. Disappointing people she cared about was difficult, but she had to do what was best. She dried her cheeks with a shirt sleeve and cast her eyes out the window again. No matter how she was feeling, the expanse of nature before her — always alive, always changing — was energizing. A fog had formed over the river, and she could no longer see across to the far meadow, much less make out the mountain peaks and sliver of ocean in the distance. But she knew they were there. They always would be, whether she was here to see them or not.

She threw back her shoulders and returned to her laptop. She would pursue those job replies, and she would do it now. Gustavus was hardly the only place on earth with a good view! Perhaps she could live in a smaller town on the coast of Washington or Oregon. Wherever she wound up, she wouldn't be alone. She would make new friends. Maybe she'd even meet a guy who was as sexy and kind and funny and honest as—

A jolt of pain shot through her middle, derailing her happy

train of thought. "Stop that!" she chided. Thinking about what *might have been* with a man she barely knew and would never see again was not only pointless, it was pathetic. Anyway, she had most likely misjudged Thane just like all the others. He was probably really a heroin dealer who ran a child porn ring out of a massage parlor in Detroit—

The doorbell rang. Mei Lin leapt up immediately, her mood transformed. Someone had come to see her! She suspected a near neighbor, since she'd heard no car, but the identity of the caller hardly mattered. The weather was tailor-made for a cup of Elsie's homemade spiced tea, and providence had spoken!

She hustled down the steps and threw open the door. Her breath caught in her throat and her heart stopped.

It was Thane Buchanan.

It couldn't be. Thane Buchanan had left two days ago.

But it was him. It was definitely him. He was here. He was back again.

Well, hot damn.

She gave a cry of joy, burst out the door, and jumped. It was a practiced move — one she had excelled at since high school. In one motion she flung her arms up and over his shoulders, body-slammed her weight against his chest, and wrapped her feet around his middle. He grunted with the surprise impact, then reflexively encircled her with his brawny arms. She'd been clinging to his neck a good three seconds, laughing all the while, before it occurred to her to wonder what the hell she was doing.

OMG! Internalized fantasies aside, the two were not technically friends. They'd never even hugged before.

Had she lost her mind?

Probably. Never mind that she'd jumped on guy friends literally hundreds of times in her life... the fact remained that all of them were actually friends. To jump on an adult man person she'd met exactly once was so far beyond the pale it was inexcusable. She should be mortified. She should be scarlet with embarrassment.

Meh. She regretted nothing.

"Thane Buchanan!" she announced, releasing him with a little push to the shoulders and bouncing back down to earth with aplomb. "You are the last person I expected to see. But I'm so glad — obviously! What's brought you back so soon? Or did you never leave in the first place?"

The handsome face with the striking blue eyes stared back at her, clearly speechless. How she did love those eyes! No one else on the planet had eyes like Thane's, except maybe...Yes! Stanley had eyes like that. Was that why he had seemed familiar to her, that first day she'd found him on the cabin floor?

Thane's jaw began to loosen. After another moment, he began to speak. "I, uh... I did leave. I went back to Vancouver... moved out of my apartment. I'm staying at my brother's place now."

"Where is that?" Mei Lin asked, her heart hammering. She couldn't keep the heady joy out of her voice if she tried, so she didn't. "You mean he lives up here?"

Thane shook his head, making drops of rainwater fly from his soaking locks and beard. "Tofino. On Vancouver Island." Damn, he was good-looking. Even better than she remembered. His hair seemed a shade darker, though—

"Oh!" she exclaimed, embarrassed for real this time. She hadn't even noticed they were standing in the rain. She couldn't imagine where he'd walked from, but he'd clearly been out — with the hood of his raincoat down — for quite some time. She stepped back and opened the door. "Come in, come in! I'm so sorry."

He laughed. It was a hearty, booming laugh, and its deep bass reverberated pleasantly through her body.

"Here, take off your coat, I'll hang it up," she offered, helping him disrobe. She really should not be this excited. She should not be staring — was she gaping? — at his powerful shoulders and solid chest and thinking about how gorgeous he must be underneath all those soft layers of cotton and fleece...

***

Thane was having more than a little trouble believing his good fortune. He had hoped that the pretty little nurse would still be in Gustavus; he had doubly hoped that if he had the gall to hitchhike to her house from the airport and wander up to her door unannounced she might actually be home. In a perfect world, she might even be glad to see him and would invite him in for a chat and a nice, hot cup of coffee.

But this? Maybe the plane had crashed or he'd been struck by a truck. The fantasy would end any moment now, and he would wake up. He'd find himself lying in mud somewhere with his head aching...

"Would you like a cup of coffee?" the imaginary woman asked. "Or maybe some of Elsie's homemade spiced tea?"

"Coffee," he murmured, staring at the vision. His mind had recreated Mei Lin as even sexier than he remembered. She wore a soft white sweater than clung to her curves and leggings that did the same lovely thing. Her dark eyes sparkled and her smile was radiant. In his fantasy, her greeting was legitimate. She knew who he was and had acted on impulse out of sheer joy. She also wasn't embarrassed or apologetic about it, which proved for sure that he was dreaming. Women always hid their true feelings — that's how they kept the upper hand.

"Come on upstairs," the vision suggested after his boots were off and his backpack and rain gear were spread out to dry. She was still smiling. "Have a seat in the living room and I'll get the coffee."

Thane followed her enticing form up the staircase and into the comfy living room he had previously only glimpsed through her porch windows. This would be the part where she started peeling her sweater off—

"How do you take your coffee?" she asked, moving into the kitchen. "I'm afraid I only have instant. Or the kind with the little bags. I can brew a pot, but it will take a while."

Thane blinked. Surely his brain could do better than this. He hated instant coffee. And why the hell were her clothes still on?

"Thane?" she asked, her voice full of laughter. "Did you hear me?"

He woke up then. Fully and completely. What was happening was real. She was real. Her sweater would not be coming off. But... Hellfire, had she actually *jumped* on him? "Instant is fine," he answered, trying hard to keep his voice normal. "Whatever you have. I don't care."

She gave a brisk nod, causing her silky black hair to swing about her shoulders. It had smelled like flowers when she'd hugged him.

"I can't believe you're back," she said gaily as she rooted around the open kitchen. "I didn't expect to ever see you again!"

Thane leaned over the counter between them and watched her hips sway as she moved. "Yeah, I know. I wrecked that whole shtick, didn't I? I'd say I'm sorry, but I'm not."

Her smile said that she wasn't either. "What happened?" she asked. "I mean, how did it go? With your non-fiancé?"

Vanessa was the absolute last thing he wanted to talk about. "Ghastly."

"I'm sorry," Mei Lin said softly, appearing to mean it. "But I still don't understand. Why are you here? I mean, I know I give awesome advice and everything, but surely you didn't fly all this way just to cry on my shoulder!"

The image that formed in Thane's head was inappropriately pleasant, and Mei Lin averted her eyes. Had she made a Freudian slip? He hoped so. "Oh, I have another reason," he said smoothly. "But it's a secret."

She stopped what she was doing and frowned at him. "Not if you want this coffee, it isn't!" she teased. "Spill it, Buchanan. I've had enough secrets lately."

"Okay, okay." He really must be dreaming. Women thrived on secrets. "I'll tell you if you promise not to laugh."

Mei Lin turned back to her work with a giggle, and his blood heated at the sound. Hers was not a girlish giggle, but a low-pitched, jolly rumbling that seemed to bubble up from her soul. "Sorry! No can do. You'd best just throw it out there."

Thane grinned. She was definitely going to laugh at him. But what the hell? "I got a call from Dave Markov last night. He was all excited because there's been a sighting up here of a very rare mammal, and he knew I'd want to hear about it."

Mei Lin turned around again.

"He knows I have a... well, I guess you'd call it a 'Moby Dick' thing for this particular critter," Thane continued. "Minus the murderous intent, of course! He didn't expect me to fly up, though. This little field trip was a spur of the moment decision; I pretty much jumped on the first plane out. And yes, I realize it was a crazy, impulsive thing to do. But after the... uh, *confrontation*, you could say I had an irresistible urge to get out of Vancouver."

Mei Lin's exquisitely shaped, dainty black eyebrows lifted. "You're talking about the glacier bear?"

Thane's mouth dropped open. Just seeing her plump ruby lips form the words "glacier bear" justified the cost of his plane ticket. "How... how did you know?" he sputtered. Then a horrible thought struck. "The word isn't out all over town, is it?"

She shook her head. "No, no. Don't worry. I only know because I'm the one who saw it."

He leaned forward, afraid to breathe. "*You* saw a glacier bear?"

Mei Lin exploded into laughter. Her reaction might have surprised him if he wasn't totally absorbed with watching her perfectly curved little body double up with mirth. "Yes, it was me," she confirmed. "I told Dave and Mary because they happened to be the first people I ran into afterwards. I had no idea it was such a big deal! He told me not to tell anyone else. But clearly, he did!"

For a long moment, Thane could do nothing but stare. Either he had just fallen in love, or he was projecting his obsession with glacier bears onto the first female he'd ever met who had glimpsed one. He didn't know which, but the effect was the same either way. Mei Lin Sullivan was now officially the most entrancing female alive.

He attempted to collect himself. But as her words finished percolating through his brain, he whirled around and headed for the nearest window instead. "You saw the bear *here?*" he demanded, his eyes scouring the misty meadow. "Where?"

Mei Lin nearly fell apart again. "No, no! It was way out in the woods... on somebody else's property."

He turned around reluctantly. "Tell me," he begged. "Tell me the whole story. *Everything.*"

"Fine," she agreed, still laughing. Merciful angel that she was, she didn't make him wait for the water to heat before she began telling her story. And what a story it was! There she had been, all alone deep in the woods when a mother bear and two cubs appeared before her. She hadn't run, of course, because she was as smart as she was beautiful. She had done everything right, and the bears had peacefully wandered away. A black cub and a blue one. Just like his favorite story his dad used to tell!

At some point she handed him a steaming mug of coffee. It smelled wretched, but even if it hadn't, his interest was gone.

"I have to see that cub," he whispered hoarsely. "Please, Mei Lin. Take me there?"

Chapter 18

Thane grumbled under his breath as he secured the last of the rope on deck while Dave drove the boat away from the dock.

"Will you stop looking so glum?" the ranger chastised with a grin. "We'll get you out there soon enough."

Thane threw his friend a sour look. It was fine for Dave to be chipper — the ranger had already had not one, but two cracks at finding the glacier cub. Thane was still waiting, and when you'd waited a whole lifetime for something, even one extra night and a morning seemed endless. Still, he couldn't blame Dave for the delay. It was entirely appropriate that the landowner's permission be acquired before Thane set out, particularly since Dave — not knowing Thane was coming — had promised the man just yesterday that they would keep the hunt between the two of them. With luck, Mei Lin would get the requisite permission on her visit to the cabin this morning, and Thane and Dave could set out first thing this afternoon.

Dave had other work to do this morning, anyway. The rebounding sea otter population of Glacier Bay wasn't going to document itself.

Thane's spirits buoyed as the boat headed out onto the open water. The ocean air was crisp this morning, and he drew in a deep, satisfying lungful as he took in the view. The broad expanse of Glacier Bay was beautifully uncrowded with vessels, even at the height of the tourist season. Since the whole area was a preserve, permits to motor into the bay were limited. Every day, a few gigantic cruise ships would sail in for a peek, but they didn't explore far before heading back out again. Most of the bay's craggy shoreline remained desolate. Few human eyes spied more than a small sample of the myriad sandy beaches, rocky cliffs, and abundant wildlife that were encircled by the ice-capped peaks towering in the distance. Yet whether humans watched or not, rare seabirds frolicked continually between the ocean buffet and their cliffside nests, while farther up in the narrow inlets, ice chunks floated and blue-white glaciers spilled from deep crevices in the mountains.

"So, where'd you end up camping last night?" Dave called out over the humming sound of the motor. The sun was in rare form today. Hardly a cloud was in sight, making the water a clear, deep blue. "Did you get in at Bartlett Cove? I heard they've been pretty full up lately."

Behind his bushy beard, Thane's lips curved into a smile. "Yeah, I heard that the campground was crowded. I could have pitched my tent anywhere, but Mei Lin wouldn't have it. The guesthouse was rented out already, but she said I'd be an idiot to camp in the rain when there was a whole extra bedroom and bathroom on the first floor of Elsie's house. I figured she was right."

Dave's mouth twisted with disapproval. "You behave yourself with Mei Lin, you hear me? She's a good girl."

Thane grinned. Dave's paternal protectiveness toward Mei Lin pleased him; it proved that his mentor was also a fan. Sadly, the only things that had transpired between himself and Mei Lin last night had been great conversation and a giant tub of popcorn. Both had been interrupted far too soon by a call from Mei Lin's parents, at which time Thane had felt obligated to quietly excuse himself downstairs. He had tossed and turned half the night looking forward to seeing his hostess again at breakfast, but then he'd overslept. When he woke, the house had been empty of all but a pot of coffee — freshly brewed, this time — and an apologetic note. Mei Lin regretted not being there to share breakfast with him, but she wanted to get to her patient bright and early. She hoped to be back soon with the landowner's blessing, after which Thane would be free to stalk the little bear family to his heart's content.

He had been sorely disappointed to miss her. But he would definitely enjoy her return.

"There's number one," Dave called out, pointing. A sea

otter was floating on its back nearby, looking like a furry log with arms. "How about you make yourself useful and keep the log?"

Thane picked up the clipboard.

"I mean it about Mei Lin," Dave added, catching Thane's eyes. "We're rather fond of that young lady around here."

Thane shook his head with a sigh. "And here I was thinking you were fond of me. Are you going to warn her off, too?"

Dave clucked his tongue with a scowl. "Just count the damn otters."

Mei Lin arrived at Stanley's cabin to find him sitting out on his porch, bright-eyed and fully dressed. An exuberant Kibbe ran out to meet her and accepted his usual tummy rub.

"Good morning, Nurse Sullivan," Stanley called out as she neared. "Would you like a cup of coffee?"

She smiled. He looked so much better. His color was good, his hair was carefully combed, and there was no trace of feverish sweat on his forehead. "I'd love one," she replied. "You're feeling well?"

He leaned over the water barrel he was using as a table, lifted a pot, and poured coffee into a second, waiting mug. "I do," he acknowledged, extending the mug.

Mei Lin took it and noticed that his hand was shaking. She sat down on the upturned washtub that had been Dave's seat yesterday and took a sip. "Still hot!" she praised. "You've been busy this morning."

He nodded, his blue eyes sparkling with pride. Mei Lin hadn't been wrong — it was his resemblance to Thane that had sparked her earlier sense of familiarity. The two men didn't really look alike apart from their eyes, but the contrast of light and dark in their irises was uniquely affecting. "Your magic pills are doing their thing, I suppose," he replied, sounding mildly disappointed. "And before you ask, yes, I took last night's and this morning's. Have to see that bear, you know."

"Yes, I know," she murmured, wondering. She owed the glacier cub a debt of gratitude. Stanley had taken enough antibiotic now that he even if did decide to stop treatment, his own immune system might be able to stave off the remaining infection. Then again, it might not. His fate would depend on his overall state of health as well as the vagaries of the particular bug. Nothing was guaranteed. "How's the wound looking today?"

"Coming along," Stanley replied, lifting a pant leg and twisting his ankle so she could see. The swelling in his calf had gone down considerably, and the hot, angry red color around the cut had faded to a dissatisfied reddish-pink. The drainage had decreased to one tiny area and even that appeared to be drying up.

"Beautiful!" she said, delighted. "Comparatively speaking, of course."

He grinned at her, and despite his wrinkled skin and coffee-stained teeth, the humor in his eyes gave him a boyish look. "I was hoping you'd be impressed."

Mei Lin's mind skipped back to Thane again. It didn't take much; she'd been thinking about him constantly for the last fourteen hours. Unfortunately, they'd spent precious little of that time together, thanks to some incredibly bad timing on her mother's part. "I am extremely impressed," she conceded. "At this rate you'll be up and stalking innocent wildlife in a matter of days."

"That's the plan," Stanley acknowledged with good humor. "Today, the outhouse. Tomorrow, the world."

Mei Lin smiled tentatively. He seemed a wholly different man from the one she had peeled off the cabin floor three days ago. But appearances could be deceiving. "You made it to the outhouse?"

"And back," he crowed. "Had to rest once or twice, but no concussive falls occurred. I count that a victory."

"As well you should," Mei Lin agreed. "As long as you're careful not to overdo. Infection can really sap the life out of you. Most people are weaker than they imagine."

He feigned outrage. "How dare you call me 'most people!' I am exceptional in all ways." His teasing tone turned serious, and his eyes locked on hers. "As are you, my dear."

Mei Lin sensed a trap.

"Dave and I had a very interesting talk yesterday."

She sighed. "Oh?"

"I understand that this nurse practitioner thing isn't just a passing thought," he said accusingly. "You've already had the training. You've even passed the boards."

Mei Lin said nothing. The strong coffee had lost its appeal.

"He told me you turned down a plum job right here in Gustavus!" Stanley exclaimed. "Elsie Dunn had folks look into it, and there's a hospice doctor in Juneau who'd love to extend his practice out this way."

"So I've heard," she replied defensively, her joy in the morning diminishing. "And I hope he is successful. There is a huge need here."

"So what's the problem?" Stanley pressed. "Can't deal with the weather?"

She frowned. "Please. I'm from Maine. Weather isn't an issue. The darkness took some getting used to, but I managed."

"So?" he barked back at her. "Don't tell me you bagged the whole idea just because of what happened with a few bad actors at one nursing home. Because that would be stupid. And you're not stupid."

Mei Lin set her cup down by her feet and rose, feeling restless. She wasn't used to being challenged so directly. At least not since she'd ditched Josh. Her family was more tactful. Her sister had always been a master at unspoken criticism; her mother talked in carefully couched, self-esteem-preserving therapist speak; and her father let his wife speak for him on any halfway sensitive matter. All three had objected to Mei Lin's dropping her nurse practitioner plans, but none of them had called her decision "stupid." Name-calling had been Josh's area, and Mei Lin didn't have to listen to him anymore. She didn't have to listen to Stanley, either.

"It wasn't *just* that," she defended. "But even if it was, I'm entitled to make my own decisions."

"And I'm entitled to call them as I see them," Stanley went on, undeterred. "So what if you couldn't tell what those nurses were capable of? Neither could anybody else who worked with them, including whoever hired them and supervised them. What makes you so special you get held to a higher standard?"

Mei Lin started to answer, but couldn't. He wasn't looking at the situation right. Somehow.

"Should everyone who signed off on their hiring resign?" he pressed. "Maybe everybody who ever worked with them and didn't suspect anything should resign, too. *Then* you'd improve patient care."

Mei Lin groaned. "Don't be ridiculous."

"That would be ridiculous," he agreed. "I've lived this business longer than you've been alive, Mei Lin. Medicine attracts some of the best people on earth and some of the worst, and I've worked with plenty of both. How many mistakes do you think you're allowed? Three? Five? You'd still have to eliminate every surgeon I know!"

"I realize that everyone makes mistakes!" she argued, frustrated. The porch was too small to pace on, so she stepped down onto the ground. "Clinical errors, unintentional oversights, the simple slip of a hand on a rough day — those things can happen to anybody. But having practitioner-level responsibility requires a certain baseline of sound judgment, and I can assure you, I don't have it! The business at Silverson wasn't the turning point for me, it was the nail in the coffin." She whirled to face him again. "The fact is, my judgment sucks. Period! Okay?"

Stanley replaced his coffee cup on the water tank and folded his hands calmly. "You think? Give me an example."

"I can give you four examples!" she spouted. "Josh, Anthony, Jeremy, and Travis!"

Stanley looked skeptical. But he said nothing. He waited.

Mei Lin blew out a frustrated breath. He was too damned good at this. Now she was stuck. "I was so convinced that Josh was a great guy I dated him for six years and then decided to get engaged and move with him halfway across the country," she confessed. "But he was really a self-absorbed control freak. Little by little, without my even noticing, he gradually became more dominating. *And* more demeaning. And like a fool, I put up with it. I put up with it all!"

"So you married him?"

"No! I dumped him and moved to Texas on my own."

Stanley shrugged. "You broke it off. And you were, what, teenagers when it started? Spare me. Go on."

Mei Lin's face grew hot. "I thought Anthony was a great guy, too, and I was twenty-four when I met him. He was a fellow nurse who asked me out on my first day of work in Dallas and we had a whirlwind thing going for about six weeks. Until the next new hire started and he dropped me like a rock. That was his pattern, you see. Falling for Anthony's BS was like a hazing ritual in that department — it was also prime entertainment for the staff. For anyone who bet I'd last a month, I paid off three to one."

Stanley clucked his tongue. "Toxic work environment. It happens. Rebound thing, besides. So... you stuck around and fought for your man? Challenged the new girl with broken bottles in the parking lot?"

Mei Lin stared at him. "Of course not! I transferred to another department. The new group was much more professional."

He smirked. "Uh-huh. Next?"

Her face got redder. Stanley's know-it-all attitude was getting under her skin, and she hardened her tone. "Jeremy was worse. Only a complete fool would have been taken in by him. And I was. I believed his whole sob story about how his ex had broken his heart, ruined his credit, and taken off with his only means of transportation. I believed him when he said that he was making a better salary now and that he could easily afford the payments on a new truck... if only he could get someone to cosign the loan for him."

Stanley winced. "Ouch. How much did that cost you?"

"See!" Mei Lin cried, feeling vindicated. "You only heard that much and you know what happened!"

"The car got repo'ed, leaving you on the hook for thousands?"

"Yes!" Her face felt like fire. She had never told anyone — not Elsie, and especially not her family — the extent of that particular debacle. The truth was too humiliating. The truth was that she was still making payments on the damn thing.

"Okay, yeah, that was stupid," Stanley agreed mildly, leaning back in his chair. "With me it was a Shelby Cobra. Bright red beauty, shiny black stripe. What a gorgeous set of wheels! I had zero chance of paying for it on a resident's salary. Ruined my credit for a decade. Guess I should have quit surgery then, huh?"

Mei Lin stared back at him. She felt like screaming, but settled for gritting her teeth in frustration. "You're missing the point. I agree: no one is perfect. But when a person repeatedly shows poor judgment in pretty much all major life areas, that means something! What it means is that they shouldn't hold life and death decisions in their hands!"

Stanley pursed his lips and considered. "You're right, nothing is as dangerous as a nurse practitioner who's naive about romance and personal finance. It's a good thing I'm a surgeon, since I'm lousy with money and have women on four continents wishing me to hell. What about the last guy?"

"Travis was a registered sex offender!" Mei Lin blurted. She'd never told anybody *that* before either. "I met him at a bus stop and we went out four times before I had the sense to check him out online! He'd spent eighteen months in jail after a sting operation caught him trying to arrange an out-of-state meeting with an underage girl!"

"Now there's a scumbag," Stanley agreed. "What made you decide to check him out?"

"I don't know! He seemed nice enough at first, but there was just—" She broke off when she realized Stanley was smirking again.

"Something that bothered you?" he finished for her. "How oddly perceptive. For a lousy judge of character, I mean."

Mei Lin turned away. He was turning her argument into mincemeat, damn him.

He chuckled a little nervously. "I'm sorry. I know that none of this is funny to you. Come and sit down again, please? Indulge a supercilious old fool with nothing better to do than give unwelcome advice."

Mei Lin felt totally off balance. She returned to her seat as requested and picked up her cup, but quickly set it down again. The rim was coated with dog drool.

"You're young," he said more gently. "You're a glass-half-full kind of person and you're idealistic about our profession, which is fine. But your expectations for yourself — and all the rest of us — are unrealistic. Some of the best trauma surgeons I know are arrogant, narcissistic jerks with completely screwed-up personal lives. But if I'm bleeding out from a car wreck, you'd better believe I'm calling whoever's best in the OR and to hell with the rest of it. And if I'm stuck in a cabin in the middle of nowhere with an infected leg and a bad attitude, the last nurse who's going to inspire me is some holier-than-thou ex-military woman who treats me like a child. What I need is a nurse who is alive, someone creative and a little unconventional. Someone soft enough to care, but with enough sass to handle wild bears and stubborn old goats alike." He softened his voice. "People like that don't wander by every day, Mei Lin. "

She looked into his piercing light eyes and could see that he meant every word he was saying. She could also see that saying it was important to him. She dipped her chin, embarrassed that her eyes were tearing. She choked out a laugh. "I'm terrified of bears."

"You're here, aren't you?" he replied. "And thanks to you,

so am I."

For a long time, neither of them said anything. He sipped at his coffee while Mei Lin dried her eyes with her sleeve. She supposed, despite herself, that the man did have a point. But she didn't want to think about herself and her professional life right now. She had come up here for other business — business that was infinitely more pleasant to think about.

She cleared her throat and changed the subject. "I have to ask you something. Dave wants to know if it's okay if he brings someone else here with him this afternoon. Another wildlife specialist."

Stanley frowned. "I thought he agreed we wouldn't tell anybody else. At least while the cub's still on my land."

"He didn't tell anyone local," Mei Lin explained. "And it happened before he'd promised you that. It was right after I told him; he was so excited he contacted a colleague in Canada, someone he knew was equally obsessed with glacier bears. He wouldn't have told Thane either, I don't think, if he suspected he'd jump on the first plane up here!" Hearing her own words suddenly made her doubt them. *Had* Dave really been all that surprised? She'd only known Thane a few days herself, but after witnessing the manic gleam the words "glacier bear" had put in his eyes, she would expect no less of a reaction. Perhaps Dave had actually been hoping his friend would join him?

She realized that Stanley was staring at her. His cheeks were flushed and his pupils had widened. "Well, you can just tell Dave, *no!*" he said forcefully. "I don't want anybody else on my property!"

Mei Lin froze. Stanley's outburst was so unexpected she wondered if something was wrong with him. She looked for any signs of a physical problem, but saw only raw emotion — specifically, fright. "That's fine," she replied softly, baffled. "Do you feel all right?"

Stanley looked away from her, his expression changing swiftly to embarrassment. "I'm fine," he said hoarsely, but in a more normal tone. "I just... I mean it. It's fine for you and

Dave to come, but I don't want anybody else out here. Will you tell him that?"

"Of course," she agreed. In addition to the flush on Stanley's face, tiny beads of sweat had broken out on his forehead. She refilled his mug with drinking water and set it down on the makeshift table. His pale blue eyes avoided hers, and as he picked up the cup, his hand shook even worse than before. Whatever had spooked him, the effect was profound.

Mei Lin's mind spun with questions, but for now, she refrained from asking them. Stanley was clearly terrified. But of what? The mere thought of one more stranger coming onto his property? But he hadn't known her or Dave either, not when they first wandered up!

Her heart felt like lead. Thane would be so disappointed. But she was worried about Stanley, too. The seemingly fearless surgeon had voluntarily faced infectious diseases, bombing raids, and armed guerillas in some of the most hostile environments on earth. All *before* he'd nearly succeeded in carrying out a slow and painful suicide.

What more could possibly frighten him?

Chapter 19

By early afternoon, the weather in Gustavus had become as perfect as Mei Lin had ever seen it. The sky was blue as a robin's egg, only a few wispy clouds drifted across its vast expanse, and the sun warmed the air around her to a balmy seventy-two degrees. What better way to celebrate than an impromptu picnic with a gorgeous guy at one of her favorite spots on earth?

She admired Thane's muscular form as he unfolded himself from the passenger side of the Subaru and stepped out onto the graveled wide spot that passed as the trailhead's parking lot. He'd been horribly disappointed when she broke the bad news, but he was trying hard not to mope, which she respected. "This is it!" she announced with cheer.

The Nagoonberry Trail ambled through forest, wetland, and fields of wildflowers on its way from a residential area to the beach, and in her healthier days, Elsie had walked it regularly. After Mei Lin's arrival the elderly shut-in had begun to enjoy her favorite walk once again, albeit vicariously. Mei Lin would return from the trek with reams of pictures and videos on her phone, and the two of them would pore through the collection together. Elsie could identify animals from their scat and tracks and birds by their song, and they had both delighted in following the progress of the wildflowers as they burst from the soggy ground and unfurled to their full splendor.

Mei Lin could hardly wait to engage in some quality nature appreciation with Thane. She hitched her can of bear spray to the fanny pack containing her water bottle and phone, then reached over the seat to grab the gear in which she'd packed their lunches. It was gone. Thane already had the larger backpack out of the car and slung over one broad shoulder, where it dangled effortlessly next to his own lightweight drawstring pack. "Oh," she said with surprise, unused to male gallantry in any form. "Thanks."

Thane didn't seem to process her meaning. He merely smiled down at her as she joined him outside the car, his face showing enthusiasm even as his eyes still glinted with a trace of melancholy.

She smiled back at him and led the way through the trees and down the path. The trail was beautiful as always. Everything was so green! Thick moss covered the forest floor and everything on it, sweeping across fallen tree trunks, rocks, and stumps like a living, breathing carpet. In temperate rain forests, trees fell victim not to forest fires but to the wind, which regularly toppled all sizes of trunks by tugging their roots from the saturated earth. The felled trees were quickly blanketed with both the moss and a variety of colorful lichens and fungi, ensuring the speedy return of their nutrients to the already rich soil. Mei Lin grinned as Thane paused by one of her own favorite stumps, which was capped with a moss so thick it looked like a giant head of green hair. Huge gray and white shelflike fungi protruded from the stump horizontally, giving a vague resemblance to eyes and a nose. "I call that one Hairy," Mei Lin said.

"Very appropriate," Thane agreed.

Catching sun above the moss was a sprinkling of forest ferns, then a variety of berry bushes and seedling trees. The mature Sitka spruce and hemlocks sported bark that was speckled with green moss and blue lichens, and their lower regions were ringed with short, spiky sticks bearing witness to limbs of the past. Up above Mei Lin's head the branches gradually began to fill out, till at the treetops a feathery sea of green nearly blotted out the sky. The trail meandered to a small clearing, where a pond of jet-black water was covered with the flat green leaves and yellow blossoms of lily pads. Mei Lin paused long enough to a pluck a few wild blueberries from the bushes that edged the trail, and Thane wordlessly followed her lead. As she watched him select just the right berries, then savor their unique sweetness with a flicker of his eyelids, any thoughts she might have had regarding the value of a full year of celibacy evaporated.

"Your turn to lead," she said cheerfully, moving behind him to pluck more berries. "See if you can locate my secret bench."

Thane accepted the challenge with a smile and set off back down the trail, his long-legged stride confident, but unhurried. Mei Lin shamelessly appreciated her new and improved view, enjoying the play of his muscles beneath his soft jersey shirt and well-worn jeans. She enjoyed it so much, in fact, that she blindly trod straight into a pile of moose scat. They talked little, enjoying the chatter of the birds and the occasional breeze that rustled through the evergreen canopy above.

Thane stopped suddenly. Mei Lin pulled up short; if she had been following two steps closer, she would have crashed into his backside. *Darn.*

"Aha!" he crowed, looking off into the distance. He smiled at her, then stepped off the main trail and headed down a narrow path that curved toward another clearing. In a few moments they reached Mei Lin's patently obvious "secret bench," which sat under the spreading umbrella of a black cottonwood tree. Thane set their backpack down on the wooden seat, stretched out his arms, and admired the view. "Nice," he approved.

"I've always thought so." Mei Lin stepped up beside him and looked out over the meadow. Her eyes drank in the beauty of the lupine flowers, their purplish-blue hues contrasting perfectly with the chorus of green that surrounded them. Beyond the wildflowers, grass, and scrubby bushes of the foreground, a line of young evergreens stretched toward the sun, silhouetted against a stunning backdrop of distant, blue-green mountains. "Shall we eat here?"

"Most definitely," he agreed. They settled on the bench and Mei Lin unpacked her takeout offering: the best soup and grilled paninis the Cafe Herbivore had to offer. She'd ordered twice as much food for Thane as she usually did for herself, and she was amused to watch him finish every bite. They ate while having a spirited discussion of the relative benefits of living in the US versus Canada, a conversation which, like most they'd enjoyed so far, ended up leaving them in peals of laughter. Mei Lin couldn't remember the last time she'd felt so relaxed and comfortable with a man — at least not one she was attracted to. She was a pleaser by nature, and the single men of her experience were so needy and demanding that any kind of relationship meant work. Being with Thane was different. He didn't seem to *need* anything from her. He was merely enjoying her company.

"Let's go see that beach," he suggested when the food was gone. "Should be around low tide now. We can check out who got there before us."

Mei Lin knew from the gleam in his eye that he didn't mean people. "Let's!" she agreed eagerly, rising. He seemed so much better, and she was having so much fun, she could hardly suppress her happiness. "I'm so glad to see you're enjoying yourself," she admitted, "even if I do make a poor substitute for a glacier cub!"

Thane grinned at her as he collected their trash and stuffed it into his pack. "You hear me complaining?"

"You're not the complaining type. But I know you're disappointed. And I'm sorry about Stanley. He's a little unpredictable. But he did practically beg me to come out and see him again tomorrow, and I intend to appeal your case. So don't give up!"

Thane shrugged. "Give up? A Buchanan? Never. That cub could pop up again most anywhere. I can hardly blame the man. If he's as keen on seeing a glacier bear as I am, the last thing he needs is more folks traipsing around his place, potentially scaring them away. That's just good sense."

Mei Lin doubted that Stanley's outburst was motivated by any kind of sense, but she didn't say so.

"Besides," Thane continued, "near misses have always been a part of the quest. It's a family tradition; my father and grandfather were even more obsessed than I am, if you can believe it!"

"I cannot," Mei Lin chuckled as they resumed walking down the trail. "But I am getting the idea that this particular disease runs in families."

"Oh, for sure. My dad used to tell us bedtime stories about glacier bears." His tone of voice changed suddenly. The shift was subtle, but Mei Lin could feel it — an undercurrent of sorrow. "He was a fabulous storyteller. When you told me about the bears you saw, it reminded me of his stories."

"All these bear stories!" she exclaimed with a chuckle. "You make me jealous. The only bedtime stories I remember my mom reading were politically correct children's books about multicultural families — which were about as exciting as they sound. My dad was better, though. He'd read us princess tales on the sly."

Thane laughed. "My mom read us books. But my Dad could tell stories straight off the cuff. Crazy stuff, and so funny... he never told any story the same way twice."

Mei Lin could hear the slightest of hitches in his voice, even as he smiled. Clearly, the pain of his father's loss must still be raw. "Your dad passed away?" she asked softly.

"He did," Thane confirmed. "A long time ago. When I was thirteen."

Mei Lin was surprised. She could not imagine the horror a child would feel at losing a parent, but still... twenty years seemed a long time to grieve. Perhaps the family quest had brought up memories he hadn't processed in a while. "I'm sorry," she empathized. "What happened to him?" Her sister's voice, which at some point had become a permanent adjunct to her conscience, immediately berated her for asking such a personal question. Mei Lin ignored it. Ri had always been so guarded that it took her forever to get to know someone, much less trust them. But Mei Lin was an open book. She'd always believed that making herself vulnerable made others feel more comfortable sharing.

"He was murdered," Thane answered flatly. He stopped, reached down to grab a stick, then poked at another pile of scat, this one half hidden beneath the broad leaves of a devil's club. "Looks like black bear, maybe a day old. Been eating blueberries."

Mei Lin's voice was faint. "Murdered?" she repeated, horrified.

Thane straightened up and tossed the stick. "Yep," he replied, not looking at her. "It was a fluke kind of thing. He was at a medical conference in Chicago, and he was kidnapped by some career criminals. One of their buddies had a gunshot wound, but couldn't go to an ER without getting arrested. They found out the conference center was swarming with surgeons, so they plucked a likely candidate off the curb and tried to force him to treat their friend. The police tracked them down and raided the place, but my dad was shot in the crossfire."

"That's... awful," Mei Lin sputtered. If anyone else had told her such a made-for-television story, she'd think they were lying. But she knew that Thane was not. "I'm so sorry."

He shrugged and started walking again. "It was a long time ago. It wasn't easy. But we dealt." After a few more paces, he dropped to a squat and examined something else on the trail. "You've got wolves here," he said more matter-of-factly. "Ever hear them howl at night?"

Mei Lin didn't know what he was looking at. Her focus was entirely on his face, which looked normal from this angle, but didn't deceive her. He was still deeply affected by his father's murder.

What question had he just asked her? She had to replay the last few seconds in her mind. "I've never heard any howling, no," she replied finally. "But I've seen wolf tracks on the beach."

"Awesome," he said more jovially, getting to his feet again. "Let's go find some more."

Mei Lin wanted desperately to hug him. He needed a hug, even if he wasn't asking for one. Many people, her sister most definitely included, considered uninvited hugs to be a violation of personal space. But Mei Lin didn't think Thane was one of those people.

She closed the distance between them and clasped him around his waist. *I'm so sorry,* she attempted to convey. *I can't do much, but I hope this will make you feel a little better. For now.* Thane's arms enfolded her reflexively, but she was careful not to overstay her purpose. After a few seconds she took a step back and smiled at him. A happy distraction was now in order. Her voice turned mischievous. "We've got a ways to walk before we get there. But I bet I can find wolf tracks before you do."

Thane's lips twisted into a grin, and his still-moist eyes sparkled devilishly. "Like hell you can."

The next few minutes found the two of them frolicking through field and forest like a couple of ten-year-olds on a sugar high. They met no other humans on the trail, which was fortunate, since their ringing laughter and occasional shrieks would have thoroughly wrecked anyone else's quiet reflection. They agreed that sprinting anywhere with enough underbrush to conceal a bear was verboten, but when it came to halting, delaying, or otherwise interfering with each other's progress toward the beach, Mei Lin soon discovered that Thane's criminal creativeness was equal to her own. They made up rules as they went, debating the specifics, but when Mei Lin's use of secret off-trail shortcuts was finally ruled out of bounds, she realized more desperate tactics would be needed. Stealing a piggy back ride seemed the perfect way to cut her losses — besides being all sorts of fun — until they drew within sight of the beach and she noticed that Thane had untied both her shoes. In a flash, he tugged the low-heeled boots from her feet, shrugged her from his back, and took off toward the sand with an evil cackle.

"No fair!" she protested hopelessly, shoving her feet back in the boots and retying them. Soaking her socks in wet sand was not an option, nor was picking her way through gravel and prickly plants in bare feet. When she looked ahead and saw him studying the ground, then sidestepping with a grand flourish of his hand, she knew her bet was lost.

"Gray wolf!" he announced proudly.

Mei Lin panted her way through the rest of the grass and brush and onto the soft sand of the intertidal zone. The difference between high and low tides was dramatic in Maine, but the Alaskan coast took the prize for having the greatest area of beach regularly revealed and concealed by the shifting saltwater. From where Mei Lin stood at the edge of the high water mark, hundreds of yards of temporarily exposed sand stretched between her and the lapping edge of low tide. Each time the water withdrew, it left behind a fresh array of colorful plants and stranded sea life, providing a happy smorgasbord for waiting land creatures.

"Big one, probably a male," Thane elaborated, pointing. The wet sand made good impressions of animal paws and human shoes alike, providing a clear record of anything that had traveled the beach since the last high tide — provided no heavy rains had intervened. The tracks at which Thane pointed looked much like dog prints, except for their impressive size and near-linear pattern. Wild wolves, unlike domestic dogs, did not waste energy with aimless meandering. "Looks like he was moving at a good clip," Thane said confidently.

"No way," she protested with equal aplomb. Never mind that she would stake her life on pretty much any professional judgment he made. She was feeling playful. "It was clearly a female dachshund. Long haired. Blind in one eye."

Thane raised an eyebrow. "Ha! Look at that stride length. No human tracks traveling with them, either."

"So she was off leash," Mei Lin insisted.

"In bear country? With one good eye?"

Mei Lin pretended to frown. "Fine! So it was a wolf."

"Thank you. Now what's my prize?"

Mei Lin could envision several options, and from the look on Thane's face, she could tell he was envisioning similar ones. They were standing close, but not close enough. The pull between them was palpable: a primal, compulsive force...

Warning signals assaulted her brain. Had she not sworn she would never do this again? Jump into yet another relationship based purely on superficial attraction? She had only known Thane a matter of hours! Her next relationship was supposed to be based on cold, hard facts. She was to ease into it one slow, deliberate step at a time. Like her now happily married sister Ri, she was to guard her heart until the man in question had been thoroughly, completely vetted. Then, and only then, would she allow herself to smile her most heartfelt smile, to reach her eager hands up to a pair of well-muscled shoulders, to lean her whole stupidly vulnerable self into an embrace that was warm... and masculine... and completely intoxicating...

Oh, to hell with it.

Chapter 20

Thane's day had improved dramatically. Never mind that the most pleasant time he had ever spent on an intertidal beach had just been interrupted by a couple with two young children and one energetic, poorly behaved labradoodle. As he and Mei Lin turned away from the chaos and began to trek the backside loop of the Nagoonberry Trail, he had to seriously wonder — again — if he was dreaming. Everything that was happening in Gustavus seemed surreal. The potential sighting of a glacier cub was a once-in-a-lifetime opportunity, but the discovery of a woman like Mei Lin was its own kind of miracle.

If you'd asked him a week ago, he'd have told a different story. Glacier bears, he would have insisted, were certain to exist somewhere, whether a human saw them or not. But a woman who didn't play head games? A beautiful, kind woman who was open and frank and uncomplicated and who *meant exactly what she freakin' said?* No way. Such women were the stuff of fantasy, like mermaids or unicorns.

And to think the little town of Gustavus had a glacier bear *and* a unicorn!

Thane Buchanan was a very, very happy man.

"So, have you ever lived anywhere else besides Maine? And here, of course?" he asked as they picked their way slowly along another meadow path, pausing frequently to pluck a ripe raspberry or blueberry. Mei Lin didn't answer for a moment, and when he turned to look at her he was surprised to see her face clouding over. A few seconds ago she'd looked as jolly as he did.

"Texas," she said finally, pronouncing the word as if it were a disease. "I didn't care for it much, but then I never got out of Dallas. I might have liked the rural parts better."

Thane considered letting the subject drop. She appeared to

be avoiding something unpleasant, and he usually let sleeping dogs lie, particularly when they were female. But Mei Lin was different, and he wanted whatever was between them to be different, too. Open, honest, and down to earth. He was so horribly weary of walking on eggshells!

He stopped moving, reached out a hand, and smoothed a stray lock of her hair behind an adorably cute little ear. "What didn't you like about Dallas?"

She hesitated, but only for an instant. Her expression remained grim, but her deep brown eyes looked up at him with an affection that weakened his knees. "It was my first big move away from home, and pretty much nothing went right," she said soberly. "I'd just broken up with my fiancé, which was a good thing. But I made some serious mistakes. I had trouble at work and I dated some real jerks. If I had to sum up the experience in one word, I'd go with 'soul-sucking.'"

"Sounds like it," he agreed softly. She hadn't given much detail, but that was all right. He was certain that as they grew closer — which he definitely intended to make happen — she wouldn't shrink from sharing whatever was important to her. For now, he just wanted to comfort her, as she had comforted him when he spoke of his father's murder. So he did.

When they parted this time, Mei Lin's beautiful dark eyes were shiny with tears. "You're good at that," she quipped.

He chuckled warmly. "So are you."

"I've always been a hugger," she said with a smile. "My mother used to worry because when they first adopted me, I would assault complete strangers at the playground."

Thane laughed. Then a long-buried memory swamped him. "You know, I think I had the same problem. I have this vague, preschoolish memory of my mother telling me, more than once, 'that girl doesn't want to marry you, honey. Now let her go!' God only knows what that was all about."

Mei Lin cracked up. She had an amazing, merry laugh that rang with an overtone of kindness. It made him want to hug her all over again. Among other things.

"I bet you got that from your dad," she surmised. "Or is your mom a hugger, too?"

"Good God, no," Thane chuckled, hard-pressed to imagine such a thing. His mother had always been remote. She didn't even hug Doug, at least not in public. "Definitely from my dad. When we were little and he came home from work, he'd always give us giant bear hugs." The familiar pang of loss stabbed at him, but his good mood transformed it into bittersweetness.

"Again with the bears!" Mei Lin said playfully. "Well, I can't knock it. You clearly learned from the best. Did he have a booming laugh like yours, too?"

Thane's heart thumped in his chest. He couldn't remember a single woman he'd ever dated who'd asked him dip squat about his father. Come to think of it, his male friends didn't either. It was understandable, particularly if people knew about the murder, to think Thane that wouldn't want to talk about his father. But he did.

"I wouldn't call it 'booming,'" he began, stepping around behind Mei Lin on the pretense of picking a berry. He preferred for her to lead. That way he could watch her hips sway. "I'm not built like him. I take after my grandfather on my mother's side — we're the big guys. My dad was built more like Jason. Tall, but lean."

"I see. And was your mom's dad also obsessed with glacier bears?" Mei Lin teased.

Thane laughed. "No, the only thing Grandpa Joe's ever been obsessed with is banking. The bear obsession is strictly a Buchanan thing. My grandpa Buck was a huge outdoorsman — spent his whole life around Juneau. And *his* dad," Thane raised his voice dramatically, "is the one who started the whole thing when he spied a real live glacier bear up in Yakutat."

Mei Lin's steps slowed. He moved where he could see her face, worried that all his family talk was beginning to bore her. She didn't look bored, but she did look pensive. "Yakutat?" she repeated, her gaze fixed on a point in the distance.

Thane looked where she was looking, but saw nothing

noteworthy. "Yep," he answered. "You know it? It's a little fishing village on the strip of coast between Glacier Bay and Cordova."

"I've heard of it. Do a lot of people see glacier bears there?" she asked. Her voice was strangely thin.

"Not *a lot*," Thane replied. "But they have as high a concentration as anywhere. That's where we'd go camping in the summers to look for one... my dad and my grandpa and Jason and me." He counted those trips among the best times of his life, and he would have been happy to talk more about them, but there was definitely something wrong with Mei Lin. The bloom of color in her perfectly shaped cheeks had all but disappeared. "Are you okay?" he asked.

"I'm fine," she said quickly. She turned back to the trail and started walking again.

"No, you're not," he argued, determined to keep the honesty thing going. "What is it? What did I say?"

She stopped then and turned to face him. Her dark eyes searched his face. She seemed bewildered. After a long moment, she answered. "It's just that your stories about your family and being a kid here remind me so much of stories somebody else was telling me. It's uncanny, really. But maybe not so uncanny as it seems. I mean, I suppose a lot of people who grow up around here, or even visit the area often like you did, must have family stories about camping and looking for glacier bears. Right?"

Thane's eyebrows rose. What an odd thing to spook her! "Well, sure. Camping out, learning to hunt and fish, those things are all normal rites of passage. And anyone local would know the glacier bear lore."

Her color returned. "Of course," she agreed, smiling again. They continued talking about families and siblings, laughing easily as they compared the dynamics of two-girl versus two-boy households and debated the influence of birth order on personality. Thane was having a perfectly delightful time — and assumed she was as well — until for no discernable reason her sparkling eyes widened and turned glassy.

Thane stopped his mouth. What the hell had he said this time? He'd been talking about the first place he could remember living, the apartment in Seattle where he and his brother had shared a tiny room with a view of the Space Needle. He'd mentioned how he could remember not wanting to move to the suburbs, because he'd overheard his dad lamenting about how it would mean a longer commute to the hospital and less time at home. What Thane could not understand was why his dad's ultimate capitulation (after Margot had bribed them all with the promise of a golden retriever puppy) should make Mei Lin look like Thane had struck her.

"Your dad," she asked with a quiver in her voice. "You said he was a surgeon?"

Thane studied her, confused. "I can't remember saying that, but yes, he was. Why do you ask?"

She didn't answer him. She looked as though he were torturing her. Her lips moved slightly as if she wanted to speak, but she couldn't seem to form any words. He reached out and put his hands lightly on her upper arms. "Mei Lin," he said gently. "What is it? What am I missing here?"

The sound of a trumpet erupted loudly from somewhere behind him, making both of them jump. "I'm sorry," he said, collecting himself. "I didn't even know you could get a signal out here. That must be Dave..." A blue-gray bear cub scampered across his mind. "I don't think he would call unless it was—"

"Answer it!" Mei Lin insisted, smiling at him now.

Her good mood seemed to have been restored, but Thane could swear that her eyes lacked their earlier sparkle. He shrugged off his pack and pulled out the phone. He'd assigned Dave's number the fanfare ringtone in expectation of good news on the job front. Potentially, this could be even better. "Yo! Dave?"

"It's your lucky day, my boy!" his mentor's voice rang out

cheerfully. "I just followed spoor from a sow and two cubs for nearly half a mile, from Smith's place straight up the creek bank. Lost them after they took off across a meadow and onto a gravel track. But guess what? That gravel track was an old park road. They've moved onto the reserve!"

Thane whooped so loudly he flushed several birds out of the nearby trees. He might have been embarrassed, but seeing Mei Lin's face brighten, he had no regrets. "Where can I meet you?" he asked eagerly. "Just tell me where the closest place I can drive to is and I'll—" Suddenly realizing he had no car, he cast a hopeful glance at Mei Lin.

His expression, whatever it was, made her crack up laughing. "Of course I'll drive you!" she answered without being asked.

Thane got the information he needed from Dave. Then he hung up his phone, dropped it on the ground, and swept the most exciting woman in Alaska up into his arms.

Mei Lin tossed aside her car keys, unfastened her fanny pack, and sat down at Elsie's desk. She booted up her laptop and stared at the screen as it flickered to life. In her haste to get back to her computer she had nearly clipped a moose calf with her fender, and she felt terrible. Her heart was still hammering from the fright, but she suspected it would be hammering anyway.

The similarities were too glaring to ignore. Stanley had sons he wouldn't admit to having and he had spent the past twenty years overseas. He was a surgeon who told stories about glacier bears to his children after hearing them from his father and his father before him, and all the men in the family had gone camping together at Yakutat. Thane had a surgeon father he hadn't seen in twenty years, as well as a brother, grandfather, and great-grandfather who were obsessed with glacier bears and had gone camping at Yakutat.

It could all be coincidence, yes. But Mei Lin couldn't stop thinking about the men's eyes: those striking, two-toned gray-blue eyes. By itself, such a resemblance would mean nothing. But with everything else combined...

She quickly navigated to the search screen. She had to know the truth. She was looking at two halves of a whole that fit perfectly together, except for one whopping contradiction: a dead man. Thane was absolutely convinced that his father had been murdered. His mother must have told him so. But why? Why on earth would any mother make up such a horrible story?

Mei Lin's fingers trembled over the keyboard. *Chicago Tribune archives.* She hit the enter key and waited again.

The situation was truly uncanny. Either the two men's stories bore an amazing resemblance to each other for no particular reason, or she had just run into a long-separated father and son who had simultaneously appeared in a random small Alaskan town where neither had any pre-existing ties.

Neither scenario was believable.

The screen changed. Mei Lin tapped on the obvious search hit and waited again. Perhaps it wasn't all that crazy. What if the latter coincidence wasn't as great as it seemed? If her hunch was correct, it would mean that Stanley had grown up in Juneau. If he'd come back to the U.S. looking for someplace to die, why shouldn't he return to his boyhood home? If he didn't want to be recognized, for whatever reason, he might not want to return to Juneau itself. But he could easily hide out at an isolated cabin in a nearby town.

The *Chicago Tribune* archive search page popped up, and she immediately began typing. *Buchanan. Surgeon. Kidnap.* She hit the enter key.

No, the second coincidence wasn't all that incredible. What was more difficult to imagine was why Thane's mother would have lied. How could any woman do such a thing to her own sons? Especially when it was clear — even twenty years later — how very much at least one of them had loved his father?

The search engine spit back its answer. Mei Lin expected either no hits, or several. She got several, all written within a week of each other. She held her breath and started reading.

When she'd finished every word, she slumped back in her chair, dazed.

Thane's mother hadn't lied. His father *was* abducted from outside a hotel in Chicago while attending a medical conference. Several witnesses had watched as the surgeon was surrounded by three men on a curb and then bundled into the back seat of a car. For two days, the local news reported no updates. On the fourth morning after the abduction, a new story made headlines. Two long-wanted criminals had been arrested and another shot and killed following a police raid at a suburban home. Another wanted man, a suspect in multiple murder cases, was already in critical condition at the time of the raid from a previous gunshot wound; he did not survive transport to the hospital. The missing surgeon had been found at the scene. It was presumed that he had been abducted in order to treat the wounded man, but unfortunately, he himself received multiple gunshot wounds during the raid. The surgeon was transported to the hospital in critical condition and, according to the next day's paper, died overnight. Whether the fatal shots were delivered by the kidnappers or the police was under investigation. Some days later, a generous obituary was published, listing Stanley George Buchanan as a board-certified trauma surgeon from Seattle who left behind a wife and two sons.

Stanley Buchanan. He hadn't changed his first name. Only his last.

Mei Lin sat and stared at nothing for a very long time. *Why?* Why would Stanley do it? Why would he pretend to be dead and then take off to another country? He must have had help from the hospital... or someone. Perhaps law enforcement itself. The article didn't say so explicitly, but it was clear that the criminals were mobsters. She could understand if Stanley had gone into some kind of witness protection program, but seeing as how dead men couldn't testify in court, that made no sense. And surely no sanctioned witness protection program would tell a spouse and children that their loved one was dead!

No, Stanley must have done this on his own. Somehow, some way, he had left that hospital unbeknownst to his family and started his life all over again. But why? Was he truly even injured? Or was the whole kidnapping scheme merely part of the ruse?

She frowned to herself, unable to believe it. Stanley cared about his sons, she had no doubt of that. Perhaps he had been trying to protect them. Had he not freaked out when he realized that he'd babbled about sons in the delirium of his fever? He had probably been denying their existence for decades. Yet he had mentioned them offhandedly again when he'd gotten excited about the bear. In a way Mei Lin took pride in that particular lapse, since it spoke to his level of comfort with her. She had promised to keep anything her patients told her in confidence, and clearly he had believed her. Of course, he had no reason to think that she would uncover his true identity. He couldn't possibly predict that one of his sons would—

Thane! Mei Lin's insides twisted into knots. The poor guy had been mourning his father all this time! But he had been deceived. Cruelly deceived. And Stanley's wife... why, she had remarried! Was her second union even legal?

Mei Lin stood up from her chair and paced. She was confused. But she was also angry. Remembering how Thane had spoken of his father with such admiration... the way his eyes had moistened at the mere mention of the man... the pointlessness of his pain made her feel physically sick. She wanted to scream and lash out at someone, and the obvious candidate was Stanley. Yet a part of her refused to believe her own leading theory. How could the man she knew cause that kind of pain to his wife and sons? She could not imagine it. There had to be some explanation. A reasonable explanation.

Good lord, girl... I'm scum of the earth!

Stanley's voice echoed in her head, mocking her. He had a guilty conscience. She knew that. But what exactly did he feel guilty about? Who the hell was Angela?

Just let me die.

Mei Lin let out a shriek of frustration. Then she shut off her computer and grabbed up her pack.

Only Stanley himself knew why he had done such a horrible thing.

And he was damn well going to tell her.

Chapter 21

Margot stood at the window of her home in Port McNeill, looking out over the hillside to the waters of Broughton Strait. She dearly loved this cozy house with its floor-to-ceiling picture window in the living room. The basement her husband puttered in might be a cluttered mess, but the formal living room was her domain. Here she could stand and gaze out at the same stretch of cool, gray-blue water she'd been staring at most of her life. She found comfort in the sameness of it, even as the town in which she'd been born and raised changed all too quickly around her. Here, in her clean and orderly living room with her dependable view, she could convince herself that everything would be fine. At least most of the time.

She heard Doug's footsteps on the carpet behind her, and in a few seconds his strong, heavy arms wrapped around her waist. He gave her a comforting squeeze, and she melted into him.

"Still worrying about Thane?" he asked as his whiskers tickled her temple.

"I can't help it," she answered. "I just wish he'd find that damned bear and come home."

"He could be there for weeks, honey. You know that. He's worked hard in school, he deserves a little fun."

"I need to see him. We have to talk."

"It can wait," Doug assured her. "He's not thinking about Vanessa now. She's not his problem or yours either."

Margot said nothing. She lifted a hand to her mouth and absently bit a fingernail.

Doug gently pulled her hand down. "You're not thinking about Vanessa. Are you?"

Margot stiffened. "I can't help it! I know it doesn't mean anything that they're both in Alaska, but I just have this awful feeling..."

He rotated her in his arms to face him, his soft brown eyes patient and sympathetic as always. He was a rare prize, this husband of hers, and she cursed her younger self to hell and back for being such a malcontent idiot. Doug had loved her in high school, but back then she'd hardly known he was alive. He was just another hometown boy, destined to work at the pulp mills all his life. She'd wanted a more worldly mate. Someone tall, dark, handsome, and exciting. *Ha!* If only she'd stayed closer to home and married Doug first, she wouldn't be tortured by the horrid, sick feelings she was enduring now.

"This isn't bad news, you know," he said quietly.

Margot's eyes began to water. He had always been so understanding. More so than she had any right to expect. "I know it isn't. It's just that..." She could not finish the thought.

He held her tighter. "I know. You're scared. You've been doing what you've been doing for a very long time now, and it's hard to think about shaking things up."

Her heart skipped a beat. Doug hadn't said much when she'd told him about the detective's call. He'd just held her and listened to her vent. She shouldn't have assumed that meant he had no opinion. It had always been his way to let sensitive issues percolate a while.

"You know what you have to do, don't you?" he whispered.

She pulled away from him abruptly, stung. If she'd thought about it, she could have predicted this was coming. But the prospect of Doug's disagreeing with her was just one of many things she'd been unwilling to think about.

"I most certainly do not!" she protested. "It's not that easy!"

"Isn't it?" Doug returned calmly. "The danger's gone now. Stanley's most likely still alive. His sons have a right to know what really happened."

"They have a right to be happy!" Margot declared, raising her voice. She hated it when they argued. It didn't happen often, and most of the time when it did Doug let her have her way. But when her husband chose to pick a battle, he was immovable, and she feared this was one of those times. "They're happy now, just as they are!"

Doug said nothing for a moment, which was a bad sign. The longer he thought about his words, the more important he believed them to be. "They could be happier. You don't know. You have no way of knowing if their lives would be better or worse."

"Oh, yes I do!" she retorted hotly. Her cheeks flared with color as years of suppressed worry and pain flooded back into her memory. "You *know* what that man put me through!"

"Even so, that's got nothing to do with Thane and Jason."

Margot's mouth stuck open. In the past, any mention of Stanley's mistreatment had elicited her husband's immediate and affectionate sympathy.

"I'm sorry, sweetheart," he said gently. "But this isn't about you. It's not about Stanley, either. It's about them. They're not little boys who need your protection anymore. They're grown men with minds of their own. Maybe they'll want to seek Stanley out, make him a part of their lives again. Maybe they won't. But don't you think it should be their choice?"

Margot's insides burned. Doug was right, of course, but that made no difference. Would the consequences of falling in lust with Stanley Buchanan never, ever stop wrenching her guts out? "Don't you see?" she shrieked, her whole body shaking. "*They'll hate me!* Every damn thing that's happened... the separation, the lies... everything will look like it's *my* fault! You know what a hero Thane's made of that man! And I'm the one who kept them apart! *My own son will hate me till the day he dies!*"

The sound of her own voice, laying bare her deepest and darkest fear, broke her down. Doug said nothing else. He merely reached out and pulled her to him, stifling her sobs against his chest.

Mei Lin made it from the Torpins' place to Stanley's cabin in twenty minutes flat. If she'd met the bears again, she would have plowed right into them. Her eyes were unseeing; her mind completely preoccupied. Even Kibbe could sense her mood, as evidenced by the fact that after running out to meet her, he accepted one quick pat on the head and then quietly slunk away.

Stanley was sitting on the porch with his binoculars, as expected. He wouldn't know, yet, that Dave had tracked the bear family off his property and onto public lands. "Well, hello!" he called out merrily. "I wasn't expecting you back so soon."

Stanley's vision wasn't the greatest. She got to within ten feet of him before her thunderous countenance made an impression. She could tell the exact moment he noticed, because his eyes widened and the sides of his beard drooped. "Hell's fire, girl. What's wrong with you?"

Mei Lin found herself at a loss for words. Never mind the time consumed by the drive and the long walk — advance planning had never been her forte. Instead, she just threw it out there.

"I know who you are, Stanley," she announced, priding herself on a reasonably calm tone of voice. "Or should I say, Dr. Buchanan."

His face paled. He stood up with a jerk. The move was unwise. A great deal of pain must have hit him unexpectedly, because he immediately stumbled. He shifted his weight to his good leg and clutched the porch railing. "He knows?" he demanded in horror.

Mei Lin was taken aback. The nurse in her wanted to check his leg — make sure he hadn't busted a stitch or something — but she was too confused to move. "Who?"

Stanley didn't answer. He just stood there, or rather leaned there, visibly shaking.

"No one knows except me," she answered, her pacifist side taking charge again. She was angry, yes, but the poor man looked weak as a kitten. "Sit down," she ordered, coming closer. "Before you fall down and injure something else."

Stanley made no move on his own, but when she put her hands on his arms he allowed her to guide him back into his Adirondack chair. She poured him a cup of water and he drank it dry before speaking again. Mei Lin took a swig from her own water bottle, then settled on the washtub beside him.

"How did you find out?" he asked finally, his voice thin.

"I met your son," she replied as a realization struck her. Did he already know that Thane was here? He must!

Stanley nodded mutely. Miserably. He showed no surprise.

"Did Dave tell you about him?" she asked.

Stanley shook his head without looking at her. "You told me."

Mei Lin lifted an eyebrow skeptically. "All I was said was that Dave wanted to bring another wildlife specialist from British Columbia."

"You said his name," Stanley insisted. "You said Thane. That was enough. I know that he's been living in Vancouver, working on his master's. Before that he worked for Fish and Wildlife on Vancouver Island." He smiled faintly. "He's always loved bears."

Mei Lin drew in a breath. Of course. No wonder Stanley had done such an abrupt reversal about having "strangers" on his property! No wonder he'd looked so frightened. One face-to-face meeting with Thane could topple twenty years' worth of deception!

"*Why*, Stanley?" she demanded, anger returning to her voice. "Why did you do it? How could you let them all believe you were dead?"

He wouldn't look at her. He sighed heavily and stared at nothing. All at once, he seemed much older. "It's a long and complicated story, Mei Lin," he said quietly.

"I'm not leaving here until you make me understand."

After a lengthy period of silence, he turned and caught her gaze. "I don't know what it is about you. I really don't. I've kept this to myself for so long... not a single slip. Then one day you hike up here and smile at me with those innocent brown eyes of yours and I'm blabbing to beat the band."

"You were delirious. At least part of the time."

"See there? Even when you're angry, you're not unkind. Makes it easier for a man to let his guard down." He smiled weakly, then sobered. "You promised me once that whatever I told you about myself — voluntarily or otherwise — would never leave this cabin. Did you mean that?"

"Of course I did," Mei Lin defended. "I haven't said a word. To anyone. I didn't ask to be put in the middle of this, Stanley. But here we are. And I need to understand."

He fixed her with those mesmerizing eyes again. "You have to believe me when I say this is very important to me. There is nothing else more important. *Nothing.*"

Mei Lin waited. A grain of guilt sprang up within her. She hadn't broken her promise to him, but what if he made her swear again, right now, that she never would? Even if it hurt Thane? She swore internally. She would cross that bridge when and if she came to it.

"I told you I was never a saint," he began.

"Repeatedly," she affirmed. "Go on."

His face and tone were dismal. "I married Thane's mother for all the wrong reasons. I'd gotten her pregnant, and I'll admit I was proud of that, in some stupid, macho way. But I also really did want kids. Not the responsibility of them — I was too selfish for that — but the fun of being a dad. I married her knowing I didn't feel the way a groom was supposed to feel about his bride, but like the self-confident ass I was, I figured I could make it work. Well, I couldn't. Turned out she wasn't all that crazy about me, either." He chuckled ruefully. "It was a miracle we had Jason, frankly. I spent most nights on the couch — when I came home at all. There were other women; we talked about divorce. But I didn't want to lose my boys, and she had a thing about admitting failure. So we both just kept up the pretense."

Mei Lin tried hard to focus. She was not a judgmental person by nature, but hearing any married man talk about "other women" had an embarrassingly primal effect on her. Namely, a strong desire to punch... something. "I know about the kidnapping," she spouted, anxious to move on. "At least, I know what the *Chicago Tribune* had to say about it. Your family seems to believe the official version. So what's the truth? Why are you here?"

A sardonic smile twisted his lips. "Those are two different questions. Let's stick to the first one. Obviously, I didn't die. I was shot three times, but my injuries weren't fatal. And as soon as I told the authorities what I knew, they were all over me."

"How do you mean?" Mei Lin asked. She thought she knew, but she was trying not to make presumptions.

His eyes darted around the clearing, and she felt a pang of empathy. No one could possibly sneak up on the two of them with Kibbe around. But Stanley had lived with his secrets so long he couldn't *not* look over his shoulder.

"They planned all along to kill me," he said flatly. "I knew that when they didn't censor themselves. I saw all their faces, heard their names. They were desperate for me to save this guy; he was clearly a powerful player in the organization. They said they'd kill me if he died, but I knew they'd kill me anyway as soon as I was no longer useful. I did my best to keep the man breathing, but I knew he wouldn't make it. I tried to buy time, asking for more supplies. Nothing short of an ace trauma team in a fully equipped OR could have saved him, but they didn't know that. The whole time I was with him, weak as he was, this guy still took meetings, made plans, talked on the phone. He even ordered a hit, right there in front of me. But no matter what I did, he kept losing blood. When he started lapsing in and out of consciousness, I figured we'd both be dead soon. Then the raid happened."

"Who shot you?" Mei Lin asked weakly, remembering the article.

Stanley's face tightened. "A guy named Tony Russo. He was the worst of the bunch, and that's saying something. First thing he did when the cops arrived was point his pistol at *me*. I'd have died right then and there if his aim hadn't been off because he was getting shot at himself. When I collapsed he got the hell out of there. Unscathed."

Mei Lin's face felt hot. She looked out a moment at the rippling creek, which was currently glinting in the sunshine. It was difficult to imagine that such injustice, such horror, could coexist in the same, beautiful world as her rainforest. "Was he caught?" she dared to ask, already knowing the answer.

Stanley laughed bitterly. "Of course not. He slipped away somehow. They caught up with him later, but nothing could be proven without my testimony." His expression darkened. "I would have loved nothing better than to put him away. To put all of them all away."

Mei Lin believed him. "But you didn't."

He turned to her with an expression she found inscrutable. It was part anger, part regret... perhaps part disgust. "What I wanted was to be the hero," he said mockingly. "Always had. That's how I ended up a trauma surgeon in the first place. My motives were never pure, you see. Not in life, and certainly not in love. I couldn't *wait* to get up on that stand, to put all those bastards behind bars. I knew they'd kill me in a heartbeat if they could, but I didn't care — that just made it all the more exciting. To me, being in the Witness Protection Program sounded like a small price to pay... a unique adventure."

His blue eyes misted over. Mei Lin could read his expression easily, now. His soul was consumed by self-loathing.

"All I ever thought about was myself," he continued. "I never stopped to think about my sons, my parents... what my exhilarating foray into crime-fighting would mean for my family. But my wife knew. And luckily for the rest of them, she was totally over my sorry hide. So much so that she could stand beside my bed as I lay there bleeding from three bullet holes, look me straight in the face, and say *no*. No, you selfish bastard. This time, you're not getting your way."

He laughed without bitterness. To Mei Lin's surprise, he seemed genuinely amused. "The woman was a gem, truly. I should have appreciated her earlier. But our marriage was already over by then. She held all the cards; I couldn't take the boys into hiding without her permission. And I couldn't testify publicly without putting my family in danger as well as myself. So all I could do was give my statement off the record. Since I was able to clear up a couple key questions and produce some new leads, the cops were happy enough with that. They falsified a death certificate, set me up with a fake identity and passport, and off I went."

Mei Lin sucked in a breath. "So your wife knew all along. She lied to her children, to your parents, everyone."

"She had to," Stanley defended. "Tony Russo was no idiot. He wasn't a hundred percent convinced I was dead, and he knew the danger of the intel I'd picked up. If and when the police acted on that information, he would suspect. And if he saw anything odd going on with my family — like my parents throwing a party the day after my funeral, or my boys trundling off to visit some mystery relative — none of them would be safe. He would use them to get to me. One way or the other."

Mei Lin stood up. Her legs felt like jelly. As the circumstances behind what had happened became clearer to her, her anger with Stanley was dissipating. But the rest of her emotions were all over the place. She could understand his wanting to protect his sons. But the cost! It seemed too great.

"For all I know, they could still be in danger," Stanley added sternly. "Tony Russo is still alive and kicking, and his brother's been in jail for fifteen years, thanks partly to my information. Guys like them have very long memories. And they *were* suspicious of my convenient death. They sent a few thugs in suits to my funeral, just to make sure nothing smelled funny."

Mei Lin looked at him with dismay. She couldn't imagine it. Thane at the tender age of thirteen — devastated, bereft — being watched for signs of insincerity by a bunch of cunning, ruthless murderers!

"So you can understand," Stanley finished, gesturing for her to sit again. "You understand why no one else can know. The man that I was has been buried for twenty years now, and that's where he's going to stay. Stanley Smith is all there is. And that's what's best for everybody."

Mei Lin couldn't sit down again. She was too tense, too jumpy. She had a strong, paranoid compulsion to scan the forest for men lurking in dark suits. Yet as much as that thought spooked her, if she suddenly *were* presented with any of the men who'd threatened an innocent, teenaged Thane, she would scratch their miserable eyes out.

"Tell me about him," Stanley said suddenly, his voice changed to a plea.

Mei Lin looked to see his light eyes firing with expectation.

"You've met him, haven't you?" he continued. "I can't ask Dave, but... I'd love to hear anything you can tell me about him. About my son."

The tender tone of his last words hit her with an almost physical pain. Her conscience was in torment. Stanley loved his son, missed him, was desperate for any nugget of information about him. But why should he get it, when Thane had heard nothing of his father... and never would? It wasn't fair. To either of them. She understood why Stanley had done what he did, but still, it didn't feel right to her. It *wasn't* right!

She couldn't think of what to say. She could sing the praises of Thane Buchanan for hours on end, but no words came to her lips. When she looked into Stanley's hopeful face all she could see was Thane's wounded one. He needed to know. He *should* know.

"I think you should ask him yourself," she answered.

Stanley frowned. "Did I not just explain that?"

"I understand what happened twenty years ago," she replied with more calmness than she felt. "But now is different. Your sons are adults, and the danger has passed."

"You don't know—"

"If it hasn't passed completely, then what's left of it is miniscule," she interrupted. "Tony Russo has no idea where you are. And he can't possibly be wasting time watching your family anymore, not across the border in Canada or all the way up here in Alaska. The benefit of righting the wrong here outweighs the risk a million fold!"

Stanley's face reddened. His lips pursed together and his brow knitted. "There's more to it. You can't possibly know—"

"Then tell me!" she said boldly. "What else are you afraid of?"

He kicked out at one of post rails, making Kibbe rise with a start. The dog surveyed his master critically, shuffled a few feet away, then lay down again. Stanley didn't seem to notice. His face was tight with frustration and his fists clenched the arms of his chair. "Don't you think I *want* to see my sons again?" he cried. "That's *all* I want! But I'm trying — for once — to do the right thing! There is no happy reunion possible here! There's been too much time and too many lies. The truth wouldn't help them now; it would only make them angry!"

"Of course it will make them angry!" Mei Lin argued, surprised by her own temerity. She wasn't afraid of Stanley no matter how many posts he kicked, but intentionally aggravating a patient over a matter which was arguably none of her business was way, *way* outside any professional code of conduct. "But I'm equally sure they'll get over it! It may take a while, but eventually they'll understand. And as soon as they do they can move on to forgiving you."

"There's no reason for them to bother," Stanley growled. "What are they going to get out of it?"

"They'll get their father back!"

"They have a father!" he shouted in return. But his voice broke before he could finish. Tears flooded his eyes. "Doug Tremain is their father now. He's been a good one, too. God knows he's done a better job of it than I ever could."

Mei Lin stepped closer to him, but Kibbe, in the uncanny way canines have of responding to human distress, was already there. The dog dropped his muzzle onto Stanley's knee and wagged his tail sympathetically. Stanley sniffed and rubbed the dog's ears with affection.

"Fatherhood is not a contest," Mei Lin said softly. "You are you, and Doug is Doug, and right now, he is irrelevant."

Stanley shook his head. "I'm not worth finding again, Mei Lin. My sons believe that I died a hero. They've got a picture in their minds of the man they think I was. Whatever they think, it's better than the reality. Why bust up the dream? I'd rather be a stone-dead saint."

Mei Lin's teeth gritted. His self-effacement now was every bit as over the top as his self-love had been back then. "You're not a hero or a saint," she countered. "But right now you are acting like a coward."

To her surprise, he laughed out loud. "Yeah. That too."

"Not in everything," she corrected. "Just in this. You're afraid to face their anger. So afraid you won't even give them a chance!"

The dig at his pride had no effect.

"There is no chance, Mei Lin," he replied with authority, even as his eyes continued to water. "And it's best to leave well enough alone. My boys are happy now. They don't hate me, and they don't hate their mother. Hating someone hurts, no matter who it is, but hating somebody you love... that's a soul-killer. No way is getting to know this cynical, dried-up old man worth that. For once I'm doing the unselfish thing. And I'd appreciate it if you'd stop arguing otherwise."

Mei Lin opened her mouth to say something, but wound up shutting it again. She could think of nothing else to say, at least not now. But that didn't mean she was dropping it. The only thing she dropped was her own hind end, back down onto the washtub. She would sit down, and she would think a while.

Then she'd start round two.

Chapter 22

Thane shifted slightly to avoid getting a kink in his leg. Waiting quietly and motionlessly was par for the course in his business, but he wished they had chosen a slightly more accommodating spot — like a nice, knee-height fallen log, or even a smooth tree trunk to lean up against. But no, the best place to view this particular bend in the stream happened to be a flat stretch of muck in the middle of a grove of sapling alders. Dave insisted that it was one of his personal hot spots for catching black bear fishing for salmon, and since it was the nearest hot spot to where the tracks they'd been following had left off, it seemed as good a place as any for a stakeout.

They'd been waiting quietly for nearly an hour now, with no luck. They'd agreed already that when the hour was up, they'd go back to tracking and trailing. Ordinarily Thane was a fount of patience, but today the forced inaction was killing him. As much as he wanted to see that cub, he could not stop thinking about Mei Lin. They had started a very good and pleasant thing this afternoon, and although he didn't officially regret interrupting it under the circumstances, he would have been more comfortable with his decision if their current odds of success weren't quite so abysmal. Dave had trailed a mother bear and two cubs to within a quarter mile of where they stood, but it was a leap to hope that the same bears would be fishing here now. They could just as easily be snoozing in a mossy daybed miles away. Or, worse yet, the particular bear family Dave had trailed here might not be the same one Mei Lin saw two days ago. Female bears usually kept to their own territories, but when the salmon were running, such boundaries tended to blur.

Dave glanced at his watch, then let out a sigh. "Well, this is a bust," he announced, albeit in a whisper. "I'm thinking maybe we should move on to that berry patch off the Lake Trail I was—"

Thane cut off his friend with a hand on the shoulder, and Dave immediately quieted and looked where Thane was looking.

The tops of the bushes beside the stream bank were rustling. Something large was definitely moving within. The men held their breath as a grunting noise met their ears. And then, as if by magic, a black bear cub popped out of the underbrush. It splashed into the stream and sniffed about, then lifted its front paws and dashed them down flat in the water. It was a mimicry of its mother's fishing technique, but on the shallow bank, the cub was more likely harassing water bugs.

A few seconds later the cub's mother appeared. She was an older female with a slightly grizzled muzzle, and as she looked up and down the stream she gave the air a few perfunctory sniffs. Bears could see nearly as well as humans, but they trusted their vastly superior sense of smell more, so with the men placed downwind, the bear detected nothing that alarmed her. She swung her head over her shoulder and made a snuffling noise. Thane's heart skipped several beats.

It would happen any second now. *Come on, little fella!* The gray cub had to be behind her still, hidden in the ferns. He heard the faintest grunt from beside him and realized it was Dave. Thane's giant paw was squeezing the poor man's shoulder in a death grip. He relaxed his hand, then tried to relax the rest of himself, as his gaze stayed riveted on the patch of brush.

The greenery rustled. A second cub popped into view, barreled into the stream, and pounced on its sibling's back. The cub beneath responded with an open mouth full of teeth, but the force of the attack sent both of them sprawling into the water, rolling sideways in undignified somersaults.

Thane's already stressed heart dropped into his boots. The second cub was as black as the first.

He and Dave watched the bears in silence for another

twenty minutes, drawing what pleasure they could from the young mammals' antics, which were not assisting their mother's quest for food in the least. She wandered off upstream by herself, looking for calmer, more salmon-friendly waters, until at last she was out of view. The bumbling cubs followed at a distance until the men lost sight of all three.

"Sorry about that," Dave mumbled as they headed back toward the nearest trail.

"No worries," Thane replied. He reached out to clap his friend on the shoulder, but Dave's preemptive wince waved him off. "They're out here somewhere."

"I must have been tracking the wrong group for a while now," Dave continued morosely. "I know just where it happened, too. I thought the first set was moving west, and these tracks seemed to be coming from the north, but I let my enthusiasm convince me they were the same. The glacier cub probably did move on west. I bet their territory ranges out closer to the bay..."

Thane listened with half his brain. The other half was devoted to a continuous playback loop of Mei Lin Sullivan, a beach covered with wolf tracks, and those glorious few moments before they'd been slobbered on by the labradoodle...

He was walking on autopilot with a stupid smile on his face when Dave received a call on his radio. The speaker was one of the assistant rangers. Standing several feet away, Thane could only pick up occasional phrases through the static. But as he watched Dave's face gradually brighten, he had no trouble getting the gist.

Don't know how credible, really... couple of hikers... foreign, spoke pretty good English... first time seeing bears... German, maybe?... not too knowledgeable, but... that's what they said... asked three times... matter of fact, you know... I didn't say much... any bear would be exciting... definitely said cubs were different colors... young ones... she said gray... word he used was "light"...

Dave was spitting out questions, fumbling to write in a notebook with a pencil with a broken lead. Thane felt his own pockets but knew he had nothing to write with either. Dave gave up, signed off, and stuffed everything back in his pockets. When he turned back to Thane, his face was glowing. "We got 'em, my friend! Hikers had no idea what they were seeing, but that's just as well. Sighted them off the Bartlett River Trail, heading away from the bay into the forest. I told you! Didn't I tell you? I said that first set of tracks was heading west, maybe a little northwest—"

Thane went back to half-listening again as they hiked back to Dave's truck with Thane leading — in double time. The more they hurried, the better chance they had of catching up with the bear family. And then, afterwards... A swish of shiny black hair loomed large in his mind... Afterwards, he would return to the house. The house where he was staying. And also the house where she was staying...

"Thane!" Dave demanded as they half-walked, half-jogged. "Take it easy! I'm older than you, remember? And my legs aren't as long, either!"

Thane chuckled. But he didn't slow down.

This time, as Mei Lin steered the Subaru away from the Torpins' place and back down the long gravel road toward town, she drove slowly. She would not near-miss another moose calf. Her spirits were low enough.

She felt horrible. First, because she'd made no progress at all in reasoning with Stanley, despite multiple, increasingly creative attempts. He did not want any contact with his sons. He didn't want them to know he was alive. And he was holding Mei Lin to her promise of confidentiality, adamantly. Of course, doing the right thing by Stanley would mean that the next time she saw Thane, she would feel like a traitor. And while she could think of all sorts of things she would like to feel the next time she saw Thane Buchanan, soul-crushing guilt was not among them.

But she would feel guilty no matter what she did. She felt

guilty enough just seeing how pathetic Stanley looked as she left him, sitting on his porch with a blanket over his knees, eagerly scanning the edge of the clearing every few seconds with his binoculars. She could have told him that the glacier cub had left the area. But she had not. Never mind that Dave had specifically asked her to pass on that information, as well as his apologies for not getting back to the cabin today. Mei Lin couldn't bring herself to tell Stanley the truth. She was too afraid that his hope of seeing a glacier bear was the only thing keeping him alive.

She was pulling back out onto the main road when her cell phone dinged. She moved the Subaru to the shoulder and picked up her phone from the console. She had a text. From Thane. Actually, she had a series of them.

She read through the first few, and her vision blurred. None of the words in the texts were tender or romantic, but the story behind them tugged at her heartstrings. He was excited, and he obviously wanted to share that excitement with her. He gave a detailed accounting of how disappointed he'd been to see the wrong bears, but how optimistic he was that some hikers had spotted the real thing. He and Dave were checking in at the lodge when he texted, but they planned to head to the river trail immediately. He did not know how long they would be out.

The text that got her was his last one.

Wait up for me?

Nearly ten minutes passed before her eyes got dry enough for her to drive again. Even then, she hesitated. Nothing she could do at Elsie's house would help anybody. She would only pace and stare out the windows, wishing for Thane to come back and hug the misery out of her, even as she dreaded the sight of him. How could she *not* tell him, whether she chose to or not? Her acting sucked. Every laugh, every smile, every kiss would be tainted by her guilty secret. Unlike some men she'd dated, Thane wasn't oblivious to her feelings. He would see the conflict in her. He would feel it.

And what of Stanley? Mei Lin had never met anyone more

consumed with self-loathing. She realized now that his moments of seeming light-heartedness had been outliers. He could give heartfelt career advice or get excited about a bear, but fundamentally, his worldview hadn't changed since she'd found him delirious on his cabin floor. He hated himself, and he believed his life to be worthless. He felt guilty about leaving his sons and maybe other things... like Angela. Who was Angela, anyway? Mei Lin still didn't know. She didn't understand him at all!

Her frustration boiled over. She banged her hands on the steering wheel and swore out loud. This waiting and worrying was no good. She had to *do* something! But what?

She had no idea what. She had no plan whatsoever.

Then again, when did she ever?

She revved the Subaru back into action and performed a three-point turn.

Chapter 23

When Mei Lin walked up to the cabin for the third time that day, Kibbe greeted her as if he hadn't seen her in months. Stanley looked at her with alarm. "What's up? Is Jesse okay?"

"He's fine." Mei Lin took off her heavy backpack and walked with it past Stanley and into the cabin. "I offered to bring your dinner up myself tonight," she called out as she unloaded the plastic containers of food Amanda had given her. Then she walked back out to the porch. She realized that her tone sounded clipped. Besides being winded from the walk, she was impatient to get on with it. Unsurprisingly, she still had no plan.

"I'm afraid Dave won't be coming by either," she admitted. "He and Thane are following another lead. Some hikers thought they saw a gray cub out at the park."

Stanley's disappointment was evident. "Oh. Where, exactly?"

Mei Lin did her best to explain what she remembered of the details.

"Well, I hope they find it," he said, smiling now. "Thane would get a kick out of that. I'm sorry I..." His voice trailed off in thought. But after another moment, he looked up at her with amusement. "I'm surprised to see you back again. I thought for sure you'd given up on me this time."

Mei Lin steeled herself. She would not be fooled by another of his superficial displays of good humor. She plopped back down on the washtub and absently rubbed at Kibbe's ears. "Who is Angela?"

Stanley blinked. For an instant he seemed genuinely puzzled, then his muscles tensed and his smile disappeared. "I don't know," he said unconvincingly. "Who are you talking about?"

"You told her you were sorry," Mei Lin explained. "Who

was she?"

His face reddened to a disturbing hue. "Is this something else I babbled when I had the fever?" he demanded. "You said you told me everything!"

She shook her head, summoning her reserves. Playing hardball was difficult for a born people-pleaser, but she was determined to get a better handle on his mindset. If he got angry with her, that didn't necessarily mean she was failing. It could mean just the opposite. "I did tell you everything, up to the point when you asked me. You didn't mention Angela until the next day, when you were having a nightmare. Who was she?"

He pursed his lips with annoyance and looked away.

"Someone you loved?" Mei Lin pressed.

He scoffed at that. "I don't think I've ever loved a woman — at least not the way you mean. That's part of what makes me such a swell guy."

"Then I'm sad for you," Mei Lin said genuinely. "I tend to err in the opposite direction, but that has its own problems. Who was Angela?"

He met her eyes. "Are you going to let this go?"

"Did you stop asking me about Mariel?"

He harrumphed. "Fair point."

"Who was Angela? Why did you tell her you were sorry?"

Stanley's blue eyes flashed with pain, and she could see that deep within him, some thread of resolution was breaking. "She's the woman who saved my life. The last time I should have died. Wait... no, that honor belongs to you now, doesn't it? Let's say the 'next to last' time."

Mei Lin scrambled to make sense of his words. "Where did this happen?" she asked.

"South Sudan," he said in a gravelly tone. "Near one of the camps the UN had set up for the displaced. The field hospitals were lucky to have one resident surgeon for tens of thousands of people; some had no surgeon at all. The injured would come in waves, depending on where the fighting was. I'd go wherever

I was needed. I'd just finished an assignment in the Upper Nile, and another doctor and I — a pediatrician — were headed back to our base camp. It wasn't far. We had a UN escort."

He stopped talking for a moment as his mind traveled far away. "I see," Mei Lin encouraged. "Moving around in an area like that must have been dangerous."

He nodded, his weathered brow creasing. "We had to stay inside the compounds. You couldn't go for a walk outside the barriers, much less take a joy ride. Being on the roads was always risky, but I was used to that, floating between camps was what I did. The organization had an SUV, and I drove it myself whenever I got the chance. It was a sorry old vehicle, beat up as hell, but at least it ran. After being cooped up in the camps, it was always a rush to get behind a wheel again. Any wheel."

"I'd be terrified to go out at all," Mei Lin admitted.

He shook his head. "The roads were dangerous for any number of reasons, but it wasn't men with machine guns that took us down that day. It was nothing but a damn pothole."

Mei Lin remained quiet. After a long moment, he spoke again.

"I wish I could say that somebody shot at us," he said bitterly. "Or that the brakes failed, or that we were rushing to save lives. But none of that was true. There was nobody on the road that afternoon but our convoy. I took that as an invitation to let loose and see what the old Expedition could do."

His tone was flippant, but fraught with self-recrimination. "It was the rainy season. Puddles everywhere. I was dodging the potholes; making a game of it like some idiot teenager. Erik was laughing and egging me on — we were both punch-drunk from lack of sleep. But that was no excuse. One of the peacekeepers could have driven us. Truth is, we were having fun — until I hit a puddle that was deeper than it looked. There was a cracking sound, and the next thing I knew, we were rolling."

His voice turned stony. "Erik was cut up bad. He bled out

right in front of me. I couldn't do a damn thing to help him. Nothing! My legs were pinned; I couldn't feel my right arm. He was a young guy, maybe forty. He'd been on assignment less than a month."

Mei Lin tried to steel herself, but her eyes grew teary anyway. She was a hopeless crier. "Your arm," she squeaked, "that's how you injured it?"

He nodded. "It was mangled. Bad enough that if I'd come in with a bunch of critically injured, it would have come off right then and there. I can't tell you how many amputations we did in the camps. We had no choice. There was never enough time — always another patient who couldn't wait, another life that would be lost." He scowled at his nearly normal-looking arm. "I only have *this*... I'm only here at all, because of Angela. Our escorts turned around and took us back to the hospital we'd just left. She was the resident surgeon there. She pronounced Erik dead and then went to work on me. Never mind that she'd been up all night, too. She spent hours. Stitched together muscles, tendons, nerves... the job would have been difficult under the best of circumstances, and she had little to work with and no backup. Just her own skill with a needle and thread. And the whole time she was knocking herself out to save my arm, she knew that it was me who'd caused the accident. That I'd been reckless and just plain stupid. She knew that it was all my fault."

"I'm sure she didn't pass judgment," Mei Lin soothed, disturbed by the film of anxious sweat forming on his skin. "You wouldn't have, either. She knew that you and that arm of yours had saved countless lives—"

"She should have let me die!" he shouted suddenly, his eyes flooding as his voice rose. "At the very least, she should have cut off my arm at the shoulder!"

Mei Lin remained silent.

His previously taut muscles went limp. After a long spell of silence, he spoke in a mumble. "Erik was her husband."

Mei Lin stifled a gasp of horror. For a moment, she couldn't breathe. Then tears spilled over her cheeks and her voice came back to her. "What happened was an accident."

"It was involuntary manslaughter!" he countered. "In this country, I could have been charged."

The word "charged" sent another icy ripple through Mei Lin's veins. She would never be able to erase the image of Julia crying and screaming as she was handcuffed and taken away from the nursing home. But this was about Stanley's demons, not hers. She cleared her throat and sat up. "You made a mistake, yes. And that mistake had horrific consequences. But you can't control the world and everything in it. Nobody gave you the option of dying instead of Erik, and nobody asked if you deserved to lose your arm as punishment, either. What happened, happened. You can apologize, and you can try to make right whatever is in your power to make right. But that's all you can do."

The speech was parroted straight from the advice Mei Lin's therapist mother had given her after the Silverson debacle. But the words had no more effect on Stanley now than they'd had on her back then.

"It wasn't one mistake," he lamented. "I've been a daredevil my whole damn life. Always looking for the next big thrill — and to hell with how anyone else felt about it." He turned and held her gaze. "I told you I never really loved the woman I married. But I believe she did love me. For a while, anyway. Whatever love she had, I killed it. I was so damn cocky... I really did believe I was immortal. I had a sports car and a Harley, and I collected speeding tickets like baseball cards. Performing life and death surgery wasn't enough for me — I had to go bungee jumping, hang-gliding, sky diving. I had to climb Mt. Rainier and surf Mavericks. Got plenty of injuries, but always bounced back. And Margot hated it all, because she worried about me. She cared when I didn't call, feared the worst when I didn't come home. Idiot that I was, I couldn't understand that. I resented it; I thought she was a nag. I led the kind of life you'd expect from a shallow, impetuous teenager —

except that I was pushing forty at the time. Eventually Margot had enough. She told me she didn't care what I did anymore. And towards the end, she really didn't."

Mei Lin drew in a shaky breath. She was feeling a strong tug of sympathy for Stanley's ex-wife, but she recognized the emotion as counterproductive. "Your marriage was only part of the equation," she reminded. "You had two sons together, and their childhood was happy. The man you're describing is not the dad they remember."

He looked at her sharply. "How do you know?"

Mei Lin felt a wave of warmth creep up her neck. She tried as hard as she could to look blasé.

Stanley laughed out loud. "So *that's* how it is!" he chortled with renewed merriment. "Well, son of a gun! I guess it shouldn't surprise me. He is a handsome devil, isn't he?"

"And how would *you* know?" Mei Lin asked with sudden irritation. "Have you been spying on him?"

"Oh, no," Stanley said more soberly. "That wouldn't be safe. But the internet is a wonderful thing. I've seen pictures. Is he as tall as he looks?"

"Yes," Mei Lin snapped. "He's also intelligent. And funny. And kind. And *honest*."

He raised an eyebrow. "Meaning what?"

"Meaning when he says he misses his dad, he damn well means it!" she fired back, surprised by her own vehemence. "Thane remembers you very well, Stanley. He loved you! I can see it in his eyes every time he mentions your name! To know that you didn't die... that you're right here, right now, and that he could so easily see you again... don't you understand what that would mean to him?"

Stanley stared back at her, stricken. His pale lips moved experimentally several times before he managed to form words. "He... he talked to you... about me?"

"He told me the whole story of your family history with the glacier bears!" she practically shouted. "How do you think I got suspicious in the first place? He remembers everything: the bedtime stories, camping in Yakutat... you'd think the guy was raving about Disneyworld! And he thinks you were *murdered*, Stanley. Murdered! He's carried that horror with him for twenty years!"

Stanley turned his face away. "He has another father."

"That doesn't matter!" she persisted. "You don't just trade off people you love like used tires! Thane deserves the chance to get to know you again! And so does Jason!"

"We've been through this already!" he fired back. "I'm telling you, finding out about me would only hurt them mo—"

Mei Lin said a bad word. She practically screamed it. "That's not the real reason and you know it! You're just plain scared!"

"I'm just plain dying!" he yelled back at her. "You want to tell them I'm alive just so they can watch me die all over again? So they can cry at another funeral?"

Mei Lin stopped yelling. She got the feeling they weren't talking about sepsis anymore. "You're just plain dying," she repeated thinly. "Of what?"

He let out a growl. A pain stabbed through her as she realized how much it sounded like Thane's.

"Cancer," he answered dryly. "They found it when I got sent back stateside, for my arm."

"What kind of cancer?" she shot back. The C word didn't scare her. She'd nursed too many survivors who died of something else. "What stage?"

He frowned at her, but rattled off his diagnosis in medical speak.

"So what?" she barked. Coming across as unsympathetic was as unnatural to her as kicking small animals, but she was on a higher mission. "That's almost certainly treatable, and you know it!"

He snorted. "Well, it's not getting treated."

"Because you're afraid," she goaded.

"Because I deserve to die, dammit!" he shouted again. "What part of *I'm a worthless jackass* don't you get?"

"All of it," she retorted.

He swore. "Look," he said after they'd both cooled down a bit, "If I'm done living, that's my business. I've been ready to go ever since the moment Erik took his last breath out on that godforsaken bloody road. Having cancer is merely a convenience. If I just bide my time, nature will take care of me all by itself."

Mei Lin seriously wanted to hit him. "Nature has nothing to do with this. And it *would* be your business... if you didn't have children. But you did, Stanley. And you *do*. Which means this isn't just about you."

His jaws clenched visibly. For one beautiful moment, she thought she'd gotten through. But in the next instant her hopes were dashed again.

"I know what's best for my sons," he said sternly. "And I need you to promise me you won't tell them anything."

She stifled another frustrated scream. "Why should I?"

"Because you already promised!" He held her eyes with the full intensity of his own. "You promised me that nothing I shared with you would leave this cabin. Do you remember that?"

She made no response.

"Don't let me down, Mei Lin," he continued. "I trusted you. I've thought about this for a long time, and I know what I'm doing. It's the best thing for everyone."

Her eyes felt hot. A pressure was building up inside her — a pressure of unshed tears and unrelieved frustration. She could not stand much more of it.

"Promise me," he said again. But this time it wasn't a demand. It was a plea.

Mei Lin stood up and grabbed her pack. "I'm sorry," she heard herself say as her feet started moving. She needed to get away. Away to somewhere she could think straight. And cry. And maybe even scream. "That's not a promise I can make."

Chapter 24

Mei Lin climbed back into the Subaru and planted her hands on the steering wheel. She didn't know where to drive. She didn't want to go back to Elsie's house or even to the Nagoonberry Trail, because in both places her emotions would be hopelessly distracted by happy memories of Thane. She wanted to be alone. All she'd done on the walk from the cabin was cry. Now it was time for the thinking part. She needed a quiet, lonely place where she could sit and concentrate. But where?

A memory flashed through her mind. She'd been told of a place just outside town... a sobering place that inspired reflection.

She drove a few miles north of Gustavus to the spot Carol McRoberts and several other locals had described to her, then she got out and started walking. The trail was only a footpath, but enough humans had preceded her to make it easy to follow. After a few minutes, she reached her destination.

Here, on a miserable night of bad weather in the winter of 1957, an Alaska Air National Guard plane had crashed. The pilot and three others in the cockpit had perished, but seven military passengers survived the night. At first light, neighboring citizens who had heard the terrifying noises were able to locate and rescue the men, some of whom they carried out on litters made of tree branches. The debris from the crash was left behind. All through the half century that followed, the surrounding forest had been gradually but steadily enfolding the scattered remnants.

The story was a poignant chapter in the town's history, and the site was touted as emotionally affecting. Still, Mei Lin had never wanted to see it. She tended to avoid anything depressing, which she supposed seemed strange for someone who had chosen end-of-life caregiving as a career. But her empathetic soul felt things keenly, and if she could do nothing to help a situation, she tried to spare herself the heartache. Why her heart would lead her to seek out such an experience now, she wasn't sure.

The wreckage materialized in bits as she approached. First to appear were shards of painted metal, twisted amidst the underbrush. Then more shreds of metal, as well as stray pieces of piping and rubber. When she reached the fuselage itself, she sucked in a breath of surprise. The plane's cylindrical midsection was battered and beaten, but largely intact. Vacant window holes gaped from its sides. Older trees had snapped and collapsed with it; now new trees stretched toward the sky, hemming it in. The red and white tail section still thrust up proudly through the leaves, and a broken wing lay crumpled across the forest floor, dressed with mossy vines.

She stepped carefully over and around pieces of gray metal entangled with furry green growth, wondering at how deftly the forest had incorporated the unnatural materials into its web. As she scouted out a fallen log to sit on, small birds flitted about overhead. Other than the crunch of her feet on a floor of brown needles and twigs, the cheeping of the birds was the only sound to be heard.

Her eyes were dry now, and her emotions less volatile. Thinking that four men had once died here was unquestionably sad. But despite the tragedy that had brought the plane to lie in this place, thinking of how its solid belly had shielded seven others from death lent the scene a bizarre, paradoxical sense of peace.

Stanley Buchanan himself was a paradox, she realized. He had led a selfish life in many ways, spurred on by his innate restlessness and a compulsion for thrill-seeking. At a minimum, he'd been a lousy husband. Mei Lin couldn't and didn't excuse that, but his self-recrimination went too far. Although he had frequently tempted fate in the pursuit of his own fun, he hadn't done so with the intention of harming anyone. He had certainly never asked to be kidnapped and shot at, and it was that unfortunate incident which had forced him into making the decision that would separate his family. He had acted unselfishly, if not necessarily wisely, in letting his sons and parents believe that he was dead. The "unselfish" part could be argued if he hadn't cared about his children, but Mei Lin knew that he did. His boys had occupied center stage in his delirium, and the honesty of that testament spoke for itself. Yet as much as Stanley loved his sons, as much as he must have craved any information about their wellbeing, he had never attempted to see them, even surreptitiously. He had denied himself that pleasure for the sake of their safety.

No, she thought as she twisted a green twig anxiously between her fingers. Stanley was wrong about himself. He was imperfect, but so was everyone. No matter what mistakes he had made, he still had much to give. His cancer could almost certainly be cured; with luck, he could live for decades. Decades that could be filled with family Christmases, Sunday dinners and birthdays, camping trips and bear quests, perhaps even time spent with grandchildren.

Aggravated anew, she tried to snap the twig. But it was too green; its stringy tendrils merely clutched her fingers tighter. If Stanley wasn't so blasted stubborn, he could be enjoying all of those precious family times! The future could bring them all so much happiness. But Stanley couldn't see it; he was too blinded by his own, unnecessarily negative perception of himself.

Hypocrite! she thought with a frown. Was this not the same Stanley Buchanan who had worked so hard at building *her* up, at making her see her own strengths and failures more objectively? Had he not harassed her about underestimating herself, forced her to see the irrationality of her self-blame, to the point where she had finally begun to think that yes, damn it, she *could* do it? Maybe she could be a nurse practitioner, and a good one? Maybe she *could* grow a pair and take a stab at what her heart truly wanted... to stay right here in Alaska? To stay and make a real difference by ensuring that every terminally ill person in the area had the option of dying as comfortably as possible in the security of his or her own home?

Mei Lin pulled with all her might until the tenacious vine at last gave way. *Ha!* She untwisted the remaining pieces from her swollen, green-stained fingers and chuckled ruefully. She hadn't even realized she'd made that decision. But now she was certain. She was going to apply for state certification, accept the town's generous offer, and give the nurse practitioner thing a go.

Thanks to Stanley Buchanan, she believed in herself again.

She rose from the log and straightened her spine. She was going to fix this fine mess of his. How she could do it without breaking promises, sowing family chaos, and hurting feelings that were already raw, she had no idea. But she believed she could do it.

Mei Lin Sullivan had her mojo back.

Thane and Dave didn't find the glacier bear on the river trail. They couldn't even find any tracks. They would have concluded that the couple had made the whole thing up if the assistant ranger — who knew nothing of Mei Lin's sighting — hadn't insisted that their story sounded credible. Dave planned to try and contact the couple himself first thing tomorrow, this time with his wife's German-English dictionary in hand. Perhaps, he grumbled, something had gotten lost in translation.

Thane's feet pressed against the passenger floorboard of Dave's truck. He'd been disappointed, but now he just wanted to get home. Thoughts of Mei Lin had consumed him all day, and as the sun slowly descended in the sky his eagerness to be with her increased proportionally. He was giddy as a freakin' teenager, and although some part of his brain told him he was being foolishly optimistic, he had no trouble ignoring it. He trusted Mei Lin at a gut level, instinctively, with a degree of confidence that was in no way objectively warranted. Something significant had started between them the first night they met; their interlude on the beach had merely confirmed it.

The drive back from the park seemed interminable as plans for the perfect evening unfolded in his mind. Their living situation could be considered awkward, since she had asked him to stay at her house before they were technically involved. But he didn't think social correctness would matter to her. Their relationship would progress as slow or as fast as they mutually decided, regardless of where they were sleeping. No, if he understood Mei Lin — and he flattered himself to think that he did — what mattered to her most was that they were honest with one another. Being a straightforward kind of guy, that would be easy for him. He would start things off nice and traditional, by buying her dinner. The restaurant at the crossroads would do fine: it looked warm and homey and was rumored to have excellent pizza. Maybe afterwards they'd pick up some ice cream at the little tourist shop next door. Then they'd go back to the house and enjoy a steaming cup of coffee. They could cuddle up on the porch with their mugs and a blanket and watch the bats come out. And then...

"You going to try again by yourself tomorrow?" Dave inconveniently interrupted. "I won't have time. Not until late afternoon."

"Uh... yeah," Thane answered absently. "I'm sure I'll get out there somehow."

"You want a ride with me first thing? Probably be good to get there early."

Thane flinched. No way in hell was he committing to getting up at the crack of dawn tomorrow. His night with Mei Lin could fall far short of his fantasy and still be highly enjoyable. But under no scenario he could imagine was he likely to get much sleep. Was Dave trying to make a point? Probably. "No thanks," Thane replied.

"Mei Lin got other visitors?" Dave asked as the truck at last pulled into Elsie Dunn's driveway.

"I don't think so," Thane answered, grabbing up his pack and opening the door before the vehicle had stopped moving.

"I'll see you tomorrow. Thanks." He exited the truck in record time and waved Dave away again with a grin on his face. Then he turned to the house.

He waited until the truck was pointed the other way, then reached for the doorknob. He was debating whether he should knock first when the door opened. Mei Lin looked him over with her dark eyes sparkling, and her perfect lips curved into a smile.

The next moment she was off the ground and in his arms. To what degree she'd jumped there, as opposed to being lifted, he wasn't sure. It seemed a mutual effort. But unlike the hug she'd delivered upon his surprise arrival last evening, this greeting came with a kiss. He was well into reimagining the ideal end to this nearly perfect day when the sound finally penetrated his consciousness. He wasn't sure how long it had been going on, but after half a dozen repetitions he was unable to ignore it anymore. *Someone* was walking down the staircase from the second floor. He and Mei Lin were not alone.

With an audible growl, he pulled himself together and set her carefully back down on her feet again. Then he looked over her shoulder at the source of his annoyance.

He had to blink three times before convincing himself he was seeing clearly. "Jason!" he shouted gruffly. "What the hell are you doing here?"

His grinning brother had the nerve to laugh out loud. "Nice to see you too, bro."

"Timing sucks," Thane accused, none too kindly.

Jason's grin didn't waver. "Hey, don't stop on my account. You know I'm all for it. Just say the word and I'll mosey right along."

"You're not moseying anywhere," Mei Lin said pleasantly, threading her small arm through Thane's own with a possessive gesture that melted him. "You're fine right here with us."

Thane shook his head and tried to get a grip. How had Jason gotten here? He could remember now, vaguely, that the Spider van he'd rented on his last trip had been sitting in the driveway as they'd arrived. Doubtless, that's why Dave had asked about visitors. Still, how had Jason known to come to Mei Lin's house? When Thane had left Tofino, he didn't know himself where he'd be staying. Never mind that he hadn't said one word about Mei Lin!

His fantasy woman began to explain. "It turns out that your equally obsessed little brother couldn't stand the thought of your seeing that glacier cub without him," she explained with a chuckle. "So up he flew. Any luck since your last text?"

Thane shook his head, then shot another look at Jason. It was true that his brother had seemed anxious to tag along, but at the time he'd said he had too much work. *Liar.* "That still doesn't explain why you're *here*," Thane continued crossly.

Jason's gray eyes twinkled at him with amusement. No doubt he was wondering why Thane had failed to mention that there was a woman in Alaska with whom he was on scalding-hot greeting terms. Well, he could keep on wondering.

"He was actually on his way to Dave's house to look for you," Mei Lin continued, her voice unaccountably cheerful. "But I told him you'd be coming here."

"But how did you run into him in the first place?" Thane protested.

"That would be my fault," explained a female voice he'd never heard before. "Jason was dropping me off."

Thane stared with surprise a second time as a small woman came the rest of the way down the staircase and slipped around Jason. She was a pretty thing with light brown skin, a mass of glossy black curls on her head, and amazing large dark eyes. She resembled Mei Lin in size, but the two women were built differently. Whereas Mei Lin was curvy and cuddly, this woman was lean and muscular. More striking still was the difference in their affect. While Mei Lin radiated warmth and good humor, this woman gave off a distinct vibe of wariness.

"Thane," Mei Lin said merrily, "This is my sister, Sriha. Otherwise known as Ri."

"I knew that," he conceded, stepping forward to shake the

woman's hand.

Ri had a firm grip, and she made a point of looking him in the eye. He was quite sure that if she ever suspected him of hurting her sister, she wouldn't hesitate to punch him in the jaw, no matter how much bigger he was. As a big brother himself, he respected her protective instincts. Not that he felt bad about harassing Jason, of course — the point was to protect one's younger sibling from *other* people.

"Ri and I met on the plane," Jason explained. "She was flying up for a surprise visit with a sibling, and ironically enough, so was I. But when the plane landed, we couldn't reach either one of you. So I rented some wheels and drove her out here. The house was empty so we waited outside."

"Then I came home and got a double shock," Mei Lin laughed. "Isn't it hysterical?"

"Hysterical," Thane repeated, unimpressed. He threw Jason a warning look. "She's married, you know," he advised, tilting his head toward Ri. His brother wasn't a bad guy, but Jason was only slightly less obsessed with the pursuit of attractive women than he was with surfing, and the last thing Thane needed — besides this unfortunate meeting occurring at all — was to have his little brother tick off Mei Lin's big sister.

But Jason was all charm. "Oh, believe me," he laughed out loud. "I found that out ten seconds after we buckled our seat belts. It only took another ten minutes to realize I've met the guy."

Thane raised an eyebrow. "Say what?"

"You've met him, too," Jason explained. "Ri is married to Dave Markov's older nephew. You remember when we were teenagers, Dave asked us if we wanted to go camping with them? They were named Wolf and Bear, which we thought was pretty funny, but instead of being hulking bullies they were these skinny little city kids. They'd never even been camping before!"

"Don't let anybody who grew up in Anchorage hear you call them a city kid," Ri teased. "Both brothers are expert campers, now. But their dad wasn't. He left their outdoor education to their Grandpa and their Uncle Dave."

Thane scratched at his beard. "I do remember that, now that you mention it," he mumbled, still annoyed. The fact that Jason and Ri were both very likeable people had no effect on his wish for them to disappear. "Wolf couldn't have been more than twelve at the time; he was only about yay high," he gestured with a hand. "Quiet type, as I recall. Bear was another story. Dave couldn't shut that kid up for anything — he kept singing those dirty little jingles you learn in primary school."

Ri laughed. "Sounds about right."

Mei Lin caressed Thane's wrist with her thumb. She was trying to tell him that she understood his frustration, which was nice. But of course she was making it worse. He opened his mouth to ask where Jason was staying, but quickly changed his mind. Jason couldn't stay at Dave's place any more than Thane could, and he would undoubtedly have no money and no reservations. Thane could loan him his camping gear and point him towards the bay, but there was still the problem of Ri, and if Thane knew—

"Since we're all practically related, I suggested a sleepover," Mei Lin announced, leaning her curvaceous hip apologetically into Thane as she said so. "You and Jason can have the first floor, and Ri can stay in the master bedroom upstairs. Plenty of space for all — and God knows we have enough food!"

Thane seriously wanted to cry. But he managed to plaster a smile on his face. Despite Mei Lin's show as a hostess, he was pretty sure that she was equally disappointed.

"Speaking of which," Ri offered cheerfully as she started back up the stairs. "I should get back to the kitchen. It's a good thing at least one Sullivan sister knows how to deal with frozen salmon!"

Thane threw a hard stare at his brother. "I'll help," Jason said transparently, grinning like an idiot. He headed up the staircase after Ri.

Mei Lin immediately melted into Thane's arms. "I'm sorry,"

she said with good humor, her voice muffled by his jacket. "I know this was unexpected. But I am really happy to see my sister. And your brother seems like a lot of fun."

Thane growled low in his throat, and Mei Lin chuckled back at him. But when she raised her head and looked at him, her expression was hardly what he expected. Her glimmering brown eyes were troubled, and by something more weighty than inconvenient houseguests.

"There's a lot I want to tell you," she said quietly. "But I'm afraid it'll have to wait."

"Because of Jason?" he asked immediately, concerned. Whatever was bothering her, he didn't like it. And if shoving his brother's interfering butt out the door would help in any way—

She shook her head. "It's not him. Or my sister, either. It's my patient up in the cabin. We have some unfinished business I need to tend to. I have to go back up there first thing tomorrow morning."

"Well, that's no problem," he said quickly. He would do anything to ease the lines of tension around her beautiful eyes, up to and including babysitting both their relatives. He could see that whatever was bothering her went deep, more so than she was trying to let on. "If there's something you need me to do... Anything..."

She kissed him again. It was a sweet and tender kiss, coming from a soul unafraid to freely share her affection. At least, it started out that way. He intended to return the gesture in kind, but somehow or other — and he swore it was not entirely his fault — they wound up in a potentially embarrassing situation right there in the middle of Elsie's foyer.

He was jarred back to his senses only after something clattered onto the tile floor of the kitchen above their heads. With an audible groan, he summoned a giant surge of willpower and set Mei Lin away from him. "You are..." he accused, breathing heavily, "so impossible to..."

"Likewise," she said maddeningly, smiling at him. She was

breathing hard, too, which had a disturbing effect on her chest. "Seriously. I can't be held responsible."

"*You* can't?" he protested. "Are you kidding me?"

She laughed. "In case you haven't noticed, *I'm* not the one who keeps breaking things off!"

Thane swore beneath what little breath he had and forced his eyes to look away from her. He no longer wondered if he was in love. He only wondered how he could survive it.

Chapter 25

Mei Lin parked the Subaru in its accustomed spot by the Torpins' house, grabbed her pack, and hopped out. She had hoped to get here much earlier, but after her impromptu house party had extended into the wee hours of the morning, it was inevitable that they would all oversleep. The dynamic of having two brothers and two sisters hanging out for food and laughs was rare fun, and they had all gotten along famously. If she hadn't been so distracted and disturbed by the burden of her knowledge about Stanley, she would have had an awesome time. Instead, every time she looked at the brothers, she felt uncomfortable. Sleep had not come easily after she had departed to her own room, and dragging her heavy skull off her pillow this morning had been equally difficult. The last thing she wanted to do this morning was to leave her happy company asleep in their beds and go argue — again — with Stanley. But she could not let things go on as they were. She could not get any closer to Thane while knowing that she was deceiving him. And she very much wanted to get closer to Thane.

"Kibbe boy!" She reached down and delivered a belly rub to the wiggly brown mutt at her feet. It was only when the panting black lab mix next to him demanded equal attention that Mei Lin realized something was off. What was Kibbe doing here? She looked around the drive. Jesse's truck was gone, but Amanda's SUV was parked in its usual spot.

Troubled, Mei Lin finished greeting the dogs and headed for the Torpins' front door. Kibbe wouldn't leave Stanley alone at the cabin. Someone must have brought the dog here. But who would have gone up to the cabin after she had left it last night? She'd done Jesse's dinner run for him. Something was wrong!

The door opened just as she reached it. "Hi, Mei Lin," Amanda greeted tiredly. The poor young mother always looked tired. Right now, she also looked guilty. "I'm so sorry. I meant to call you. You don't need to take care of Stanley this morning. He showed up here early, asking if Jesse could give him a lift to the clinic."

Mei Lin blinked with surprise. "He walked all the way here? How could he?"

Amanda shrugged. Somewhere inside the house, a baby began to crank. The voices of the two older boys could also be heard, gradually increasing in volume as they competed with the droning din of the television. "I wouldn't have thought he was up to it, either. But there he was, and Kibbe with him. I made him sit down long enough to have some breakfast, and then they were off."

Mei Lin still could not believe it. "But... did he look okay? Why did he want to go to the clinic?"

"He didn't say," Amanda answered. "He wasn't very talkative. I got the idea his leg was hurting him. But he was walking on it, for sure."

Mei Lin didn't like what she was hearing. Within the house, the boys' voices rose to arguing level. The baby screamed.

"I'm sorry," Amanda apologized. "I have to go. Why don't you give Jesse a call? He should be down at the dock, still. Maybe Stanley told him more."

Mei Lin thanked the young mother and said goodbye. The dull ache of worry in her stomach had graduated to a burn. Why would Stanley want to go to the clinic? Was he so upset with Mei Lin that he didn't want to see her at all? Even if that were true, his actions made no sense. He could have posted a note on the trail telling her to go away; he could have asked for Sandra Gruber to come up and see him instead. But no, he'd walked down to Jesse's himself. Even though he knew perfectly well that walking so far not only put undue stress on his healing wound, but also risked a dangerous degree of exhaustion. No matter what remedy he sought at the clinic, in balance he would be doing himself harm. Not to mention the idiocy of his coming alone, when if he'd waited just a few hours more, someone could have brought him down in the wheelbarrow!

Mei Lin jumped back in the Subaru and made her way out of the drive as quickly as possible while dodging the scampering dogs. She could feel her pulse pounding in her temples. She was afraid.

That's not a promise I can make. Her last words to Stanley pummeled her conscience. She *had* promised him, days earlier, that she would never break his confidence. Then last night she had essentially reneged. She was trying her best to be fair to Stanley, but keeping the truth from Thane felt horrid. Before she'd realized the connection between the men, she'd been so happy. Her feelings for Thane had come on quickly, but that didn't mean they weren't real. She felt an innate connection with the animal-loving giant, a bond of understanding and affection that was already stronger — incomprehensibly — than anything she'd felt for her ex-fiancé.

What she and Thane had together could be amazing, she was sure of it. All she wanted was *not* to screw it up! But did that justify her betraying Stanley's confidence? Was she looking out for Thane, or for herself?

She drove straight to the clinic and ran inside. Sandra was behind the desk, giving instructions to Lilly. "Has Stanley Smith been here this morning?" Mei Lin gushed, interrupting. "I'm so sorry, but it's important. Have you seen him?"

The nurse practitioner raised one thick eyebrow. "He hasn't been here. Today or any other day that I know of."

Mei Lin turned to the young receptionist. "You opened the normal time?"

Lilly nodded her head. "I've been here since seven-thirty. I don't know Mr. Smith, but I didn't see anybody here until eight, and I knew all of them."

Mei Lin wanted to cry, but she had no time. "Thank you. Again, I'm sorry." She knew that they had questions, but she couldn't wait. She bolted out of the clinic and drove to the dock.

Yesterday's warm, sunny weather felt like it had been a

dream. This morning's sky was an unrelieved, uniform gray. And although no rain immediately threatened, the air was cool and damp. Mei Lin parked at the dock and jogged up to where Bill Hoskins' sport fishing boat was tethered. Both Jesse and Bill were standing nearby.

"Amanda told me about Stanley," she related to Jesse between panting breaths. "But he didn't *go* to the clinic! Neither Sandra nor Lily ever saw him. Did you take him somewhere else?"

Jesse's clear blue eyes widened. "No. I dropped him off right out front, maybe seven-fifteen. That's what he asked for. He said he'd just sit and rest until they opened. Amanda had set him up with coffee and some extra muffins..." He swore. "I should have known he was up to something. Didn't make any sense."

"What did he say to you?" Mei Lin demanded.

Jesse shook his blond mane. "He didn't say much of anything. When he got to my place, he was pale and breathing heavy. Amanda made him sit down and eat, but he hardly said a word. Just that he wanted to see the nurse practitioner as soon as possible. I didn't understand it, but seeing as how he was going for medical attention, I didn't argue with him." He swore again. "I should have known."

"No," Mei Lin assured. "If anyone should have known better, it was me." She made no effort to explain herself. She was too close to breaking down into a full-fledged cry that would help no one.

"Well, where do you think he went, if not into the clinic?" Bill Hoskins asked. Mei Lin had never talked to Bill about Stanley, but she wasn't surprised that he'd already heard about their reclusive neighbor's illness.

"No idea," Jesse replied. "But he couldn't have walked much farther on that leg of his. Not when the day before yesterday he could barely make it to the outhouse! He's better, but he's not *that* much better."

"No, he's not," Mei Lin agreed, her concern only growing.

"Are there any trails out by the clinic? Could he have just headed off into the woods?" Her mind spun with images of Stanley walking until he collapsed. She would never have guessed he would take such drastic action. But how well could any person understand the emotional chaos inside another's mind?

Bill shook his head. "There's houses all around there. But no trail that leads anywhere in particular."

"He could have hitched," Jesse suggested. "If he could make it to the main road, I'm sure he could flag somebody down."

"But where do you think he'd want to go?" Bill asked. "Somewhere he didn't think you'd take him, obviously."

"He probably thought the clinic was the *only* place you'd take him," Mei Lin said miserably. "He must have wanted to go somewhere else, but he didn't want either you or me to know about it." Her stomach lurched. Gustavus was the kind of place where almost any hitchhiker had an excellent chance of being picked up by somebody. The permanent residents were friendly and accommodating, and even the seasonal residents picked up on the vibe. Violent crime was rare; so rare that the town didn't even have a local police force.

"If he hitched with a local, odds are the word would get back to you," Bill suggested, scratching his beard. "But it could take a while. And if he hitched with a tourist, we'd never know."

Mei Lin grew more desperate. Where could Stanley possibly have wanted to go so badly?

"There's something else," Jesse said, his voice raw. "The way he said goodbye to Kibbe. It wasn't... well, I thought it was odd. But I didn't think... I mean—"

"I get it," Mei Lin broke in. Stanley had told his dog goodbye. Goodbye forever.

Hot liquid surged up behind her nose and eyes; it was all she could do to withhold the explosion. How could she have been so deluded? Stanley might have worked a miracle on her own sense of self-worth, but she had failed to do the same for him.

He had come to Gustavus to die, and that's still what he wanted. If he had consented to a temporary reprieve, it was only to give himself one more chance at seeing a glacier bear.

Suddenly, as she stood shivering there on the dock, bracing herself against the cold wind that blew off the waters of Icy Strait, she understood.

The glacier cub. Of course he still wanted to see it! The man was obsessed. He could have his throat half slit with a razor already, and he would stop in mid cut to catch a glimpse! And yet, like a fool, Mei Lin had told him just last night that the cub had moved off his property. She had also left him worrying that she could betray his darkest secret at any moment...

No wonder Stanley had left the cabin! It was the only way he could remain in charge of his own destiny. If he went off after the bear himself, alone and on foot, he'd stand a good chance of killing himself through exposure and/or exhaustion, but what would he care? He was already content to die a slow, protracted death from an entirely treatable cancer. Why not clock out via a quicker, more thrilling route... while pursuing one of his life's greatest quests in the bargain?

"I know where he might have gone," Mei Lin announced.

"Where?" Jesse asked.

She fought off another strong heave that would have ended in uncontrollable sobs. "Glacier Bay."

"I still am not really understanding this," Ri exclaimed as she pulled on her boots in the moving car. "You think the man is looking for this bear, the same as Thane and Jason are, but you also think he's suicidal?"

"Yes," Mei Lin answered, not really listening. She hadn't had time to make sense when she'd told Ri to grab her rain and hiking gear and jump into the car. The men had only just left a few minutes before she'd got home, and Mei Lin needed to catch up with them. By this time Stanley could have already started down the trail, collapsed into a heap, and rolled out of sight beneath the ferns.

It was a little over nine miles from the center of Gustavus to the national park's headquarters and visitors' center. They crossed over the park boundary about midway through the trip, and the flanking forests grew increasingly dense as they drove. Ri stopped asking Mei Lin questions the first time the Subaru's tires squealed, and now they rode in silence.

Mei Lin hadn't been to the bay in several months now. Toward the end of Elsie's life she had stayed close by the house, even when friends had offered to spell her. But earlier in the season, when Elsie was a little more spry, Dave had bundled his elderly friend up in blankets and taken both her and Mei Lin on an all-day boat ride up to see the tidewater glaciers. Elsie had been as excited as a small child and had loved every minute of that very cold day, perhaps because she knew it would be her last trip of the kind. They had heard the thunderous roar of calving glaciers and the rowdy calls of nesting seabirds. They'd seen humpback whales spout, sea otters frolic with pups on their bellies, and harbor seals bask in the cool sun while floating on shards of ice. They had even spied two young black bears prowling along the shoreline. It had been one of the most amazing days of Mei Lin's life, and as her patient's condition worsened she couldn't recall it without tearing up. These days, she was more sanguine. *Life is for the living,* Elsie had so often said. *To not live it to its fullest is a crime.*

Mei Lin smiled to herself ruefully as she imagined Stanley and Elsie coming face to face. Wouldn't her Elsie have a thing or two to say to him!

"Where are we, exactly?" Ri asked cautiously as Mei Lin pulled off into a small parking area in the trees.

"This is the Bartlett River trailhead," Mei Lin explained. "I don't see the Spider. I bet they drove on up to headquarters first, to see Dave." She drummed her fingers on the wheel anxiously as she considered. "Listen, Ri. I've got to find the men to explain what's going on, but Stanley could have started down this trail hours ago. He could be a hundred yards away from us, collapsed in the middle of it, right now. Would you mind checking it out? Just maybe walk the first half hour or so, and if nobody's caught up with you by then, come on back. I don't think Stanley could have made it much farther. But if you meet anybody on the trail you can ask them if they've seen a man around seventy, walking alone."

"Got it," Ri said confidently, stepping out and adjusting her pack. "Half an hour, then turn around." She looked at her phone. "Looks like a decent signal right here, anyway. I'll call you in an hour, if I don't find something before."

"I'm sure we'll catch up with you before then," Mei Lin assured, wanting to hug her. Ri had always been the adventurous sister. Still, up until a year or so ago, Ri would have been no more equipped than Mei Lin to head off on a wilderness trail in bear country all by herself. Living in Alaska with a volcanologist for a husband had made a difference.

Mei Lin waved goodbye to her sister and pulled out of the lot. She drove around another bend, swerved to avoid hitting a slow-moving porcupine on the berm, then cruised along the shore of Bartlett Cove to the building she remembered Dave's office being in. But neither the truck he usually drove nor the Spider were parked there. Figuring the men must have gone to the visitors' center, she impatiently reversed direction.

"Yes!" she proclaimed triumphantly as she reached the main parking area and located the Spider. She parked right next to it, then headed toward the largest of the wooden buildings clustered near the beach. "If they're chasing after Dave, they could be anywhere," she muttered to herself, pulling out her phone. Neither Thane nor Dave had answered earlier, but that meant nothing. On these roads, signals came and went as they pleased.

The phone had only just started to ring when a deep voice called out to her from the real world. "Mei Lin! What are you doing here?"

She looked up to see Thane and Jason both, smiling as they walked toward her from outside the main entrance. They were decked out in rain gear and carrying full packs. She pocketed her phone and ran towards them, the full weight of her worry crashing down as she realized everything that lay at stake. Thane had Stanley's eyes, no question, but Jason — aside from his age and more abundant hair — was practically a dead ringer for their father.

Mei Lin flung herself into Thane's arms without apology. She needed his strength and comfort too much to deny herself either, but she did manage to keep it short. She pulled herself away from him and then hastily gave both brothers a simplified explanation of the crisis. Her patient, who was also obsessed with glacier bears, had disappeared. Most likely, he was pursuing the cub where the German couple had reported seeing it, information that she had foolishly relayed to him last night. But he was sick and weak and such a quest could definitely kill him, a fate which he might not care about, but which Mei Lin most definitely did.

The men didn't bother with nonessential questions. They asked for a description of the man and when he had likely started out. Then Jason took the Spider and headed for the river trail to catch up with Ri, while Thane took Mei Lin's hand and began walking with her toward the public dock. She was so relieved at the men's quick understanding of the situation that she wanted to cry — again. But she did not. "Is Dave at the dock?" she asked, realizing she didn't know why they were headed there.

"Oh, no, he's halfway up the bay by now," Thane answered soberly. "I'll make sure they radio him, but first we need to know if Stanley got in a boat."

Mei Lin hadn't considered the possibility. "Why would he?"

"If he knows the area," Thane explained, pausing as a brood of sooty grouse chicks followed its mother across the trail, "or even if he bothered to look at a park map, he'd know that that trail runs right along the shore of the cove. With an injured leg, it would make more sense to reach the place the German couple mentioned by water. He could have tried to get someone with a boat to drop him off, or he could have rented a kayak. Either way, the staff up here will likely remember him."

Mei Lin wanted to kiss him. Her desire along those lines was pretty much continuous, but it hit her especially strong now. She managed to resist, however, in order to keep moving forward. The trail on which they were walking was a well-worn one, close to the lodge, and it was flanked with a variety of colorful berry bushes and interesting birdlife. But this was no time to indulge in sightseeing.

They emerged from the forest onto the shore, and she drew in a great gulp of cool air. The vast, gray-blue waters of the Sitakaday Strait stretched out before her, with a view of green trees and mountain peaks beyond. She only wished she could enjoy it at her leisure.

"I'll talk to the people on the dock," Thane said. "There are only so many boats he could have hopped on at that hour. Why don't you check at the visitor information station? They would know if he rented a kayak."

Mei Lin nodded and headed off toward the small building. A college-aged summer staffer stood up to meet her. "Can I help you?"

Mei Lin gave a quick description of Stanley, and the girl immediately looked down at a logbook on her desk. "There was a guy here who fit that description, yes," she said uncertainly, describing the clothing worn by the man she had seen. "But we have his name as George Grayson."

Mei Lin didn't know whether to cheer or curse. How like Stanley to dream up yet another fake name! "I'm sure that's him," she insisted. And she was. Besides the use of his middle name as his first and the Freudian reference to the color of a glacier cub, the staffer had perfectly described Stanley's favorite coat and hat.

"I have to wonder why you're asking," the girl said with concern. "I was a little worried about him, honestly. He sat through the orientation and he seemed to know what he was doing with the kayak, but he didn't look well. He was pale and kind of sweaty... I don't know. You could just look in his face and see that something was wrong. I asked him over and over again if he was sure he felt up to paddling, because you know these waters can be dangerous. But he just kept insisting he was fine and said he didn't plan to go too far. Still, he rented the kayak for the whole day. It made me nervous. I watched him paddle out that way..." She looked increasingly worried the more she talked. "Maybe I should have refused to rent to him. But he met all the criteria..."

Mei Lin asked for a description of the kayak, assured the poor girl that none of this was her fault, then hurried to catch up with Thane. She relayed the information in a rush. "Can we follow him on the water?"

Thane nodded. "We'll radio Dave; see if he can scare us up a decent boat. Then we can search the shoreline. He could have beached his kayak anywhere between here and the estuary at the end of the trail." He caught Mei Lin's gaze, and for a moment it was as if Stanley's own eyes were looking at her. "You up for a boat trip? And possibly a hike?"

She held the telling gaze with her own, her voice as confident as she could make it. "Absolutely."

Chapter 26

The humming vibration of the small boat's motor made the binoculars in Mei Lin's hands shake. Or perhaps her hands were shaking anyway. She was glad to be moving finally, to be doing something. But she still felt frustratingly helpless.

Thane had contacted Dave, and things were starting to happen. A ranger had been dispatched to catch up with Ri and Jason and provide radio contact for the group as all three searched the nearly two-mile length of the Bartlett River Trail for any sign of Stanley. Another ranger piloted the vessel that carried Mei Lin and Thane along the corresponding shoreline. Stanley had only been in the park a few hours, Dave had explained, and they had no objective reason, yet, to believe that he was either lost or in imminent danger. But if he could not be located soon in any of the expected places, an official search and rescue team would be called.

Mei Lin understood the need to prioritize missing persons cases by their respective risk. It was the height of the tourist season, after all, and trained search and rescue dogs in particular were in high demand. But the certainty in her gut was punishing. She *knew* that Stanley's life was at stake, right now, no matter how the situation appeared objectively. "Do you see anything?" she asked Thane, unable to trust her own watery, burning eyes.

"Not yet." One hand held a pair of binoculars to his face; his other arm was around her shoulders. "Are you cold?" he asked gently. "I can feel you shivering."

"It's... not the cold," she answered. Thane still had no idea of his relationship to Stanley, yet he could not be any more helpful to her, and the same was true of Jason. The bittersweet irony of the situation made her want to cry all over again, but she had a more selfish reason for appreciating the men's good hearts. If only they could find Stanley safe and sound, he would be forced to meet both his sons face to face. Certainly then, Mei Lin hoped and prayed, he would be moved to tell them the whole truth himself, relieving her of her impossible burden.

Thane asked for no further explanation of her shivers. He merely gave her shoulders an affectionate squeeze and dropped a kiss on the top of her head. "We'll find him," he said tenderly. "Don't worry." He surveyed the shore another moment, then turned back to her. "What you need to watch for is a kayak that's drawn way up into the brush," he advised. "The tide's coming in this morning, and he would have known that. If he did see something and decide to pull out, he wouldn't leave the kayak on the beach. If he did, it'd be out to sea with the humpbacks by the time he returned." He pointed at the line on the shore where the vegetation began. "Only safe place would be all the way off the sand. If he's smart, he'd look for a halfway decent-sized tree to anchor it to, besides."

Mei Lin nodded with understanding. She was not encouraged. The amount of vegetation along the shoreline varied, but if anyone wanted to conceal a kayak in the brush, it would not be difficult. She raised the binoculars to her eyes and concentrated. The scream of a gull close overhead made her jump, but she kept her eyes on the task. Their boat passed a group of kayakers laughing and pointing to something happening in the water, most likely the playful antics of a sea otter. If she were making this trip for pleasure she would be looking for such animals herself, scanning the deeper waters of the strait for the telltale plumes of whales and dolphins. But there was nothing pleasurable in watching the steady passage of more and more shoreline, none of which yielded any visible sign of a single, bright blue kayak.

"I can't believe he could have paddled even this far," Mei Lin said miserably as the search dragged on. "People can do crazy things by running on sheer adrenaline, I know. But there's always a limit. Having a serious infection is more debilitating than people realize. The body uses tremendous stores of energy, even if the person is doing nothing but lying in bed. People start to feel better when their pain lessens and their fever comes down, and they think they can just get up and go... but they can't."

She struggled to keep her voice steady. "His arms would take him farther than his legs, particularly since he'd already walked so far. But he couldn't paddle in these currents for hours! He just couldn't. Maybe we should—"

"Hold up," Thane shouted suddenly, gesturing to the female ranger driving the boat. The motor quieted and their progress slowed. "Look there," he told Mei Lin, pointing.

She didn't need binoculars to see the blue kayak perched on the sand of a beachhead well ahead of them. It wasn't hidden in the brush. It wasn't hidden by anything. It was sitting out in plain view, swaying slightly as its tail end was lapped by the rising tide.

Thane spoke to the ranger again, and their boat made its way toward shore. Mei Lin stood and stared at the empty, untethered kayak as her heart dropped into her boots. "This is a good spot," Thane said calmly. "Jer should be able to get us in close enough to where we can walk to shore. She'll radio the others, and we can track him from here." He gave Mei Lin's shoulders another reassuring squeeze. "You must have given the man pretty good directions. By water, this is about as close as you could get to the point on the trail that the German couple described."

Mei Lin nodded dumbly as their boat drifted toward the sand, then stopped a few paces short of it. Thane slipped over and into the shallow water without hesitation, then held out his hands to her. The rubber boots that covered his giant calves were well above the water line, but Mei Lin's ankle-high duck boots would not be. Wishing, once again, that she could enjoy this experience under different circumstances, she climbed down into his arms and let him carry her — as if she and her pack together weighed nothing — to dry ground. She heard him have further words with the ranger before the boat pulled away, but she found herself unable to move. She merely stood, staring, at the abandoned kayak.

Stanley's jacket lay over the seat.

She felt Thane's presence behind her. "He left his coat," she said flatly. "He must have been warm from all the paddling." *Or else his fever is back*, she left unsaid. A relapse of infection was unlikely, but possible. Stanley could have skipped two more doses since the last time she saw him. "He knew enough to pull out at this exact spot," she said grimly. "But he didn't secure the kayak. So either he thought he wouldn't be gone long..." she fought against the choking feeling in her throat. "Or he didn't plan to come back at all."

Thane's strong arms pulled her back against his chest, then wrapped around her. "I know," he said softly. "I've passed the information along. Now, you and I need to get going."

She nodded, squeezing her eyes shut against the ever-threatening flow. He released her, then pulled the kayak up off of the beach and tied it. He removed Stanley's jacket and stuffed it in his own pack. "You'll need to stay behind me," he told her as he studied the ground. Uphill from the kayak, Stanley's boots had made obvious impressions in the sand. But as the terrain changed and the vegetation became more dense, Mei Lin lost sight of them. "Tracking and trailing *people* isn't my specialty," Thane continued as he picked his way slowly through the brush ahead of her. "But you could do worse."

Mei Lin was having trouble speaking again, which was just as well. She could not begin to explain to him how important his presence here really was — over and above the comfort he provided her.

"You should call out to him," Thane advised.

Mei Lin considered. She could not rule out the possibility that Stanley, if he could still move at all, would respond to her voice by moving the opposite direction. At a minimum, he was frustrated with her because she'd refused to give him the assurance of confidentiality he wanted. More likely he was both angry and scared, convinced that she had already betrayed him.

Still, calling out to him was worth a shot. If he had collapsed somewhere, either from exhaustion or delirium, he might lack the presence of mind *not* to answer.

"Stanley!" she called out hopefully. "It's Mei Lin. Can you hear me?"

Both she and Thane went quiet, listening. But the only sounds to be heard were the whistling of the wind in the trees and the distant drum of a woodpecker. "Keep trying," Thane advised, his tone optimistic. "We're not that far from the trail. So far he seems to have been following the path of least resistance."

They continued moving slowly, with Mei Lin calling out every few moments, until seemingly out of nowhere they emerged onto a well traveled footpath running parallel to the shore. She did not need Thane to tell her that they had reached the Bartlett River Trail. She looked up and down the narrow lane, but saw no other people. "Is this where you and Dave came looking for the bear yesterday?" she asked.

He nodded. "Stay here a second." He walked away from her, carefully studying the brush on either edge of the trail. As he moved, he spoke into his radio. Mei Lin couldn't understand the garbled response, but she thought the speaker sounded like Jason. After what seemed like an eternity, Thane returned to her and put the radio away. "Do you remember exactly what you told Stanley? About the location of the bear?"

"I just passed along what you texted to me," she explained. "About the nearest mile marker post."

Thane lifted a hand and pointed to a red-painted stake planted on a bend in the trail a few yards south of them. "That's it."

Mei Lin sucked in a breath and hastened to the mile marker. Then she turned toward the dense woods opposite the beach and peered through the gloom of the tightly spaced tree trunks. Stanley had to be in there somewhere. She called out again, but heard nothing. "He *must* have been right here!" she exclaimed. "And not all that long ago, given how far he would have had to paddle. Can you track him into the woods from this point? Or do you think he stayed on the trail?"

Thane's striking blue eyes studied her with a disturbing hint of pity. He shook his head. "I don't think he stayed on the trail. Jason and Ri started at the south trailhead, and they've passed this point already. They've also met two groups of hikers coming from the opposite direction, and no one has seen him."

Mei Lin knew that Thane was trying to tell her something. Something she wouldn't want to hear. "You think he left the trail, then? Probably from a point right around here? "

Thane nodded. "There's no way to know for sure. But if this mile marker was his goal — and the location of the kayak makes pretty clear that it was — he'd have no motivation to push much farther either up or down the trail. He'd do exactly what Dave and I did yesterday. He'd hunt around this area for signs of an animal trail. Wildlife do use the human trails — the path of least resistance always appeals — but they have other, less obvious highways as well. If seeing bears is his priority, he'd look for a likely trail and follow it into a less trafficked area. Then he'd hunt for a comfortable sit spot with a good view of any bears that might happen by."

Mei Lin looked again, but the sheer density of the rainforest confounded her. These woods were different from those in Maine, where one could wander beneath the trees with relative ease, crunching through a carpet of dead leaves and pine needles with little concern aside from poison ivy. Here, the clumps of bushes, maze of fallen tree trunks, and plethora of ferns, vines, and underbrush made it difficult to walk, period — and ridiculously easy to hide. "And would he find such a path?"

"He could find one of several. And he could spend hours following different ones and staking them out." Thane's voice dropped, and he eyed her with uneasiness. "But... unless the man is partially deaf, he'd most likely still be within earshot."

Mei Lin nodded with bleak understanding. "He isn't deaf as far as I know. Which must mean that either he's deliberating ignoring me" — her voice quavered — "or that he's unconscious."

"Those aren't the only possibilities," Thane answered. "But I'd say they're the two most likely."

"So what do we do now?" The words were choked. This was all her fault! She shouldn't have left things between her and Stanley as she had. She should have stayed with him, she should have promised... Or at least she should have tried harder and longer to reason with him!

Thane's arms reached out to her again, and she buried her face in his chest. His touch felt divine, and yet... she felt like she was cheating him. Would he be so eager to comfort her if he knew everything that she was thinking? Everything that she was keeping from him?

That cheery thought was the last straw. Her composure broke. She sobbed against the slick fabric of Thane's waterproof jacket while he stood silently, holding her. She had wanted so badly to fix this mess. For Stanley and for Thane. Yet all she had done was make things worse! She'd lost Stanley's trust, with potentially dire consequences, even though she hadn't said a word. And the longer she dared keep Thane in the dark, the more she involved him, unwitting, in the search for his own father, the more deeply her deception would hurt him, too!

She wanted very much to let out a bloodcurdling, frustrated scream. But she managed to let her sniffles and gasps for breath suffice. After a few more moments of self-indulgent venting, she pulled herself together and stepped away from him.

She had no plan of action. When did she ever? "What do you think we should do?" she asked again, her voice stronger.

"Talk to him," Thane suggested gently. "Keep calling out, whatever you think might sway him. If Stanley doesn't want us to find him, we're in for a challenge. I'll try my best to pick out his trail, but with Dave and me tromping all over this area yesterday, the chance of that is pretty slim. The others are on their way back here now, and they can help us search bush to bush if we need to. Our best bet will be the rescue dogs. It just may take a while to get them out here."

Mei Lin got the picture. The hairs on her arms prickled at the thought of Stanley's being close enough, right now, to overhear every word they were saying. It seemed incredible, but at the same time, she knew he couldn't have the endurance to walk far. What was he thinking? Why had he left his jacket in the kayak, when it was almost certain to rain? Was he off his meds? Had he packed any food? Had he wanted to find the glacier bear, no matter what it cost him... or was giving himself this one last chance just a perk on the road to his ultimate goal?

She feared she already knew those answers.

"When you and Dave looked around here before," she asked, trying hard to focus, "did you find any particular place that might appeal to another bear hunter as a good spot for a stakeout?"

Thane lifted his gaze to the wall of tightly packed spruce and hemlock trunks that edged the trail. He shook his head. "The only clearings I remember were a good distance from here, and they were boggy. If he were very lame, he couldn't make it even if he did know how to find them. Right around here it's all flat, so one fallen tree trunk near an existing path makes just as good a sit spot as another."

Mei Lin's hopes drifted lower. As if acting on cue, the gray skies that had been holding their peace all morning chose that moment to let loose. Large, pelting raindrops fell from above to make a loud pattering sound on the surrounding foliage. Thane reached out to pull the hood of Mei Lin's jacket up over her head, then did the same with his own. He put a hand under her chin and tilted her face up to his. "What are you thinking, exactly?"

Mei Lin jerked her chin down again and leaned into his chest. She couldn't bear to look at him. She had been stalling this moment as long as possible, hoping for a miracle. But the time had come to take action. Never mind whether that action felt entirely right. She no longer had a choice.

"I know him, Thane," she began. "He thinks his life isn't worth living anymore. And I can picture him so clearly... lying out there in this rain without a jacket, shivering from cold or fever or both, with his leg aching terribly. He's breathing heavy, so exhausted he can barely move, and he couldn't get up again if he tried. He figures he'll die of exposure eventually, and that's just fine by him. If he's heard me calling, he doesn't care. We argued yesterday, all day long. I said absolutely everything I could think of to change his mind. But I couldn't do it."

She summoned her strength and lifted her chin. She needed to look Thane in the eyes... his father's eyes. She wanted to savor the tenderness in them before both men came to hate her. "I *can't* change his mind," she repeated with conviction. "But you can."

Chapter 27

Thane looked down at the bedraggled bundle of femininity in his arms and felt a disquieting mix of pity, lust, and confusion. He was trying his best to help her. He could see that her feelings for this cantankerous hermit of a patient went deep, and he admired that even as it baffled him. Did she not nurse the dying for a living? Such personal involvement must come at a huge emotional price. But perhaps her beautiful, giant heart could do nothing else.

If he could spare her the pain of losing this man, he would move mountains to do so. He'd been pleased that his particular set of talents had come in handy thus far. But with no dogs and no clear trail, there was little else that Thane or anyone could do now besides set up parameters and then painstakingly search each designated area. He would personally poke under every bush within a five-mile radius if it would make Mei Lin happy... except that now she had started talking nonsense.

"What do you mean?" he asked. He couldn't imagine why she thought he could talk a patient of hers into anything.

She remained in his arms even as the rain fell steadily all around them, dripping off the brims of their hoods and oozing between their jackets. "Thane," she answered, her voice suddenly steely. "You told me that your father was kidnapped by criminals who needed a surgeon, and that ultimately he was shot and killed."

He lifted a wary eyebrow. Mei Lin didn't seem hysterical, but her change of topic was bizarre. "Um... yeah," he replied uncertainly.

Her fingers tightened on the back of his rain jacket. "Your father didn't die," she plowed on. "He survived the shooting. But he was still a dead man, because the criminals knew that he had critical information about their operation. The authorities got to him in the hospital that night and tried to convince him to go into the witness protection program so he could testify. But he wouldn't do it. He had a wife and children and he didn't want to disrupt their lives or put them in any kind of danger. So they made a compromise."

Thane was speechless. He could think of no sane reason why Mei Lin would be spinning some bizarro version of *his* family history, particularly not right now. Yet on she plunged, talking more and more crazy.

"Your father wouldn't testify in court, but he did tell the authorities everything he knew. In exchange, they protected him by falsifying a death certificate, hiding him out while he recuperated, and then giving him a new ID. When he recovered he took a job overseas, performing surgery in third-world countries and in war zones. He did that work for nearly twenty years, until an injury forced him to retire. He—"

"Mei Lin!" Thane interrupted finally, setting her away from him. He didn't want to be gruff with her, but this was too much. She was scaring him. How the hell, in the space of a few short minutes, had she gone from being his dream woman to being insane? Why was she so fixated on *his* father? This wasn't only crazy, it was creepy.

"He retired and went back to his home, Thane. He came back here, to Alaska, where he grew up. He bought a cabin off the grid and he got ready to die..." Her voice broke and her eyes filled with tears.

Thane stood motionless. He couldn't decide whether to pull her close and comfort her or turn and run. What she was saying about his father wasn't true. But neither was it so implausible that no sane person could believe it. She clearly did believe it. But why? "What makes you think you know all this?" he demanded, his voice louder than intended.

"Because he told me!" she answered with equal volume.

The birds stopped chirping then. The rain stopped falling. The earth stopped moving. In the whole world there was only her face, her eyes. He could feel heavy breaths moving his rib cage, but everything else he ever knew, ever felt, was suspended.

Very slowly, Mei Lin moved closer. She wrapped her tiny arms around his waist, pressed her face against his sopping raincoat, and squeezed. "I'm so sorry," she soothed. "So sorry to do this to you, this way. Please don't be angry. Please try to see the good part. Because there *is* a good part. A very good part, I promise you."

Thane still couldn't move. With her touch, the birds had started chirping again, and his body had returned to the forest. But his brain was turning somersaults. *He told me. Your father. He came back here... he bought a cabin. He didn't die... Didn't die...*

"Stanley," he heard his own lips mutter. "You said your patient's name was Stanley."

"Yes!" Mei Lin agreed, tightening her hold still further. "Yes, Thane. It's him, and it's all true, I swear."

He felt raw inside. Ripped open. Disemboweled. He shook his head involuntarily. "It can't be."

"But it is," she insisted.

He felt a spurt of horror. Was everything that had happened between him and Mei Lin just a set up? Had she known who he was all along, sought him out, grilled him for information? He grabbed her arms and set her firmly away from him again.

"Please don't look at me like that," she pleaded.

Could she read his mind, too? "You knew who I was!" he accused. "Did somebody hire you to find me?"

She shook her head in obvious disbelief. "Of course not! You're the one who showed up randomly on *my* doorstep, remember?" she proclaimed, her gorgeous round cheeks flaring with indignation. "I had no idea you were connected to Stanley in any way until yesterday at the beach... when *you* started talking about your dad!"

The beach, his ailing brain repeated. *Ah, yes. The beach.* He had enjoyed the beach. And he had talked about his dad. But only because she had asked him questions!

"None of us would be the wiser in this whole insane

situation if it weren't for that silly gray bear cub!" she exclaimed, not giving up. "Don't you see how it happened? Stanley went ape when I told him what I'd seen — he started spouting off all these fond memories of camping trips and bedtime stories... Imagine my surprise when you started telling me the same ones!"

Thane felt very odd. He didn't want to believe the worst of Mei Lin, but then again... he did want to. Because if she was a nutcase or some clever operative either one, he could forget all her nonsense and go back to his normal life. But if she was genuine, if she was telling the truth...

No. She couldn't be.

"I didn't think too much of the similarities between the bear stories," she continued, her words flowing rapidly. "I mean, that *could* have been a coincidence. But when you said that your father was a surgeon, it all seemed a bit much. As soon as you left with Dave, I got online and searched for an article on the kidnapping, and then I saw the name: Stanley Buchanan. I went straight out to Stanley 'Smith's' cabin and confronted him, and he didn't even bother denying it!"

Thane's grip on normalcy was loosening. He was falling into the abyss. He remembered exactly what had happened on the beach — it was only yesterday. *Your dad...* she had asked him as they paused to pick berries. *You said he was a surgeon?* A sudden breeze had tousled her dark hair, buffeting her pretty face. She had been looking at him with a queer expression. A puzzled, slightly freaked-out expression.

Dear God. She didn't know, did she? Not before then. He'd left her shortly after that, and he hadn't come back until evening. *There's a lot I want to tell you,* she'd told him just after their siblings invaded. *But I'm afraid it'll have to wait... It's my patient up in the cabin. We have some unfinished business I need to tend to...*

His body felt cold. It all fit, dammit. Every last bit of it. Mei Lin wasn't lying.

But if she was telling the truth, that would mean... He

stiffened. *No.* All it meant was that some man claiming to be Stanley Buchanan was living in a cabin in Gustavus.

"Are you all right?" Mei Lin whispered anxiously, moving closer. "Please tell me you're okay. I really am sorry to have to tell you like this. It's just that... we don't have much time. He didn't want you or Jason to know because he thinks you'll hate him, even though he really did do it to keep you both safe. He isn't a perfect man, Thane, but he loves you. He loves both of you very much. When he was delirious, his boys were the first thing on his mind."

Thane couldn't think clearly. Her words penetrated in fits and starts. He got that she bought this man's story hook, line, and sinker, but he didn't have to. He wasn't going to.

We don't have much time, she was saying. About that much, she was probably right. He lifted his head and scanned the green, soggy forest through the dashes of water falling from the sky. Somewhere in this vast sea of vegetation, a man was out in the rain without a coat. He was ill and exhausted. He might even be dying. Whoever the hell he was, Mei Lin cared about him. That was enough. For now.

"You do believe me," she said softly, almost begging. "Don't you?"

"I believe you," he said easily. *You've just been had, that's all.* He threw his arm around her shoulders and gave her a friendly squeeze. "Let's keep looking."

Mei Lin felt like crying again. But after the last jag, her reserves were empty. Thane didn't believe her. His perfunctory, dismissive hug had confirmed it. He wasn't angry, so he must not think she was lying. More likely, he thought she was delusional. Never mind the illogic of that scenario. She supposed that under the circumstances, it was the easiest thing for him to believe. But it wouldn't save his father's life.

"Stanley won't respond to me," she repeated. "He's mad at me for betraying his confidence. Besides which, he still wants to die. There are only two people in this world who have the power to convince him that his sons would *want* to know him, that they won't hate him, that there could be some purpose for his future. You need to call out to him, Thane. You and Jason, not me."

He stared at her with a vacant expression. The damnable rain kept coming. It was lighter now, but enough had already fallen to soak through Stanley's clothes.

"You have his eyes, Thane," she said, her sense of desperation increasing. "I noticed that first thing, long before any of the rest of it came out. You don't look much like him otherwise, but I nearly did a double take when I saw Jason. He looks so much like your dad. Or at least, what I imagine Stanley looked like when he was younger."

Thane did not respond. But it was obvious that her words disturbed him. He must have seen enough pictures of his father to be aware of the family resemblances. She kept talking. "He said that his grandfather had seen a glacier bear in Yakutat. He mentioned having cousins up there. Someone named Uncle Regis, maybe?"

Thane's eyes widened. How she wished she could remember more details! "He talked about how much he loved taking the two of you out on bear quests. He said he would tell stories where the boys looking for the bear were brothers, one with brown hair and one blond. I assume Jason was blond when he was little, right?"

Thane still didn't answer. His face had gone white.

"One story was about the boys hiding their food in a tree, but I can't remember anything else. He only talked about having sons when he was overexcited or feverish. Otherwise, he denied it. Adamantly. When I mentioned to him what he had said while he was delirious, he got frightened. He's spent the last twenty years pretending to be somebody else to protect his family. He couldn't tell the truth to anyone. He believed that a man named Tony Russo wanted him dead and wouldn't hesitate to use his family to flush him out. The criminals were skeptical that Stanley had died in the raid. They even sent some men to his funeral, to see if any of the family's reactions seemed insincere—"

"Stop!" Thane thundered, his face now suffused with red. He stared at her for a long moment, his eyes wild and unseeing, before his shoulders slumped and his gaze fell away. "Please, Mei Lin. Just stop," he said in a hoarse whisper. "Okay?"

Mei Lin stopped. She wanted to touch him, but she didn't think it was a good idea. The poor man was reeling. What he probably needed most at this particular moment was some space.

She stepped away. Her heart pounded in her chest; raindrops pattered onto her hood. She moved to the mile marker, then looked around for a stick. Once she'd found a suitable tool, she looked from the red stake to a recognizable tree stump in the distance and drew a mental line between the two. Then she began to move along it, using her stick to part the underbrush. Any place large enough to hide a huddled man was suspect. "Stanley!" she called out. "It's Mei Lin. Will you answer me? Please?"

She had not been searching long before she realized that Thane had joined her. He had a stick of his own and was moving along a parallel path. "Stanley!" he called out suddenly, making her jump. His voice was tremulous, uncertain. She didn't speak to him, but kept on with her work.

"Stanley Buchanan!" he called again, this time with an edge of frustrated anger. "Are you out here? Can you hear me?"

She paused to listen for any response. All she heard was the thudding of the rain.

On Thane's next shout, his voice broke a little. And so did Mei Lin's heart.

"Dad?"

Chapter 28

Mei Lin continued to poke her stick into anything she couldn't see through — dense bushes, leafy plants, the dark caverns formed by fallen trees and their broken, moss-covered appendages. She could see no sign of Stanley or any other human. What bothered her more was that she could hear nothing, either.

As unsure as she was whether Stanley would respond to her calls, she'd been certain that a direct plea from either of his sons would undo him. If only he was conscious, his physical weakness should render him even more vulnerable to his emotions. Only a man of stone could fail to be moved by the pain-filled longing in Thane's voice — even if it was eclipsed, much of the time, by a more obvious frustrated anger.

No, she told herself miserably, Stanley couldn't possibly be ignoring his son's cries. He was either unconscious, incapable of responding, or both. He was already weak when he left home; by now he would be dehydrated and exhausted as well. Throw in a little recurrent fever and the man was a walking recipe for light-headedness, dizziness, and mental confusion. Even without a relapse of infection, he could have weakened himself to the point of passing out. And if the worst were true — if his infection had never completely cleared and was spreading through his bloodstream — he might once again be flirting with potentially fatal septic shock.

Was he confused and disoriented from the illness when he'd left his jacket in the kayak? Or was that the deliberate act of a man hell-bent on dying by exposure? Mei Lin didn't know. She wasn't even sure which was worse. All she knew was that they had to find him.

A man's voice in the distance startled her into silence. But her hopeful elation was short-lived. The voice that called to them from up the trail was far too hale and hearty to have come from Stanley, even if it did bear a clear resemblance in timbre.

"It's Jason," Thane announced. He turned and carefully backtracked toward the trail, and Mei Lin did the same. Within a few moments they reached the mile marker and met up with both their siblings and a younger male ranger.

Ri stepped up to Mei Lin and enfolded her sister in a hug. Ri said nothing, which was typical, but Mei Lin had only to look at the supportive, empathetic expression in her sister's dark eyes to know that the other search party had found nothing. While the men compared notes, Mei Lin stood silently and listened, paying particular attention to how Thane acted with Jason. She had no idea whether he would share his newfound knowledge with his younger brother. If he didn't, should she? She didn't know Jason well enough to guess how he would react.

"Dave says the state troopers have been notified and the volunteer search and rescue in Gustavus is on the way," Jason told her.

Mei Lin nodded without speaking. She appreciated Jason's helpfulness today more than she could say. He barely knew her and Stanley meant nothing to him — yet just like Thane he'd immediately offered to help, tossing aside his personal plans without complaint.

"They bringing dogs?" Thane asked.

"We hope so," the young ranger answered. He looked barely out of college, but had a definite air of confidence about him. "The dogs are in high demand this time of year, but we'll get them here as soon as we can."

Neither of the brothers made any response to that, and Mei Lin's minimal sense of relief disintegrated. Dogs, like everyone and everything else, could only be brought into Gustavus by boat or plane.

Stanley had only so much time.

Her eyes grew blurry with tears again and she swore internally, determined to keep herself in check. Emotional outbursts weren't going to help the situation. Only physical effort could do that. As the others discussed how to plot out a search grid, she returned to the imaginary line she'd started on earlier and got back to work.

She had only just reached her previous stopping point when a subtle, but distinctive sound drew her attention. It was a slapping, drumming, sort of sound. The sort of sound that would usually make her fear attack by some unseen but rapidly approaching animal. But this sound came with a clear note of deja vu, and instead of being frightened, her heavy heart leapt. She stood on tiptoe and lifted her chin. She couldn't see the trail itself from where she stood; anything beneath shoulder height was hidden by the underbrush. But she could see the heads of the others also turning toward the sound. Seconds later the tops of some of the bushes between her and the trail began to rustle. Then, like a torpedo, a smallish form burst out of the greenery, knocking both leaves and small branches askew in its eagerness to reach her.

"Kibbe!" she cried, dropping her stick and attempting to embrace the squiggling, sycophantic little canine. "How did you get out here? And how did you find me?" The answer to her second question was obvious. He was a dog, wasn't he? He had followed her scent.

Loud voices from the trail soon answered the first question. Jesse had brought him after receiving a call from Dave. Kibbe was no trained tracker, Jesse explained to the others, but hell — what dog couldn't catch up with its own master?

Mei Lin hurried over to the others with the excited mutt at her heels.

"I didn't even know he had a dog," Thane exclaimed, his voice brighter. "But I'm glad Dave thought of it!"

The optimism in his voice buoyed Mei Lin's spirits more than she could say. "Won't the rain make it harder?" she asked, even as she remembered how easily the dog had tracked her just now.

"Nah," Thane answered, bending down to greet the dog

himself. "A little bit of wetness actually refreshes a scent. Brings it out. As long as we don't get torrents, this little guy should be able to smell just fine."

Mei Lin smiled. The rain had been constant, but at least it was mostly light. "Well, let's do it!"

None of them needed to do anything. Kibbe was already sniffing in earnest, his tail wagging frantically as his nose surveyed the ground all around the mile marker.

"Stanley probably spent some time right here," Thane said thoughtfully, watching the dog. "Before he decided which direction to head."

Mei Lin held her breath. Kibbe was milling about like an ant, seemingly without purpose or direction. He kept seeming to find something and moving forward quickly, only to stop and turn sharply or backtrack altogether.

"See that? He knows his master was here," Jesse said confidently. "Come on, boy. You can do it. Which way did he go?"

Kibbe began to strut a straight line north up the trail. "Oh no," Mei Lin worried. "He isn't tracing Stanley backwards to the kayak, is he?"

"Let's see," Thane answered as they followed a few paces behind the dog. When Kibbe stopped short to examine a clump of devil's club on the forest side of the trail, all the humans paused and held their breaths.

Then, without warning, the dog plunged headlong into the brush. His lithe brown body disappeared from view almost immediately, leaving a rustling of the leaves above him as the only sign of his passing. Thankfully, that alone was enough for them to see that he was moving quickly, pushing deeper into the damp, thick forest.

Thane hastened after him, and Mei Lin followed.

Thane kept his gaze on the stirring vegetation, uncharacteristically heedless of where he stepped. He was trying hard to stay focused, but his head was all over the damn place. Mei Lin wasn't crazy; he knew that now. Her story was wildly unbelievable, but then so was any other explanation for the situation. In fact, every one he'd conjured up so far made even less sense.

He didn't die.

That concept had taken root now, and as it festered in his psyche it created an intolerable mixture of elation and horror.

He had a wife and children... he didn't want to put them in any kind of danger...

Thane could understand that much. He wanted to believe that it was love and concern for him and Jason — neat and tidy — that had prompted this miserable travesty. But he didn't really believe that. Life was never that simple. Thane had a mother, too, didn't he? Stanley had had a wife. But what kind of marriage? How many mornings, when they'd still lived in the Seattle apartment, had Thane awakened to find his father snoring on the couch? How many times, after they moved to the house in the suburbs, had he wondered how long a marriage could last when the parties had separate bedrooms?

What part had his mother played in this insane drama? Had she been hoodwinked along with the rest of them?

A familiar image loomed up in his memory, bringing with it the usual pang. His mother, dressed in a plain black shirt and pants, crying buckets as she stood by her husband's grave. Her mascara was grossly smeared, making her look like some freakish circus clown. She was no one Thane even knew. She was not his mother, and whatever she was crying about, it wasn't his father.

They even sent some men to the funeral...

A wave of queasiness engulfed him. She knew then, didn't she? Of course she did. She must have known everything... all along.

A short, sharp bark commanded his attention. Leaves rustled ten feet or so in front of him, but he could see nothing.

She knew. All the niggling questions that had plagued him

since he was a boy — that giant cloud of uncertainty and confusion — all of it twisted up and funneled down into one cool, hard line of reasoning. *She knew that Stanley was still alive.* Yet she had wanted Thane and Jason to forget him. She had wanted to erase the man — permanently — from all of their lives. Even after the boys had grown up, when they could have understood the truth, she had continued to lie to them. She was *still* lying to them!

The dog whimpered. Thane moved closer to the sound. His face felt hot; something pounded inside his skull. His dad was just ahead. He really was. Right there under those jiggling ferns.

He didn't die.

At least, he didn't die *then.*

Thane's limbs felt leaden. He saw flashes of Kibbe's brown fur through the leaves, along with some dark blue fabric. He stepped closer, and the toe of his boot struck something solid. He parted the brush with his hands and looked down.

It was a leg.

He pushed the ferns roughly away. A man was lying sprawled on the ground. He was wearing boots and rain pants, as well as several layers of shirts, but he had no jacket, and his head was bare. His clothing was soaked; his skin sickly pale. His eyes were closed and no part of him was moving.

The dog nuzzled at his master's inert arms, licked the whitish face, and whimpered again.

Oh, God, no. He can't be dead. Not now.

"Dad!" Thane heard himself shout. He tore off his gloves and touched the man's cheek with the back of his hand. The pale skin was cool and slick with rain. He could see no flaring of the nostrils or movement of the chest. But when he grasped the man's arm, he was relieved to find the limb limp and pliable. "Can you hear me?" He put two fingers in the hollow of the man's neck beside the Adam's apple and prayed to feel a pulse. "Jason!"

Did he feel a blip? "Jason, come here!"

A female presence appeared at his side; a small hand pushed

his large one out of the way. "Let me check him, Thane."

The presence soothed him, even though for a moment he couldn't place the voice. He couldn't look at her because his eyes were glued to the face on the ground. The rest of him was paralyzed.

"He's alive," her heavenly voice proclaimed.

His brother appeared behind them. Thane couldn't see Jason, but he knew he was there.

"He's very cold," Mei Lin murmured as she examined her patient. "But I don't think he's injured. I think he collapsed from fatigue. Can you help me turn him?"

Thane and Jason both reached in and helped Mei Lin position the man more comfortably. Kibbe whimpered and dashed about nervously, disrupting the nurse's efforts with a curious nose. Thane continued to stare at the face, of which he now had a clear, front-on view.

Dad.

It was him. The man he remembered. His hair was sparser and grayer, his face thinner. His whole body seemed small. His skin was deeply wrinkled, with unfamiliar scars along one brow bone and the base of his neck. Instead of laughing and joking and scuffling in play, he was gray and cold and wet and lifeless. But it was him. It was definitely him.

My dad. Our dad. He's alive.

"Thane?" the tiny, sweet voice took some time to penetrate his skull. "Thane!"

With an effort, he tore his gaze from the face of his father and turned it instead toward Mei Lin. Her brown eyes were almost feverishly bright, but her voice was calm and steady. He had emergency training himself, but he ceded to her medical judgment. She was a nurse, and her brain — at least — still seemed to be fully functioning. "Yes?" he answered.

"We need to move quickly." She looked over her shoulder and shouted at someone behind her to call a medevac. "Right now we need to get him dry and keep him warm."

Jason's voice floated over them both. "The ranger has a tarp and emergency blankets."

"Perfect," Mei Lin replied. She turned back to Thane. "Can you carry him back to the trail?"

Thane found the question mildly insulting. He scooped up the figure and stood, staggering slightly. The misstep was mental rather than physical; he couldn't believe his father was so light. The sound of his own childish laughter teased his brain, and in his mind's eye he saw the floor where the ceiling should be. Thane used to beg his dad to hold him by the ankles — upside down. How long had it been since he'd thought of that?

"You okay, Bro?" Jason's voice asked.

"Of course I am," Thane replied, more gruffly than intended. He took a step forward.

Jason's broad shoulders instantly appeared in his way. "Better follow me," his brother ordered. "Unless you want to do a faceplant."

Thane grumbled, but complied. Jason was right; he couldn't possibly see where he was stepping, and a stumble could be dangerous.

By the time they reached the trail, the ranger had a tarp laid out on the ground. He and Jesse stood on either end of it, holding a second tarp above to shield the area from the rain. Thane laid his father down on the dry tarp.

"Get those wet things off him as quickly as you can," Mei Lin ordered, opening the pack on Thane's back and pulling out the jacket Stanley had left in the kayak. "We'll put this back on him and then wrap him in the thermal blankets."

Thane felt like he was all thumbs as he and Jason attempted to remove the sopping clothing from Stanley's pale, limp body. The task was more difficult than he might have imagined, and when someone offered him a penknife he took it without question and expedited the process. Once or twice, he believed he saw Stanley's lips move, and he kept one eye out as he worked, praying he had not imagined it.

He had not. All the jarring and manipulation must have had

some effect, because just as they finished wrapping Stanley in a cocoon of thermal emergency blankets, his eyelids began to flutter.

Thane almost said "Dad," but stopped himself in time. Jason didn't know — he couldn't let his brother find out like that! "Stanley!" he said instead, patting one pale cheek. "Can you hear us?" He was sitting on the tarp, cradling his father's torso against his own chest for warmth. Beside him, Jason had Stanley's lower body across his lap, protected from the cold ground. Mei Lin crouched just outside the cover of the tarp, watching anxiously.

The eyelids fluttered for some time before making any progress. But at last Stanley's blue eyes became visible... at least most of them. Squinting through a narrow slit, his bleary gaze rested first on Jason, then moved up to Thane. Neither man said anything as the corners of Stanley's pale, whitish lips tilted slowly, unbelievably, into a smile. A hoarse rumbling came from his throat, followed by two faint, but clearly distinguishable words.

"Handsome devils."

Chapter 29

Mei Lin was scared.

Stanley had been found and the medevac plane was on its way, and she was very grateful for both those things.

Still, she was terrified.

His body temperature was disturbingly low. He could be in shock. And whether that shock was septic or not, it was still very dangerous. Stanley's pulse was rapid and weak, his respiration shallow. His color did not speak well for his heart or circulation, and his mental state was questionable. He had regained consciousness only very briefly, and although the words he had spoken might have indicated that he was aware of his surroundings, Mei Lin couldn't swear to that. Since then he had slipped into a fuzzy, in-and-out state where he could barely focus his eyes — and any further speech seemed beyond him.

She stood now in the parking lot by the trailhead, watching with a pained sense of helplessness as Stanley's stretcher was loaded into a van. Everything was happening so quickly; the events of the last hour felt surreal. Rescue team reinforcements had met them on the trail and helped to transport Stanley back to the road on a litter, where Sandra Gruber had begun proper medical treatment, including oxygen and IV fluids.

No one had asked Mei Lin if Stanley *wanted* treatment. There was no discussion of how he had refused a medevac earlier in the week, much less any worry over whether he had ever signed a Do Not Resuscitate order. Not even Sandra Gruber, whose assistance Stanley had refused a mere three days ago, seemed to have any qualms about following the standard life-saving procedures now that he was unconscious. Mei Lin felt a niggling, irritating prick of guilt about that... but not nearly enough to affect her actions. A lot had happened in those three days. Had Stanley truly set out on this bear hunt with the intent of suicide, or was he merely being his usual, reckless self? Mei Lin didn't know. What she did know, even if no one else yet did, was that unlike the last time he couldn't speak for himself, Stanley now had next of kin in attendance.

The stretcher was secured in the van and Sandra Gruber climbed in beside it. The nurse practitioner would travel with Stanley to the Gustavus airport, where he would be loaded onto a waiting medevac jet for the fifteen-minute flight to Juneau.

Mei Lin's medical services were no longer required.

As the doors of the van closed, she realized that her arm was intertwined with Thane's. She had no memory of gluing herself to the man's side; his comforting presence just seemed to draw her in. "Are you all right?" she whispered quietly up towards his ear. He had said nothing to anyone about being Stanley's son... at least not that she had heard. She had no idea where his head was at; for the last few hours she had barely been in touch with her own.

Thane nodded silently. His eyes watched the van as it pulled out of the lot and disappeared down the road.

"Are you sure?" Mei Lin asked gently. He had so very much to take in — and virtually no time to absorb it.

"Will he make it?" Thane asked, his deep voice falsely stalwart.

Mei Lin flipped back into nurse mode. It was a defensive response, rather than a choice. She couldn't answer that question truthfully as herself without dissolving into a salty puddle on the asphalt. But Nurse Sullivan could handle it. "The next twenty-four hours will be critical. But for now, he's holding his own."

Thane nodded at the non-answer. Mei Lin wrapped her arms around his waist and held him tight.

"I've got four tickets to Juneau on the next flight out," Ri announced, phone in hand. She had appeared in front of them quite suddenly, as had Jason. "Do we want them? We'd need to leave right now in order to get back to the house and pack and still make it to the airport in time. Otherwise, we'll likely be hours behind him."

Mei Lin blinked at her sister dumbly. How could Ri know that both Mei Lin and Thane would want to follow Stanley to Juneau? For that matter, why was Ri talking about herself and Jason going along?

"Yes," Thane answered immediately. "Book them. We can make it."

Mei Lin nodded in agreement, and Ri stepped away and spoke into her phone. Jason remained where he stood, and as Mei Lin lifted her gaze to his face, she noticed the intent with which he watched his brother. Jason couldn't have helped but notice Thane's concern for Stanley. What had he made of it?

Jason's clear gray eyes flickered to Mei Lin, transmitting a plea she couldn't ignore. He wanted to talk to his brother. Alone.

Mei Lin smiled weakly and — with way more effort than it should have taken — detached herself from Thane's side.

Thane felt the sudden loss like a draft of cold air. His father had been taken away, and now Mei Lin had left him, too? He turned to follow her but was stopped by the firm clamp of a hand on his shoulder.

"Bro," Jason's voice demanded. "Talk to me."

Like a coward, Thane avoided his brother's eyes. How could he ever find the right words? He doubted there were any. But Jason had a right to know. What if they never saw Stanley alive again? Jason *had* to be told, because he would need to go to the hospital as well as Thane. But wait... wasn't he already going? Why was that?

The grip on his shoulder tightened and gave him a shake. "Thane!"

Reluctantly, he met his brother's gaze.

"You think I'm blind?" Jason accused shortly. "You think

I'm stupid? I *know* who he is!"

Thane's heart skipped several beats. He stared back without comment. Jason's eyes were misty with emotion — a sight Thane hadn't witnessed in years.

"I thought I heard you say 'Dad,'" Jason whispered hoarsely. "I figured I'd misheard you. But the way you looked at him... as soon as I saw his face, I knew. For God's sake, I wasn't a baby when he—" His voice came close to breaking, and he swallowed and collected himself. "I *do* remember the guy, you know. Just because I don't bring it up all the time..."

"I'm sorry," Thane murmured, feeling like a fool.

"So how is it possible?" Jason demanded. "How long have you known?"

Thane shook his head forcefully. "I didn't... Mei Lin figured it out yesterday. She only told me right before we found him."

Jason was incredulous. "So why is he here at all? Does Mom know? *What happened?*"

"I can try to explain, if you want me to," a soft voice answered. Mei Lin had rematerialized, bringing with her a wave of pure, blissful calm. "I'm sorry, Jason," she continued. "I didn't have time to tell Thane everything, either. It's all happened so fast, and I was worried about St—" Her beautiful round cheeks flushed. "Your father," she finished gently. "We need to hurry if we're going to catch that plane. But we can talk on the way. I promise, I'll tell you both everything I possibly can."

Thane studied his brother's face. The shock, trepidation, anger, and cautious elation he saw there perfectly mirrored his own emotions. He swung an arm behind his brother's back and clamped an affectionate hand on his shoulder.

"Sounds good," he told Mei Lin.

Margot hung up her phone with such a forceful stab of the finger that she broke off what was left of her nail. "Dammit!" she fumed, missing her old landline purely for the satisfaction of slamming the headset onto the receiver. "Now Jason isn't answering either! Where are they?"

"You know where they are," Doug said calmly, lifting her suitcase into the back of her car. "They're out in the woods, out of cellular range. Where would you expect them to be? They're not going to find that bear in a shopping mall."

"But what if they've left already? What if they're on their way back here right now, and we pass each other in the air?"

He grinned at her devilishly. "Then we'll have a second honeymoon in Alaska. Just you and me."

She could not help smiling back at him. He was always so positive about everything. "You do think I'm doing the right thing? Don't you?"

"You know you are, honey. We've been over this."

"I know!" she exclaimed with frustration. "But it still seems so... hasty."

Doug loaded his own suitcase next to hers and closed the door. "That's because you know it will be hard, and you're not looking forward to it. That's understandable. But it's also the perfect reason to get it over with as soon as possible. They could be up there a week or more, and we both know you'll go crazy every day until you get this settled. Besides which," he took her hands in his. "I really want to go, myself. You realize we haven't been up to Alaska since Buck died?"

Margot nodded sadly. Doug had accompanied her to both of her in-laws' funerals, but those had been somber occasions. Stanley's parents had been good to her, despite the rocky nature of her marriage to their son, and she had genuinely adored them right back. Taking the boys up to Juneau for visits had always been a joy, and truthfully, she did miss the place. But still...

She shuddered with angst. "My God, Doug. How can I possibly enjoy any part of this? The boys are going to be furious. They'll blame *me*, and they'll hate *me*, and he'll come off smelling like a rose! I'll be lucky if they ever talk to me again!"

Doug's expression became stern. "Margot, we are both

getting on that plane, and that's all there is to it. You could argue with yourself for two more minutes or two more weeks, but we both know you'd wind up making the exact same decision. There's no reason *not* to get it over with as soon as possible." His expression softened, morphing into a lopsided grin. "Particularly since the sockeyes and pinkies are running."

Margot let out a chuckle. He *would* think of that. She was still terrified and she would probably second-guess herself a dozen more times, but thanks to Doug's steadying influence she knew she would stick to her decision. "You know you're the best thing that's ever happened to me," she said affectionately. "Right?"

Doug's grin widened as he leaned in for a kiss. "Yeah," he replied smugly. "I know."

Chapter 30

Thane sat in Stanley's room in the critical care unit of the regional hospital in Juneau, staring at the inert figure in the bed and wondering if the plethora of machines that blinked and clicked all around them were actually doing anything. He wondered why all medical places smelled alike. He also wondered why he, who had no problems camping on permafrost, couldn't endure one night in a climate-controlled hospital without feeling like he would freeze to death.

He'd had time to wonder about all sorts of things. Stanley had been unconscious upon his arrival at the ER, and he'd pretty much stayed that way as evening turned to twilight and he was moved to the CCU. They'd all taken turns sitting with him while the brief Alaskan night passed by, but although Stanley occasionally stirred and moaned, not once had he opened his eyes. Now the long hours of dawn had begun, and Thane watched the figure on the bed with trepidation. The staff had insisted that Stanley could regain alertness at any time, that he was not in a coma but was experiencing the deep, restorative sleep of a body overspent. Thane wanted his father to wake up. But despite all the time he'd had for contemplation, he had no idea how he would feel when it happened.

Mei Lin had explained to him and Jason why Stanley did what he did, or at least she had passed on what Stanley had told her. She'd admitted that there was more to the man's biography than she was telling, but insisted it would be better for Stanley to explain some things for himself.

The rudiments of the situation were clear enough. Thane was not judgmental by nature, and he bore no ill will over the decisions his father had made at the time of the kidnapping. He knew that if he himself were a parent, he would do anything to protect his children. But understanding Stanley's actions from

Stanley's point of view did nothing to stop the searing, burning sensation that festered in Thane's gut right now.

He'd been lied to by the people he loved the most. He'd missed out on twenty years — *twenty years!* — that he could have spent with his father. His mother had not only been complicit in that, she'd probably been happy about it. And now, just when Thane had a theoretical shot at making up for lost time, his father had to go and nearly kill himself! Had Stanley even missed the sons he'd left behind? Didn't he *want* to know the men they had become?

Thane's stomach cramped so painfully he let out an audible groan. He hadn't had an ulcer since his undergrad days in Okanagan when he'd lived on black coffee and junk food. How could another one erode itself in a day? Why the hell did he even care so much? Why could he not just write off this pale, writhing man as not worth the grief and go along his merry way? If it weren't for Stanley Buchanan's damnable theatrics, Thane could be cuddled up in front of a warm fire with Mei Lin right now. Wonderful, beautiful, sexy Mei Lin, with whom he'd had zero time alone since realizing he wanted her more than he'd ever wanted anything—

"Th-Thane?"

He froze. The pale man in the bed had indeed been writhing. Now he had spoken. He had twisted onto his side and was staring directly at his visitor. His eyes were wide open and his skin had regained some color.

"Yeah," Stanley's hoarse voice croaked. His dry lips curved into a grin. "I'm talking to you. I'd know you anywhere, Son."

Thane bent forward. He felt like standing up, but if he did the man would be talking to his waistline. He could think of no response, so he made none.

Stanley continued to smile. His eyes were shot with red as much as they were blue, but his dark pupils danced with glee. "I've missed you."

Thane cleared his throat, loudly. His face felt hot. "Likewise," he croaked in return. They stared at each another for a long time. Stanley's expression didn't waver. He looked so... happy. "I... uh... I'm glad you're awake," Thane offered awkwardly. "Jason's here."

If it was possible, Stanley looked even happier. "Bring him."

Thane moved to the door, opened it, yelled, and then realized he probably shouldn't have done that in a hospital where other patients were sleeping. *Oh well.* He returned to find that Stanley had squiggled around enough to stare at him while he was standing. "You're feeling better?"

Stanley made a shrugging motion, as if the subject was of no importance. His grin turned slightly wicked. "Mei Lin likes you."

"You think so?" Thane replied, bemused. His face felt like it was on fire. "And how would you know?"

Stanley made a gurgling noise that was probably a chuckle. "I know women."

Thane heard himself chuckle back. "Well, I hope you're right. I like her, too."

"Good." Stanley beamed. He was still beaming when Jason burst through the doorway and appeared at Thane's side. Stanley adjusted his gaze and smiled broadly. "Jason," he announced. "I've missed you too, my boy. You look just like me, you know. Like I used to look, anyway. You're making the most of it, I hope."

Jason blinked. Thane wondered if he was having the same "hot eyes" problem.

Stanley's gaze shifted to take in each man in turn. "Yep. Handsome devils, the both of you. I knew it." He looked thoroughly pleased with himself. Then his expression turned more sentimental. "You were good boys, always. I'm so sorry. Sorry I wasn't there. I wish I could have been. But I couldn't."

"We know," Thane proffered, realizing even as he said the words that he didn't entirely believe them. There must have been some other way. If he'd been allowed, maybe he could have helped his parents to find it. But thinking that way served no purpose.

"Well, you can be here now," Jason said with some belligerence. "So don't give us any more of this 'I'm not worthy' crap. You're getting better and we're working this out. You owe us that much, don't you think?"

Stanley's smile faded a moment as he appraised his younger son. Thane wondered how much of his brother's personality had been apparent by the age of ten. Did Stanley know what the rest of the family already knew — that Jason didn't anger easily, and that he only used that particular, chilling tone when defending something he really cared about?

Stanley stared at both his sons for a long time. When he spoke again, his tone was even. "I'm *not* worthy. That's the truth. But if the two of you want me to stick around a while, I'll do my best to oblige."

"You promise?" Jason demanded. Thane could see a definite wetness around his brother's eyes now. He was glad he wasn't the only one.

Stanley nodded once. Then his brow creased. "I can't promise there won't be any danger to you. Probably not much, after all this time, but—"

"You think we want to hear about that?" Jason interrupted. "We're grown men, for God's sake! We can take care of ourselves. Those idiots in Chicago are probably all gumming their food by now. And look at this guy—" he jerked an elbow toward Thane. "He look defenseless to you?"

Stanley smiled again. "Not hardly."

"Damn straight!" Jason proclaimed. Then, Thane noticed, he smiled a little.

"So, we're agreed," Thane proclaimed, his heart lightening. "First step is, you get better and get the hell out of here. Hospitals give me the creeps."

Stanley jumped slightly, as if he'd remembered something. "You see the bear?" he demanded.

"No," Thane replied. "Not yet, anyway. Did you?"

"No," Stanley answered, even as tiny lights began to dance in his eyes. "But I'm gonna. I'm going to see that glacier cub if—" He stopped himself, then swung his gaze to Jason. "If it *almost* kills me."

Jason's eyes were definitely wet now. In solidarity, Thane wiped his own face with his sleeve.

"We'll see it together, then," Jason proclaimed in his normal, mellow voice. "It could take years. But we'll do it."

"All of us," Thane reiterated. "The three Buchanans."

Stanley looked back at Thane with a grin of pure wickedness. "And maybe more."

Mei Lin was sure she was going to expire from anxiety. When Thane had yelled for Jason, it was impossible to tell if the news was good or bad. But only two people were allowed in the CCU rooms at a time, and she couldn't have stopped Jason's going even if she'd wanted to. A nurse aide had come up to her and Ri in the waiting room a few moments later and explained that Stanley had regained consciousness and was talking, but that it would be best if he and his sons had some privacy for a while. Since no higher authority would tell them anything, Mei Lin and Ri couldn't help but wonder if the words Stanley was saying were expected to be his last.

When, nearly a half hour later, the brothers' loud voices could be heard traveling down the hallway towards her, Mei Lin felt giddy with relief. Why, they almost sounded like they were laughing!

"Is he all right?" she demanded, meeting them at the door.

Thane smiled and pulled her to him. "He's going to be. Don't worry. He wants to see you, but we were told only five more minutes or so. Then they're going to make him stop babbling so he can rest."

"He did get jabbery there for a while, didn't he?" Jason said merrily.

Mei Lin couldn't see their expressions because her face was still buried in Thane's chest, but the mirth in their voices delighted her. Stanley would make it after all. *Thank God!* She reveled in Thane's embrace, wondering again how it could be that — in such a short period of time — his touch could come to feel so completely, incredibly *right*. Even now, as he released her, she was reluctant to let the feeling go. "Go on," he told her, his smile bright. "He really does want to see you."

Mei Lin threw an apologetic glance back at Ri, her wonderful sister who had left her summer marine biology research in Resurrection Bay to fly to Gustavus for a surprise visit, only to wind up holding Mei Lin's hand through a rescue operation and a miserable overnight hospital vigil. Poor Ri had had only two nights to spare and would have to fly out of Juneau later today. But she waved away her sister's apology with a smile. *I owe you one*, Mei Lin's answering look promised.

Mei Lin was halfway out the door when she heard Jason swear. She turned to see him frowning down at his cell. "What?" Thane asked.

"Mom. She's been blowing up my phone for days," Jason explained with an exasperated voice. "I don't know what her deal is. She wanted to tell you something in person — something so important that she was going to drive to Tofino until I told her you weren't there anymore. Then when I told her I was coming up here myself, she lost it — started giving me all kinds of crazy about why I shouldn't come. She called again yesterday right in the middle of everything and I just put it on silent. Apparently, she's kept trying. Has she been on you, too?"

Mei Lin waited while Thane checked his own phone. It took him some time to find it, since it was buried in his pack. "Hell if I know," he said with a shrug, tossing it back where it came from. "My battery's dead."

Mei Lin headed back into the hallway, her anxiety increasing again. Thane's mother had known all along that Stanley was alive. She had been a part of the deception — arguably, the more active part, since she'd been the one left behind to tell the lies. Margot Buchanan had a good reason to do what she did. But would Thane forgive her as easily as he appeared to have forgiven his father?

For some reason, she feared not. Which was probably why she had mentioned Margot as little as possible when she'd explained what she knew to the brothers. At the time they were too stunned over their father's actions to give much thought to the role their mother had played. But they *would* think about it. And when they did, thorny questions were bound to follow.

She slipped into Stanley's room. He was awake and seemed to be expecting her, and she crossed immediately to his bedside and took his hand. He looked drawn and weak as a kitten, but she smiled anyway, having feared far worse. Her eyes flooded with tears, and she made no attempt to control them. She could cry if she wanted to. She wasn't Stanley's nurse anymore; she was simply his friend.

"There's my girl," he said indulgently, pressing her hand. "I'm sorry I've ruined all the good progress you were making." He gave a nod towards his wounded leg, which at the moment was covered with blankets. "If it's gone septic, it's my own fault. Truth is, I tricked you. I stopped the antibiotic days ago — soon as I found out Thane was in town."

Mei Lin drew in a shuddering breath. "Stanley! But why?"

He shook his head and looked away. "Because I'm a coward. There's no other excuse for me. I was convinced the boys would hate me. I hated myself for what happened — why shouldn't they? I couldn't imagine any other reaction. And I... well, I just couldn't face it. I wanted to remember them happy. Thane in particular. Did you know, when he was little and I'd come home, his eyes would light up like candles? I wanted to keep that with me. The thought of seeing that same face all grown up and filled with hate... I couldn't bear it." He shivered a little; Mei Lin could feel the vibration in his hand. "I couldn't do it. I just couldn't. I wanted to run away. So, I did."

"That was cowardly," Mei Lin agreed, even as she cradled his hand gently. "But we all make mistakes. You've done plenty of brave things, too. Trying to do what was best for your family in an impossible situation was one of them."

He sniffled. "I don't think I'll ever really feel right about leaving them. Never mind that I would do it again."

"I understand," Mei Lin assured. "And I believe they do, too."

He turned his head to look at her, and the misery on his face slowly eased into a smile. "I couldn't believe it, you know. When I saw them. I thought I'd just go look for the bear — keep looking until the end of me. I'm not sure what happened, really. I remember renting the kayak and paddling off... but everything after that gets hazy. I remember that I was cold, and that I could hear Thane calling to me, but I couldn't move. I thought I might already be dead. Next thing I know, he's looking at me. His face is right there. It's a man's face, but... there were those same candle lights, twinkling at me! I couldn't believe it. Then Jason was there, too... like a younger me. My sons were men. Fine-looking men. And the expression in their eyes... well, I could only think I was in heaven." He chuckled to himself. "And believe me, thinking that was as big a surprise as anything!"

Mei Lin laughed with him. "Do you remember what you said to them then? You only managed two words: 'handsome devils.'"

He laughed out loud. "Well, they are, aren't they?" His lips screwed into a smirk. "But I don't need to tell *you* that, do I?"

Mei Lin made no reply. She merely smiled, then wiped away tears with her free hand.

"No, I can see that I don't," Stanley continued smugly. "Love's a beautiful thing, isn't it? At least so I've been told." His expression clouded. "By the way, you didn't happen to mention to the boys what I told you about their mother... how she refused to let me take them into the witness protection program?"

Mei Lin shook her head. "I didn't say anything about her. You didn't tell me much anyway, and... I figured the details should come from you. Or her."

He nodded. "Good. I told them it was my decision. That's

all they need to know."

Mei Lin tensed. "They're going to want more details eventually, Stanley. They're going to feel a real need to understand what happened. The kind of marriage you had... well, that's an important part of the story. What happened doesn't completely make sense without it."

His face hardened. "I'll figure it out. They're old enough to understand that we were practically divorced at the time. But it's better if they think I never even considered testifying and going into hiding as a family. They can't know it was their mother who refused. I don't blame her, mind you — but they might. And I can't bear thinking that by returning from the dead, I've put a wedge between her and them. They've forgiven me so much already, what's one more sin in my column?"

"But it's just another lie," Mei Lin argued. "Don't you think—"

"Please, Mei Lin," he interrupted. "Let me do this. Didn't you just say that telling my story was my place?"

She nodded miserably. He didn't understand — no doubt *couldn't* understand, what a painful position he was putting her in. Keeping such a secret would mean lying to Thane. Even if he never realized what she knew, never asked her a thing about it, it would still be a lie of omission, because she knew he would *want* to know. The thought of saddling their future with such a deception made her feel sick inside. What she and Thane had together was so good, so honest! Their openness was a part of who they were. But what else could she do? It was not her secret to tell.

"Thank you," Stanley said sincerely. "It's all I've been thinking about since I saw them — how to make things work without hurting anybody. I had this glimpse of heaven, you see... at least until my leg started hurting." He turned to her. "You think I'll lose it?"

"I don't know," she answered. "The doctors haven't talked to me."

Remarkably, Stanley laughed. "Well, it would serve me right,

I suppose. But you know, it hardly matters. I have my boys back, Mei Lin. My *men*."

"Yes, you do," she choked out. She could barely see. She wiped her face again. "Everything's going to be okay, Stanley. You just have to focus on getting better."

He nodded. "I made that decision already. As bad as my leg hurt — and my head too, come to think of it — once I'd seen them, I knew I wanted to live. I had to see them again. I wouldn't let myself leave them... again."

"You won't," Mei Lin agreed. She straightened her spine. "Because you're going to get better. Not only from this, but you're going to treat that cancer, too."

He looked at her speculatively. "That sounds like an order. I might even consider following it. *If* it came from a nurse practitioner."

"It will," she answered firmly. "So get ready."

He grinned. "All right. But I won't be one of your hospice patients, missy. A little surgery, a little chemo... Hell, I figure I can swing another decade."

She grinned right back at him. "I know you can."

Chapter 31

Doug held open the door of the main entrance to the hospital, and Margot hastened inside. It was early morning, but the sun had been up for hours already. She knew, because she'd barely slept a wink all night. They had flown from Vancouver to Juneau yesterday, but to her consternation she hadn't been able to contact either of her sons all afternoon. Since she didn't know exactly where they'd gotten to, she and Doug had settled into a motel in Juneau until one or the other deigned to answer her. The next to last thing she had expected was to receive a text from Jason in the wee hours of the morning explaining that both of them were in a hospital waiting room. The last thing she had expected when she called back was to be told that the patient they were visiting was their father.

"The CCU is that way," Doug pointed out helpfully as she stared at the directional signs without seeing them. She still couldn't believe it. Stanley and the boys *had* run into each other. It was incredible. It was ridiculous. She still didn't understand how it had happened. Jason had been in no mood to explain it to her in the middle of the night and Jason never explained anything adequately anyway. All she knew was that Stanley had been out hunting for one of those silly blue bears again and that this time he had nearly died in the process. The last part in itself was no news — Stan was always nearly dying in the process of something.

She stormed down the hall and swung open the door to the CCU waiting room. She had let Doug get a few more hours of sleep before waking him up and rushing over, but the uncertainty of the situation had been killing her. God only knew what Stanley had told Thane and Jason. What were they thinking had happened all those years ago? How much did they know of her role in it?

She was terrified.

The waiting area was smaller than she'd expected. The only people sitting in the uncomfortable-looking upholstered chairs were two twenty-something women. Thane and Jason weren't there. Margot felt like screaming, but to her surprise one of the women stood up and smiled. "Are you Margot Tremain?" she asked. She was Asian, with pretty dark eyes that floated over Margot's shoulder as her husband followed her into the room. "And Doug?"

"Why yes, we are," he answered pleasantly.

"Hello," the young woman greeted. She had a lovely smile. There was a warmth about her that was comforting, particularly to a person in Margot's frantic state. "I'm Mei Lin Sullivan, and this is my sister. We're friends of your sons. I'm sorry you missed them — they just stepped out for a quick breakfast. I'm not sure where they went exactly, but I'm sure they won't be gone long."

"That's all right," Margot heard herself say, even though it was hardly what she was thinking. "We can wait. Is... Stanley Buchanan still here?"

Mei Lin nodded. "He's in room four." Her dark eyes held an eerie sort of sympathy, and Margot's heart began to palpitate. How much did this girl know?

"I'd like to see him," Margot said. "Are there... any restrictions, or anything?"

"Only two people can be in his room at a time," Mei Lin answered. "We've been taking turns all night, but a little while ago they wheeled him off for some tests. I was just about to check and see if he was back."

"I'll go, then," Margot said quickly. She hadn't thought much about seeing Stan, but now it seemed important. They needed to talk. Alone.

"Go on then, honey," Doug suggested, giving her arm a squeeze. "I'll just park myself right here."

Margot nodded gratefully to him as he took a seat. "Thank you," she said to Mei Lin, who showed no signs of trying to follow her, but seemed content to wait with Doug. Well, good. Perhaps Doug could strike up a conversation and find out exactly who the women were. God knew no explanation would be forthcoming from either of her sons!

She strode out the other door and found room number four. Looking through the glass panel, she could tell that its occupant had returned, and she opened the door and stepped in without hesitation.

Her gaze locked immediately with that of the ex-husband she'd neither seen nor heard from in twenty years. For a moment, time stood still. The sense of deja vu was crushing.

"Hello, Stanley," she said, her voice sounding no different than if she'd run into a neighbor at the market.

"Hello, Margot," he returned in kind. His lips tilted into a small smile, but the expression was guarded. "You're looking good."

She nodded. "Thank you. You look like hell."

He laughed out loud, and Margot smiled back at him. She always could make Stanley laugh. When she wanted to.

"Are you all right?" she asked.

He shrugged carelessly. "I could be worse. At the moment I'm just happy to be here."

They stared at each other for a long moment.

"Tony Russo is dead," Margot announced, breaking the silence. "The danger is over, Stan. For you and the boys. Finally."

His eyes widened. "Are you sure? How do you know? Who told you?"

"The Chicago PD. I only just found out a few days ago. They would have notified you too, but they had no address." She sighed a little. Then she moved closer. "I have no idea how you came to run into the boys or what you've told them, but believe it or not I was about to tell them everything. Ever since I got the call from the detective, I've felt so... unsettled. There's no reason, anymore, to keep up the facade. Doug and I talked it through, and we decided that Thane and Jason should know that you were alive. The detective suspected you were up here somewhere, and we figured they might want to try and find you. We had no idea they'd succeed without trying. How did it happen, exactly?"

Stanley shook his head. His face was so very pale... she hadn't been joking when she said he looked terrible. His once-smooth skin was wrinkled and pitted, and he was practically crisscrossed with scars, especially his right arm. She wondered what had happened to him. But she didn't really want to know.

"*They* found *me*," he answered. "But I don't think they intended to. It just sort of happened. We were all out looking for the same glacier bear."

Margot laughed. "Of course you were. How poetic."

She hadn't meant it unkindly, and Stanley didn't take it that way. "Margot," he said seriously, sitting up a little. "I told them that I refused to testify, that I didn't want to go into the witness protection program. I explained that I thought you'd all be safer if the rest of the world believed I was dead, and so I decided to make that happen. I told them I made the decision myself. That I never gave you any choice about it."

A dry lump swelled in her throat. "Funny. That's not how I remember it."

His blues eyes — those fantastic, beguiling eyes! — held hers with force. "Sure it is," he said firmly.

Margot felt something inside herself crumple. Damn the man! This would all have been so much easier if he was a scoundrel through and through! But life was never that simple. Stanley wasn't a bad man; he never had been. They had only been bad for each other.

"I understand you remarried," he said with cheer. "How fortunate we were able to divorce before I died. Convenient, that."

"Indeed," she agreed, smiling back through a haze of moisture. "And thank you." The legality of their divorce was questionable, given that someone somewhere had fudged the dates to make the dissolution precede the kidnapping. But it had stood up well enough. Stanley had insisted that her future not be hostage to a phony death certificate, and she had good reason to appreciate his foresight.

"So you found a better man," Stanley said philosophically, smiling at her. "I'm glad about that, Margot. I really am."

She knew that he meant what he said, and she appreciated that as well. "A better man for me," she qualified gamely.

He threw her a mischievous look. "Our Thane's got himself a good one. Did you meet her out there? Mei Lin?"

Margot cocked an eyebrow. Thane? Involved with the woman outside? Well, there was no reason he shouldn't be. There had never been anything between him and Vanessa, a fact she had cause to celebrate, in retrospect. It seemed funny, now, to think how desperate she'd been to tell Thane her news: that Vanessa wasn't mentally ill after all... just unexpectedly manipulative. The girl had gotten herself pregnant by a married man, then decided that Thane should be the baby's father. The little witch seriously thought she could lure Margot's tender-hearted son into bed and then guilt him into being a parent, even if he did discover the truth!

The mere thought of it still set Margot's teeth on edge. She could understand Vanessa's wanting a family, and any idiot could see that Thane would make a great dad. But still, how *could* she? Margot had practically considered her a daughter! The worst part was that Vanessa's horrid scheme might even have succeeded, if Thane hadn't had the sense to keep his hands off her.

Her kind, sensitive Thane... he was worth a hundred Vanessas. And he deserved a woman just as straightforward, down to earth, and loving as he was.

Margot returned her attention to Stanley. "You know this girl? Mei Lin?"

"I do," he answered proudly. "Good as gold and smart as a whip, besides. She saved my life, actually. At least once! Possibly twice — I'm not entirely sure what happened this last time. But trust me, she's a keeper."

Margot nodded, remembering the woman's sweet smile and the way she had practically radiated warmth. *Yes.* Someone like her could be just what Thane needed. What he deserved.

"Mei Lin knows what really happened, by the way," Stanley continued. "I mean, about my death and all. We had some good long talks while she was nursing me back to health out in my cabin. But don't worry — she won't spill the beans. I've asked her to stick to our story. I don't want the boys to blame you, Margot. For any of this."

Margot's chin lifted. She felt much better, suddenly. Stronger. So far, this little venture of redemption she'd set herself on wasn't turning out at all as she'd planned. But perhaps it could turn out better.

"No, Stanley," she proclaimed. "I'm not going to have you lying for me. And I'm not going to impose the burden of our dirty secrets on that poor girl out in the waiting room, either. If you want her and Thane to have a chance together, they can't start out with a lie between them. There have been enough lies, don't you think? Too many, and for too long. I want it to stop, and I'm going to end it myself. *Today.*"

"But surely there's no harm in—"

"Of course there is!" Margot said fiercely. "If it had been up to you, you would have testified, and Tony Russo would have gone to prison. The boys and I would have gone with you into witness protection, and you would never have been separated from them in the first place. I'm not saying that would have been better for them; I still don't think it would have been. But we both know it was *my* choice. I didn't give you any alternative."

Stanley's face drew tight with concern. "But it was my fault it happened in the first place. I don't want them to be upset with—"

"It was not your fault!" she said emphatically. "And if I ever made you feel that it was, I'm sorry. It was just damned bad luck, for all of us. You did what you thought best, and so did I. Maybe I was wrong. And maybe when I tell the boys, they'll think I made a terrible, horrible mistake, and they'll be furious with me. But you know what?"

He blinked at her in surprise. "What?"

"That's a chance I'm willing to take. I love them. I've loved them every day of their entire lives, and I've let everything I do — *everything* — be guided by what I thought was best for them. I'm not perfect and I'm not 'cool' and I know that I irritate the hell out of them sometimes. But they know I love them. And I'm just going to have to count on that to be enough."

She stopped and took a breath. She didn't know where she'd found half those words, but she was glad she had said them.

"Everything's going to be all right, Stanley," she said more calmly. "Eventually."

Pale and pathetic as he looked, he smiled back at her with the same slaphappy, devil-may-care grin that had started all this trouble in the first place.

"You go, girl," he replied.

Epilogue

Two months later

Mei Lin shrieked with happiness as Thane's strong arms lifted her off the ground and swung her around the driveway in a giant circle.

"I got the job!" he announced unnecessarily. His hearty, booming laughter carried out across the meadow, flushing a flock of sparrows from the nearby bushes and out into the open blue sky. "I got the job!"

She laughed with him, barely able to catch her breath until — after she'd delivered a few affectionate pounds on his shoulder — he finally agreed to put her down. "That's wonderful!" she praised between pants.

"I'll be based in Juneau, of course, but it's a field job, so it's flexible," he crowed. "I can spend the weekends out here, at least, and maybe do some telecommuting as well, when the weather's bad. Besides which," he added, smoothing a lock of hair tenderly behind her ear, "You can always come out to Auke Lake and stay with me. That invitation stands permanently open." He raised his voice again. "That is, if you ever lose that slacker of a house guest of yours!"

"I resent that!" Stanley's voice called from the back deck, out of sight. "Who do you think does all the cooking around here, anyway?"

Mei Lin chuckled. "He's doing really well lately. It won't be long at all until he can go back to the cabin. He may be ready before they finish the road, even."

"Just make sure he waits till it's done," Thane returned more quietly. "If he wants to live without power or water that's his business, but you need to be able to drive up there easily."

"And he needs to be able to drive out," Mei Lin said

cheerfully. She was delighted that Stanley had bought a truck of his own. He was indeed a social person by nature, and she suspected that his self-imposed isolation had taken more of a toll on his psyche than he realized. But that wasn't going to happen again.

"Not that I'm against him moving on as soon as possible, you understand," Thane said, pulling Mei Lin in closer. "Frankly, I can't wait. I really do want you to come and stay at the lake house sometimes. It's beautiful in the fall."

Mei Lin didn't need convincing. She had already enjoyed several visits to Thane's grandparents' old home. They had kayaked for hours on the smooth, inky lake, admiring the stunning view of the Juneau ice fields in the distance. It was a terribly romantic locale. Then again, with a man like Thane in a place like Alaska, what wasn't?

They found themselves happily preoccupied again... and they stayed that way until the disembodied voice called out from the deck again.

"You coming up?" Stanley shouted impatiently. "I want to hear about this job!"

Mei Lin and Thane reluctantly drew apart from one another. "Couldn't he walk around to the side deck by himself if he wanted?" Thane asked in a low voice.

"Of course he could," Mei Lin replied. "His leg has healed nicely and he's getting stronger. I suspect he's just trying to be polite."

"Helllloooo?" Stanley yelled facetiously.

"Yeah," Thane chuckled. "That must be it."

Mei Lin threaded her small arm through his giant one and swung him towards the door of the house. She thought of it as her house now, rather than Elsie's, which she still felt a bit guilty about. But as Carol and Jeanine and everyone else in town reminded her, the house belonged to the town now, and she was a bona fide lessee. Her certification with the state had come through surprisingly quickly, and though no one in the immediate area needed hospice at the moment, she had found herself plenty busy. Sandra Gruber had wasted no time in transferring the majority of her elderly patients into Mei Lin's care, insisting that the newcomer had more up-to-date training in geriatrics. Mei Lin had felt a little guilty for the sacrifice until she realized that the older woman had simultaneously acquired both a small fishing boat and a new puppy. Evidently, Mei Lin's professional entry into the community was indeed a boon for everyone.

The second Mei Lin opened the door of the house, a flying ball of brown fur hurtled out and crash-landed against Thane's shins.

"Kibbe boy!" he greeted gaily. "How's city life been treating you?"

"He goes bonkers over everyone he meets," Mei Lin answered for the dog. "Still basking in his hero status, you know."

"Well, he deserves it!" Thane laughed, squatting down to deliver the obligatory belly rub.

"Did I tell you that Ed's dog is pregnant again?" Mei Lin asked. "He swears he's going to get her spayed after this 'accident.' But I've been thinking it might be nice to have one of Kibbe's little brothers or sisters bouncing around. What do you think?"

Thane grinned broadly, as she knew he would. He loved dogs, but had lost his last one shortly before starting grad school. They both knew, with no words needing to be spoken, that any puppy of hers would be his, too... someday. Their relationship was in its early days yet, and neither was inclined to rush things. But they were very, *very* happy.

"Let's do it," Thane replied. "After all, Kibbe needs family, too, right?"

"Everybody needs family," Mei Lin returned.

Thane's answering smile was crooked, but obliging. He and Jason had had a tough time at first, dealing with the reality of their parents' decisions. They were particularly hard on their mother. But Margot had persevered, and it was hard for the brothers to hold a grudge when the older generation set such a stunning example of forgiveness. Who would have expected that Stanley and Margot would get along better, twenty years after their divorce, than they ever had when they'd been married? And who would have thought that Stanley and Doug, two men as different in personality as night and day, would bond so quickly over a shared love of fly fishing?

Mei Lin couldn't have asked for a better outcome for any of Thane's family. Nor could she make any complaints about her own streak of luck. Silverson Elder Care had finally deigned to settle with the Gonzalez family out of court — for a very generous sum. And as thrilled as she was to rid herself of the fear of being dragged back to Texas, she was even happier to close the book on her own internal angst. She truly believed, now, that she had made the right decision. What happened to Mariel would not happen again.

"What's going on down there, eh?" Stanley called out — with shameless suggestiveness — as they lingered at the door.

Thane rolled his eyes. "He is *so* bad."

Mei Lin chuckled. "You love it."

"Time's wasting, you know!" Stanley persisted in yelling, even as his voice got hoarse. "If we don't get going soon, that glacier cub will be heading into hibernation!"

Thane's answering grin swelled Mei Lin's heart. He would never give up, she was certain. No one had seen hide nor hair of the legendary creature since the day of the German couple's still-questionable report. Dave himself had searched high and low relentlessly, along with Thane and Jason and Doug. Ri and Wolf had even come out one weekend to join the party. And as of yesterday, Stanley had finally been given the all-clear to indulge in brief stakeouts himself. But the crafty cub continued to elude them.

"I'm afraid I have a confession to make," Mei Lin whispered. "I've been halfway hoping you guys don't catch up with that cub — at least not right away."

Thane stared down at her with feigned horror. "What?

Treason!"

"Well!" Mei Lin defended, chuckling as she snuggled into her happy place. "I can't help it. The little guy worked one miracle already, bringing us all together, and his disappearing again now... well, it just seems right, somehow. If he makes his mark, then lopes off into legend, shrouded in mystery, the Buchanan family quest can continue indefinitely! On and on... generation after generation... am I making any sense, here?"

She couldn't see Thane's reaction, which was the one and only bad thing about being wrapped in his arms with her cheek nestled close to his heart. But the low rumble of his laughter told her he understood.

About the Author

USA-Today bestselling novelist and playwright Edie Claire was first published in mystery in 1999 by the New American Library division of Penguin Putnam. In 2002 she began publishing award-winning contemporary romances with Warner Books, and in 2008 two of her comedies for the stage were published by Baker's Plays (now Samuel French). In 2009 she began publishing independently, continuing her original Leigh Koslow Mystery series and adding new works of romantic women's fiction, young adult fiction, and humor.

Under the banner of Stackhouse Press, Edie has now published over 25 titles including digital, print, audio, and foreign translations. Her works are distributed worldwide, with her first contemporary romance, *Long Time Coming*, exceeding two million downloads. She has received multiple "Top Pick" designations from *Romantic Times Magazine* and received both the "Reader's Choice Award" from *Road To Romance* and the "Perfect 10 Award" from *Romance Reviews Today*.

A former veterinarian and childbirth educator, Edie is a happily married mother of three who currently resides in Pennsylvania. She enjoys gardening and wildlife-watching and dreams of becoming a snowbird.

Books & Plays by Edie Claire

Romantic Fiction

Pacific Horizons

Alaskan Dawn
Leaving Lana'i
Maui Winds
Glacier Blooming
Tofino Storm

Fated Loves

Long Time Coming
Meant To Be
Borrowed Time

Hawaiian Shadows

Wraith
Empath
Lokahi
The Warning

Leigh Koslow Mysteries

Never Buried
Never Sorry
Never Preach Past Noon
Never Kissed Goodnight
Never Tease a Siamese
Never Con a Corgi

Never Haunt a Historian
Never Thwart a Thespian
Never Steal a Cockatiel
Never Mess With Mistletoe
Never Murder a Birder
Never Nag Your Neighbor

Women's Fiction

The Mud Sisters
Soccer Mom in Galilee (as Rachel Stackhouse)

Humor

Corporately Blonde

Comedic Stage Plays

Scary Drama I
See You in Bells